Praise for Peter Mehlman and his first novel, *It Won't Always Be This Great*

"It turns out that not only can Peter Mehlman write funny television, he can write a funny book. Who knew?"
—Julia Louis-Dreyfus, star of *Veep* and *Seinfeld*

"Anyone who writes for television gets frustrated that they can't write like Peter Mehlman. Now he's going to make novelists mad too. Mehlman's writing style is completely unique and creates an intimate bond between the narrator and the reader. You finish the book feeling as though you've made a new friend."
— Aaron Sorkin, Academy and Emmy-award winning screenwriter, producer, and playwright, whose works include *A Few Good Men, The West Wing, The Social Network, and The Newsroom*

"Equal parts moral dilemma, subtle social commentary, and journey of self-discovery, Mehlman's tale of a man forced outside the comfort zone of his 'respectable, decent, low-impact, relaxed-fit, gluten-free world' is both laugh-out-loud funny and deeply moving."
—*Publishers Weekly*

"Overflowing with humorous, strange, and insightful social observations, the novel is told with Mehlman's particular sensibility...In a refreshing twist, Mehlman creates a narrator who still loves and respects his wife, Alyse. Even after 24 years, he's still trying to impress her."
—The Huffington Post

"As the nameless narrator tells his story to a college pal lying comatose in a hospital bed, there are clear echoes of *Catcher in the Rye* and the inspired nothingness of *Seinfeld*. Throw in some catch-me-if-you-can themes from one of the greatest Russian novels—Fyodor Dostoyevsky's *Crime and Punishment*—and basketball references with echoes of Updike's Rabbit Angstrom, and this jokey dark comedy can claim serious literary inspiration."

—*LA Weekly*

"Here's a book that's *not* about nothing. Former *Seinfeld* writer and co-executive producer Peter Mehlman released his first novel, *It Won't Always Be This Great*. The novel's tale, narrated by a Jewish podiatrist living in New York, begins with an uncharacteristic act of vandalism, and spirals out of control from there. There's a false arrest, flirtations with an attractive young patient, and the looming threat of the narrator being found out. And while Mehlman says *Seinfeld* didn't inspire the novel any more than any of the many other parts of his life, there's plenty of neurotic humor for fans of that era of his work to dig into."

—*Hollywood Reporter*

"The Peter Mehlman I met in person years ago cannot be the same Peter Mehlman who wrote this brilliantly funny, effortlessly insightful, and unexpectedly moving book. Somebody please tell me which Peter Mehlman I'm supposed to be raving about because I really want to get this blurb right."

—Steven Soderbergh, film producer, screenwriter, director, *Erin Brockovich, Traffic, Ocean's Eleven*, and others

"Thanks to Peter Mehlman, former *Seinfeld* writer and producer, the terms 'shrinkage' and 'yada-yada' became a part of the popular vernacular."

—NPR's *Fresh Air*

Also By Peter Mehlman

It Won't Always Be This Great, A Novel

Mandela Was Late: Odd Things & Essays From the Seinfeld Writer Who Coined Yada, Yada and Made Spongeworthy a Compliment

#MEASWELL

a Novel

PETER MEHLMAN

#MeAsWell, A Novel
Copyright © 2019 #MeAsWell LLC
All rights reserved.

Cover art by Peter Mehlman
Cover and interior designed by Siori Kitajima, SF AppWorks LLC

Cataloging-in-Publication data for this book is available from the Library of Congress:
ISBN-13: 978-1-950154-09-8
ISBN-10: 1-950154-09-2

Published by The Sager Group LLC
www.TheSagerGroup.net
info@TheSagerGroup.net

#MEASWELL

a Novel

PETER MEHLMAN

THE SAGER GROUP

Artifex Te Adiuva

*To Arthur Ashe, Howard Cosell, Tony Kornheiser, Philip Roth, John
Updike and, mostly, Rose and James Mehlman.*

A Midsummer Day, 2018

Arnie Pepper walks through National Airport after a flight spent plotting his defense against the present.

At the luggage carousel, a phrase drifts into his head. *Emotional baggage claim.* He pulls his notebook and pen from the inside breast pocket of his sports coat and jots it down for use in a future column, then calculates the odds of ever publishing a future column.

Three to one against?

The usual herd of lawyers hovers around baggage claim, attaches dropped between their shoes, all of them aging in double-time under the weight of families, homes, cars, credit limits, unworkable escape fantasies from self-made problems. This is a moment in their personal lives. They're here. Existing. A day like any other.

Returning his notebook to his pocket, Pepper guesses he's the only soul in this hallowed American airport who will remember this day forever.

Dodging his own dread, he switches thought channels, picturing his suitcase tumbling down the chute, a gleeful, canary-yellow specimen from AWAYTRAVEL. Purchased eight months ago, it's wildly visible, lightweight, able to dart over floors like Allen Iverson and equipped with a phone charger he'll never use.

Iverson. Damn...always a sports reference.

The opening notes of "Brown Sugar" ring out from the phone of a guy in his early 70s still hanging on to some shredded past and putting it out there for all to hear. It's a world, Pepper thinks, where people curate their own self-delusions. *Curate. What's the half-life of that pompous, trendy verb?* Watching the guy spastically search for the button that will cut off Keith Richards, Pepper remembers his cellphone is still switched off against an invading world.

Twenty-four hours ago, Pepper was as content and carefree as a white, wage-earning, statin-popping, middle-aged American male could be. Thirty-nine years ago, when he began his career at the *Washington Post*, he'd have never guessed that a sixty-one-year-old widower and single parent could lead a life as joyful and enviable as his: being paid by an august, indispensable newspaper to fly around the planet witnessing events he (sometimes willingly) would have paid to attend, mingling with superstars (sometimes deservedly) worshipped by millions.

Yesterday, around five in the afternoon, he was in his element, hanging with a bunch of like-minded colleagues behind a batting cage at Marlin's Park in Miami, doing as they had done for years, slinging gossip and trash talk. At some point, a reporter from the Miami Herald noted how every time he saw Larry King attending a game at Dodger Stadium, he seemed to be sinking lower and lower into his seat. "It's like he's melting in super slow motion," he said.

"Hey," Pepper shot back, "I hope I look as good as Larry when I'm 400 years old."

Big laughs all around.

The conversation turned to another LA team, the Lakers, who'd recently acquired LeBron James. "He's on the Lakers, but he plays for Nike, the Greek Goddess of Sweatshops," Pepper said.

Bigger laughs.

On a roll now, Pepper veered into a conversation he'd recently had with Pat Riley...

...which led to his third joke, the trifling crack that is now threatening to torpedo his career, his reputation, everything that made his life worth living.

The target of the joke was nobody, really. A notoriously soft, contact-phobic NBA player who would be starting the season on the injured list.

"My question is," Pepper said with a flawless, comic pause, "How long does a guy usually stay on the injured list for a hysterectomy?"

His audience of rumpled colleagues immediately lost it, laughing so wantonly loud that several players halted their warm-ups to look over.

In a rare move, manager Don Mattingly marched over and warned: "Whatever the joke is, it better be really funny."

A kid from the AP spoke up. His retelling was clunky, but Mattingly laughed so hard he nearly choked on his chaw of Red Man tobacco.

The other press guys, only slightly reduced to adoring fans, relished their moment of comradery with a genuine, living, major league manager. Pepper, decades into knowing Mattingly as a generic kid from Indiana with great hand-eye coordination, just smiled. Maybe if he hadn't taken a moment to reword the joke in his head, Pepper would have noticed an unfamiliar reporter among the group—a young ex-jock-looking guy with a thick neck, patchy beard and 2.7 million Instagram followers—busily snapping photos, thumbing his cell phone and sharing the joke with an angry world.

A day later, in Delta Airlines' baggage claim/holding cell, Pepper concludes that, even a year ago, his joke would have been amusing and then forgotten. But not now. Not in *this* now.

Rumination must be popping off Pepper's scalp as a toddler stares at him. The little guy is adorable in a future-ugly-adult kind of way, so Pepper winks at him. The boy cries into his mother's leg, leading Pepper to turn away and awaken his iPhone. The thing starts dinging like crazy. Dozens and dozens of text messages. He scrolls through, looking for one from his daughter. Nothing. He has not heard from her since her distressed call this morning.

Why hasn't she contacted me since? Did she find out yet about my mess?

Thea's 9:12 a.m. call came as he was about to interview the late-arriving Derek Jeter in his stadium office.

"Ugh, Daddy, I feel nauseous ad nauseum," Thea said. "Have you ever blown an interview?"

She's twenty-five and is working as a reporter for National Public Radio, but when she calls him "Daddy," he still goes gooey. *She's my daughter.*

"Yes. Hundreds of them. Why?"

"Did I catch you at a bad time?"

"No, honey. It's never a bad time. I'm just about to interview Derek Jeter. You've met him."

"Oh, yeah, I kind of remember him."

Pepper smiled. His daughter "kind of" remembers the Yankees legend.

"What's up, honey?"

"The short, embarrassing version? I'm doing a piece for 'Weekend Edition Sunday'—"

"Lulu Garcia Navarro. Best host ever."

"Yeah, she's great. Anyway, it's about a Buddhist who runs a meditation center for kids at Ketcham Elementary in Anacostia. He's got about forty kids who come in at 7 a.m. and go dead silent in meditation for twenty minutes. I saw them. It's mind-blowing."

Mind-blowing. A word picked up from her mother who died twenty-one years ago. When she was just a toddler. "Sounds like a great story. What went wrong?"

"After the class, I'm interviewing Perry—"

"Perry is the name of the Buddhist?"

"Yes. The interview is going great. He's thoughtful and charming, with the ethereal smile of someone truly enlightened. He even reveals to me that, since many of the kids are doing better in school since they started meditating, he got a sizable grant from the city to expand his work to other schools."

"So you got a *scoop*, that's great."

"Yeah. But about twenty minutes into our interview, I mentioned a quote from the Dalai Lama, and Perry went *off*. It's like he morphed from gentle holy man to Joe Pesci in *Goodfellas*."

"What did he say?"

"He said, 'The Dalai Lama is an asshole.'"

"Yikes."

"I thought he was kidding, so I said, 'Don't worry, I won't use that sound bite in the piece.' But then, he ranted about how the Dalai Lama's an 'unholy, horny fraud who just hangs out with his following of bimbo Hollywood actresses, trying to get in their pants.'"

"Wow. That's a great quote."

"Right? Then he bowed his head, chanted his mantra and looked up with his unearthly smile, like nothing had ever happened."

"Sounds like Perry the Buddha might need an exorcist. How did the interview end?"

"It didn't. He told me to wait a minute, and he'd be back. And then he scurried away. I think he might have gone outside for a smoke.

"Jesus! You're still *there*? Is there another exit you can use?"

Years of encouraging her to be the fearless woman she is, and I'm telling her to scurry away.

"No Daddy, I gotta finish the interview. It's my first national story. Which is probably why I quoted the Dalai Lama. That was so show-off-y. I'm such an idiot."

"How could you know that would set him off? Besides, you're not an idiot. I had your blood tested. You came up negative for idiot."

"We may need a second opinion."

"Okay, listen. Try hitting the reset button on the interview. Pretend the Dalai Lama rant never happened. When he gets back, try to lighten things up with, you know...a distraction."

"A distraction? Like what?"

"Like, subtly flash your Super Bowl XLVII Souvenir Pepper Spray-Key Ring in front of him. He's from DC, maybe he's a Skins fan."

"So I should punt on the he's-a-psycho story?"

"Yes, but just for now. You didn't prepare for that angle, so it would be risky to pursue right now. You can always gain his trust with a puff piece, and then do a follow up and nail him."

"Hmm."

"Whatever happens, sweetie, you'll be fine. It's no big deal."

"So I should file this under 'Half-White Girl problems?'"

Thea rarely mentions her bi-racialism. Pepper was spared having to respond when Jeter walked in with his Yankee Yearbook smile. "Thea, Derek's here. Talk later. I love you."

An off-the-record chat with the Marlin's owner, about whether Major League Baseball or the NFL was dying faster, ended forty-five-minutes later when Pepper said, "Well Derek, that wasn't totally unenlightening." Jeter laughed. Pepper left, un-muted his phone and found the storm he never saw coming had made landfall.

Now it's seven hours later, and Pepper glares at a frequent flyer awash in liters of cologne. He supposes he should be more selective about what bugs the shit out of him, but then again, pet peeves are about all anyone has control over anymore.

A limo driver resembling a Latino Wolf Blitzer and holding a sign reading "BURTON" comes over. "Hey, Arnie Pepper! Love your column! Who do you like in the NFL this year?"

"Put your money on the referees ruining the whole season," Pepper says.

A pinstripe suit approaches the driver. "That's me," he says, pointing to the sign. "I'm Burton."

"Welcome to Reagan Airport, Mr. Burton."

Pepper inwardly snorts. He still can't get with the name change. *It's NATIONAL Airport, asshole.*

In advance of the '84 Olympics, he interviewed Reagan. The commander-in-chief's helium-filled decrees and untethered detours made Pepper peek around for a ventriloquist behind the Oval Office curtains. When Pepper finally thanked him for his time, President Ronald W. Reagan said, "Well, thank you for coming by, Mr. Ambassador."

A sportswriter interviewing the president required the presence of only a third-string-staffer from the White House Comms Office, a serious woman whose face screamed: *Please, not a word about that*. Pepper nodded, seeing no need to alert the national desk about America's lack of a conscious president. The White House reporters undoubtedly knew, no need to hear it again from someone in sports, a section they viewed as the newsroom equivalent of preschool.

Thirty-four years later, the babbling heads on cable news recall Reagan as a cowboy visionary. Pepper recalls an amiable guy with neon VACANCY signs in his eyes.

A young Muslim woman edges past Pepper, trying to get closer to the carousel, angling her body as if boxing him out for a rebound. Funny. *She's dressed according to ancient Muslim custom, covered head to toe. And carrying a South Park backpack. Isn't South Park everything Muslims get all bent out of shape about? Maybe it's her way of sampling Western culture. Or maybe reassurance that there's no C-4 under all those stifling clothes.* He feels sorry for this girl, slogging through the mud pie of an angry, dim-witted, unlimited-breadsticks America, never knowing when some "USA!"-chanting meathead acting as Jesus Christ's press secretary will attack her for kicks. Can't blame Arabs for hating Americans. Look at the Jordanians: Because of us, they can't even name their national airline Air Jordan.

Pepper grabs his notepad and writes *Air Jordan*.

He thinks Thea would love that line. *Why hasn't she called, anyway?* He wants to call her just to hear the rowdy laugh inherited from her mother. He wants her to call to let him know she's okay. And to let him know that he's okay too, that she's

not mad at him, that all this ado is about not much. *She's prob-*
ably on deadline at work, he reassures himself.

Pepper sees fatherhood as a never-ending job interview, an
ongoing effort to make a good impression on his own daughter, to assure her, over and over, that he's the man for the job.
Now, his softest soft spot is flashing DISQUALIFIED by virtue
of one little joke.

She heard about it. She's avoiding me. She'll hate me for the rest of
my life.

Self-absorbed synapses reroute Pepper's thoughts: *I named*
my daughter after Althea Gibson, for Chrissake! How could anyone call
me sexist? If the feminists kept score of sportswriters like the psychotic
rubes at the NRA do with senators, I'd be in the top one percent. Hell,
Martina still sends me birthday cards! Lisa Leslie and Cheryl Miller
came to my book signing in LA! Mia Hamm sent a bottle of champagne
to the publication party! And by the way, who wrote the first column
stating that women soccer players peeling down to their sports bras is
a valid form of expression? Me! Brandi Chastain sent me a condolence
card. Jesus. How did she find out about that? I stand out among women
athletes as a paragon of what a male sportswriter should be. And even
if that's overstating it, it's still kind of true. I've been on the right side
of their every issue: Title IX, equal prize money, predatory coaches, you
name it. My radar for topics concerning female athletes has always been
top drawer, even on issues no one else would touch: I was the one re-
porter who saw Fu Yuanhui bending over in pain at the Olympic pool
in Rio and eased over with my translator after the relay and flatly (but
nicely) asked her, "Are you, by any chance, on your period?" A zillion
other journalists there, hundreds of them women, and I'm the one to
think of popping that question. I raised a daughter by myself. I know
what it's like to hit an all-night drug store at 2 a.m. to load up on indus-
trial strength Motrin. So this little Chinese girl blinks at me then smiles
adorably and says, "Yes, I am menstruation"—in English! Then, she feels
emboldened enough to announce to the media pool that she swam badly
because she was sick from her period. Boom! She's an international star
for breaking a sports taboo. Which, by the way, is one of the things the

Olympics should be about instead of all that tripe about "playing for my country." What does that even mean? It's terrific that Lindsey Vonn wins a bronze after having her knees remodeled forty times, but how does it benefit America? Do thirty million tape-delayed viewers suddenly donate to The United Way? And what if Lindsey happened to say, "I won this one for myself," as opposed to winning it for our brave soldiers fighting in overseas shitholes for our freedom? Would the great American experiment have collapsed? Now, if Obama had bet our nuclear arsenal in a game of HORSE against Putin, that would've been playing for your country. Of course, Obama would have kicked Putin's butt. I saw him play. Nice rotation on his shot. Huh, Obama would probably stick up for me in this mess. Maybe not. When we golfed, he gave me good-natured grief about my column but hell, he didn't invite me to play twice because he thought I was a crappy journalist. Then again, do I really need character references at this point in my life? Actually, it would be good if I did. They'd be lining up. Yeah, I think they'd be lining up. I know Popovich would stick up for me. Who did Pop consult when he considered hiring Becky Hammon as the first female assistant coach in the NBA? Exactly. Me. Because I don't ask dopey jock questions, he respects the hell out of me. Actually, Pop owes me a dinner, though I'd never let him pay. Ethics, people! And speaking of dinner...Mikaela Shiffrin and I had a two-hour lunch at Pyeongchang, totally off the record, just because she liked my questions. I'm not pro-women? After I blew the lid off the Olympic "That Time of the Month" story, I was so jazzed and so strung out on non-Hodgkin's jet lag, I stayed up all night researching a follow-up story about how no tampons are manufactured in China because of some crazy Beijing thing with the breaking of the hymen being equivalent to losing your virginity. I still don't totally grasp—Oh my God, I just remembered: I made that joke after her press conference about how Fu should run off and join a menstrual show. The press corps cracked up. There was zero blowback. Was my joke today more offensively sexist than that?

And while we're talking pro-feminist track records: Who told the world class dummies at ESPN to hire Doris Burke? Me! They'd never even heard of her when they started their tokenistic effort to hire a woman for a role beyond sideline reporting on NBA games, which, by the way, is the most retarded job in the history of television. In fact, after I told them to hire Doris, I suggested they hire Sarah Silverman for the studio show. She loves basketball and is the funniest human being on this steaming, humorless planet. How does ESPN respond? They look at me like I'm a door-to-door Jehovah's Witness. Is there a Jehovah's Witness Protection Program? I should write that down. Anyway, it's not like discussing NBA players requires a Ph.D. All these guys do is play basketball, practice high-fives and rub lotion on their legs. Previously, ESPN asked me to recommend a color commentator. Who did I tell them to hire? Jeff Van Gundy! Now he's the only monster talent on their palsied broadcasts, the only voice immune to clichés: "He has a nice touch for a big man." Of course he does: He plays basketball fourteen hours a day. Or: "He got slapped and still made the basket. What concentration!" Concentration? What else would be on his mind in the middle of a shot? The annexation of Crimea? Hey, speaking of Crimea, I once heard a rumor about an NBC Olympics producer selling bottles of an undetectable PED to any athlete on the hunt. Did I spread the rumor? No. I reported it out, found it scurrilous and put the kibosh to the chatter. Reporters trading in that junk? Reprehensible. A long time ago, a colleague I won't name left a locker room and told me a certain famous quarterback had an unbelievably tiny dick. I lit into the reporter, saying that spreading crap like that is a violation of what we do—and besides, you can't tell if it's really tiny because there are growers and showers. A year or two later, a woman who dated said quarterback told me he has "a micro-penis." Okay, some gossip is true. But I stood up for professionalism. Journalistic principles matter, even if they're horseshit principles. Anyway, ask Billie Jean or Martina about me. When it came to writing about LGBT and whatever the last letter is that they added on, I raised awareness (hate that expression) in several columns. Not to mention issues dealing with Blacks, Latinos, Jews and all the other groups that should stick up for me like they once stuck up for each other. Arthur Ashe and Billie Jean supported each other. Hank Greenberg and Jackie Robinson. Clemente and...everyone. Now, every group is in it for themselves, competing for number one in the victimization standings. Anyway...ESPN, that solid waste factory? I appeared on their sportswriters show, filled in for Kornheiser as host on PTI, and the producers loved me. Not enough to give me a show of my own, but some people weren't meant to be overpaid by a notoriously stingy company. I write full sentences. Carefully worded, well-thought out sentences. An important job for which I've gotten awards and prizes and all kinds of honorary bullshit. And yet, now I stand accused of being anti-women? Please. It's like when Cosell called that Garrett guy on the Redskins a "little monkey" and got slammed for racism. Imagine! Cosell, the only sports media guy who immediately(!) said Ali had a right to his name when even the Times kept throwing in "also known as Cassius Clay." I interviewed Howard after "the monkey incident" at his apartment on East 69th down the hall from Liza Minnelli. His resentment at being accused of racism...that's where I am today. Kornheiser, Kindred, Israel, Deford, Murray, Lipsyte and me—the only print journalists Cosell respected. And I'd like to think a piece of that was how we covered women, even if it wasn't. What about the column I wrote after that dope at the Times painted Lolo Jones and Anna Kournikova as losers? Lolo made three Olympic teams, for Christ sakes. Two summer, one winter! Sure, Kournikova never won a tournament, but she got to number eight in the world! Imagine being the eighth best woman tennis player on the planet. Plus, she made bazillions in endorsements. In what perverse rendering of America is a top ten tennis-playing mogul a loser? Same for Danica Patrick. She never won Indy or NASCAR or whatever other races white trash America gets all frothy over, but she drove 150 miles an hour, put millions of ignorant fat asses in the seats, and made boatloads of loot! That's a loser? No, that's misogyny against incredibly accomplished women. The fact that they're all gorgeous is immaterial. (Danica taking her helmet off and tossing her hair...sexiest thing EVER.) I got huge response on that column. I heard Michelle Obama clipped the piece and gave it to Sasha and Malia. NOW cited me as an example of "forward thinking in the primitive tar pit of Sports Journalism." Yeah, it meant so much to me, I remember the quote verbatim. Hey: Maybe I should lie and say that Betty Friedan also called me to compliment the piece? The great thing about the dead is you can misquote them all you want. Oh wait—did she die before the piece ran? Doesn't matter. It's *enough that Lolo herself called me on my HOME PHONE to thank me. Too bad Kournikova didn't but everything rolls off the backs of those Russians. Look at Sharapova. Sportswriters ask a klutzy question, she goes titanium blonde, refocusing on tennis balls and endorsement money. Lucky her, secure in the belief that money is the root of all wealth. I respect her asylum in capitalism, part of why she trusts me as much as any woman can trust a guy shoving a recorder in her face after she's been humping it on red clay at Roland Garros for three hours. Hell, the trust women athletes have put in me? Well, if beautiful Flo Jo planned to come back from the dead for the 2024 Paris Olympics, she'd give me the exclusive. I mean, you cannot be serious! After all the courageous, principled stands I've espoused in one of the world's great newspapers since 1980, 2018 rolls around and I make one (undeniably) funny, (barely) off-color hysterectomy joke—AND THAT'S IT? One reporter posts my joke on Instant Graham or whatever it's called, it goes viral, and boom? My career goes down the toilet? It's insane! And yet, here I am, up to my neck in a deranged cultural war where I don't know where the lines are or if there are lines anymore or if there ever were lines. Maybe I just imagined lines all these years. Or maybe I'm drowning in some fatal spike of national ignorance. Or maybe I'm just old and lost, over my pitch count and out of print.*

Pepper's inner rant is ended by the baggage carousel buzzer blaring like a breach at a nuclear plant. Pepper's joyous yellow suitcase is among the first to tumble down the chute, as if it had cut the line by sheer force of personality. He grabs it, absorbs its energy, and jukes through the crowds untouched, a vision of OJ Simpson in the old Hertz auto rental commercials.

Hanging with OJ at the '84 Olympics was fun. Attending a day of his trial for the murder of his wife, less so. During a sidebar in Judge Ito's chambers, Simpson waved Pepper over, gave him a mortifying hug and started gossiping about sports media people as if life hadn't gone the least bit berserk. In acutely self-conscious horror, Pepper faked some chit-chat while avoiding livid glares from the Goldman and Brown families. That night, Pepper called his own wife, Jane, and told her about the moment, how he kept checking back in with reality by glancing at Simpson's right hand, the one that massacred two people.

Jane took some time before asking, "Why would you want to check in with reality?"

Jane's question still haunts him. You never know when someone will say something that will torture you forever.

Exiting the terminal, humidity slaps Pepper's face, his nearly forty years here still no match for DC's livid barometer. He sweats more lately, a by-product of age and the profusion of meds taken by American men with health insurance. He wonders if this perspiration is flop sweat. Larry Bird once told Pepper he gleaned a lot about opponents from their sweat, flop sweat smelling rank, athletic sweat almost sweet. Bird has a certain genius, but Pepper won't mop his brow and take a sniff.

Thea said she wants to send her armpits to Alaska for the summer. She got her sense of humor from Jane who, by the way, would have laughed her head off at my hysterectomy joke. Nothing shook her. Can Thea really be offended?

Pepper heads to a taxi stand. Not long ago, he'd park in the long-term lot, but since people stopped reading and advertisers moved their con elsewhere, the *Post* saw cabs as a cost-cutter, along with reining in reporters' travel overall. Pepper misses the days when he could just go to LA and lightly fish for a story or two.

Which reminds me: Can I get a little rhythm for the night at the Forum when I chatted up Penny Marshall, and said she should make a movie about women who played professional baseball during World War II? I mean, what other sportswriter—

Pepper's thought is hijacked by a grainy voice.

"Holy shit. *Arnie Pepper!* This is so random! I just read your post on Instagram. You're lighting it up."

Pepper sizes up the lank, bearded kid who has approached him. He could be an owner of a trust fund-backed typewriter shop in the groovy Shaw section of town. Pepper doesn't recall being so slack in his own, unwieldy 20s.

"I bet your sportswriter buddies thought your little joke was *hilarious*," the kid says.

There's acidy micro-aggression in the words "little joke." Something about this encounter doesn't feel random.

"Look, pal," Pepper says. "It wasn't my 'post.' I don't post. Or Tweet. I don't even know what Instagram is. It sounds like a cocaine delivery service, but I'm sure it's a lot worse than that."

The kid is not amused. "But you did make the joke that was in the Instagram post, right?"

Pepper looks back at the terminal, hoping a better answer than the truth will fly through the automatic doors. "Look, uh, what's your name?"

"Bruce," the kid says, with rehearsal in his voice. "Bruce Bader Ginsburg."

Jesus. Get me out of here.

"You seem a bit testy, Arnie. I know Delta Airlines sucks, but..."

Pepper flinches. "How did you know which airline...?"

The kid smiles like he knows the secrets of the universe. Pepper feels his blood pressure rise. He almost says, "Listen, asshole..." but he's noticed that assholes don't mind it anymore when you call them assholes. He sees the kid peering at this collar.

"What are you looking at?"

"You have a long, loose thread on the top of your lapel."

Pepper feels for it but comes up empty. The kid slides his backpack down his left arm and says "It's more toward the back. Allow me."

Bruce circles behind him. Pepper hears an odd rustling noise, followed by a firm pat on the back. He spins around and is met with an odorous billow from a blank, white spray bottle in the kid's left hand.

"Ah! What the—???"

Bruce raises his arms, as if in surrender.

"Don't worry, Arnie. The smell dissipates...Eventually."

"Oh my God..."

"No, no, Arnie. Chill. It's just artisanal estrogen mist."

"What?"

"With a drizzle of Malaysian sterilization powder. It's all organic, non-GMO ingredients."

Frantic, Pepper notices an iPhone camera lens above the pocket of the kid's checked shirt. *Is he filming this whole thing?* "What's wrong with you?"

"Nothing's the matter with me, Arnie. I'm just another woke, crime-fighting first responder letting you off with a warning: Chill on the misogyny, dude."

"Misogyny?"

"Yes, misogyny. One would think you'd recognize misogyny. You know, as a man with a daughter."

A panicked fever flies up Pepper's spine.

"I googled the shit out of you, bro."

Pepper arches up and growls. "Listen, you warped millennial asshole—"

Just then a Tesla with tinted windows skids to the curb. Jumping in, the kid says, "Off the record, Arnie? The hysterectomy line? *Hilarious.*"

The door slams, and just like that Musk's guilt-free toy for coastal elites silently flies toward I-95 and out of sight.

Pepper stands there, momentarily frozen. His legs feel fossilized. He does a palsied knee-bend, arches his back and slowly takes tiny steps as if walking on ice.

From behind he hears a voice, "Excuse me, sir."

Pepper's body does an involuntary Lutz. The refined-looking woman standing before him is Kirsten Gillibrand, the senator from New York and crusading sexual harassment scalp hunter.

Holy shit! Is she here to bury me like she did Al Franken?

"Sorry to alarm you, but if you don't already know, there's a sheet of paper stuck to the back of your sport jacket."

He tries to look mortified in a good-natured way.

"Oh, gee. Really? Thank you. Must be some kind of prank by, you know, one of my colleagues."

"Maybe you should find some new colleagues."

"Maybe you should too, Senator."

Gillibrand uploads her campaign smile. "Touché."

Pepper's reassured by his witty come-back. *You're okay. Paranoid, but okay.* As the Senator eases by him, he wonders if she can smell the mist still coating his nostrils. He takes off his jacket. The 8.5" x 11" paper hanging from the back collar bears the typed-in name **Arnold Pepper**, his home address, occupation, date of birth, and an in-the-ballpark forgery of his signature. The heading of the form reads: DO NOT RESUSCITATE.

The taxi driver has a four-pack of an energy drink on the passenger seat, wincing after a sip. *When did sugar and caffeine become so joyless?* For this poor Somali or Namibian or Liberian, his American misery probably started when those Silicon Valley pricks stuck Uber decals on every other car. Pepper feels for his cabbie the dreary affinity of job obsolescence, this weary foreigner with the rutted face of a million National Geographic photos, now driving cautiously around the traffic circles that trim the life expectancy of Washingtonians in peptic clumps.

Estrogen Mist. Is there really such a thing? He considers asking Siri but doesn't want her thinking he's lost it. The Malaysian Sterilization powder doesn't worry him. Thea is enough on the children score, and, honestly, the odds of him impregnating anyone, considering his twenty-two years of halfhearted, sporadic dating since Jane died—

He aborts that thought, then guesses he's set the single-day record for saying, "I don't want to think about it."

Does the Elias Sports Bureau keep track of that?

Speaking of: Who on TV reports the only truly revealing baseball stats? Hands down, Jessica Ramirez. I wrote about her when she was at Stanford, then touted her as a TV analyst. Boom: ESPN hires her. The list of women I've championed...

The cab driver opens a second bottle of energy drink, but somehow drives even slower.

Did I call her Jessica Ramirez? Jesus. It's Jessica Mendoza. No excuse, but I haven't eaten since breakfast.

He's about to tell the driver to take a detour to a gourmet shop near the *Post* with a fantastic Baguette Happy Hour. But he remembers that Style section editors carbo-load there around this time and...*Damn*: It dawns on him that he wants to avoid coworkers. This is followed by a new and brutal realization, one that drops him into the deeper fear of feeling exposed for what he isn't: a man with a dark side. Even if he's not fired, he knows something is going to happen. He imagines being bundled for the rest of his life with the infamous predators of America who stayed on at their jobs with depravity clouds over their heads. That chubby load of a congressman from Texas, Farenthold, stayed around months while a zillion sexual harassment claims strafed him. He probably walked around the office happily oblivious to the sideways looks of all his young aides and pages.

Sociopaths are crushing it these days. How do you join up?

On M Street, a maniac in a Buick Encore tailgates Pepper's taxi, honking and flashing his lights. The African cabbie's gentle driving enrages a (hopefully) dying segment of hyper-victimized white men. Pepper turns around and sees the Encore's Virginia plate: P MGNET.

Warped self-images, suddenly something to advertise.

"Pay no attention," Pepper says. "You're a terrific driver."

"Thank you, Sah," the driver says, terrorized.

After two more blocks, the cabbie retreats to an open space of curb. The Encore rages past, the driver screaming in such warlike fashion he nearly runs a red — coming to a burning stop inches from a double-decker tour bus. The black, female bus driver glares out the window. A bony middle finger flies out of the Encore. Pepper watches like it's another busted play on Monday Night Football. No one gets any satisfaction.

If only the bus had pancaked the asshole.

The cabbie is still trembling as he turns onto Wisconsin Avenue, where Pepper has lived, in four locations, his whole time in DC. He'd chosen it at first because it seemed auspicious—he'd graduated University of Wisconsin. He took it as a good omen that, plopped among Northwest avenues named after Northeastern states, there was Midwestern Wisconsin Avenue. A mistake, he's come to think, naming avenues after states that hate Washington, especially the deep southern states, all smelling like Pizza Huts, making their own rules on guns, gays, and abortion, railing against imagined enemies, making sure their women know there's a price to pay for having fun.

Do they have active shooter drills at the NRA?

Out of bottomless nostalgia, Pepper stayed put on Wisconsin Avenue. One of his problems now, like many reporters who make a living watching the world, is failing to notice himself in it. He tries exercising mindfulness but winds up too focused on reminding himself to be mindful. Maybe, he wonders, his lifelong nostalgia production is dwindling. Then again, maybe he'll eventually feel nostalgic for this godawful day. Probably not. Nostalgia for college is easy. The present is too fraught to even to identify a moment worth relishing.

Over the years, several colleagues have been alums of local universities. Georgetown, GW, Maryland, AU. They all say Pepper was lucky to have gone to Wisconsin, far away enough to spare him from having college friends hitting him up for playoff tickets or autographed sticks from toothless Canadians or requests to ask a 320-pound black guy with six percent body fat if he'd attend a bar mitzvah. David Israel, formerly a killer sportswriter for the *Washington Star*, told Pepper he'd worked at the *Chicago Daily News* after graduating Northwestern. It became immediately apparent he had to cut off all contact with college friends. "They'd actually hit me up with requests like,

'Come on, just ask Refrigerator Perry to come to the reception. All he has to do is pose for a few pictures, maybe dance one hora and that's it. Do this one favor for me!' That's when I realized that college is where you meet the people who will haunt you for life."

Pepper has exactly one college friend living in Washington, his best friend in the world and fraternity brother, Jerry Corbin, now Jillian Corbin, Montgomery County Prosecutor. She was godfather and is now godmother to Thea. Pepper had suggested going with "godparent," but Jillian refused to distance herself from her new gender. After that, Pepper smoothly adapted to his friend's transition. Pretty smoothly. When she legally changed her name, Pepper mused aloud about how transgender people always seem to choose a new first name with the same initial. "It's like, 'I'm willing to swap out my genitalia, but those monogrammed towels? No way. That's where I draw the line.'"

Jillian laughed so hard she literally threw up.

As the taxi nears Pepper's Friendship Heights condo, he thinks of talking to Jillian about his situation. She's a brilliant lawyer and (un-shockingly) well-versed on matters of gender. It couldn't hurt to explore what his overall attitude should be when pleading his case to his boss.

Apologetic but not desperate?

Strong but not militant?

Ironic but not glib?

Affecting but not maudlin?

Just be himself, whatever that is?

People die from the fall off tightropes. It's not like Pepper will be testifying before the Senate for a seat on the Supreme Court, but still—he needs help.

And what about Pat Summitt pointing out publicly that I was the only male columnist to describe her as an all-time great basketball coach with no modifiers like "woman" or "female?"

As the cab approaches his condo, Pepper sees a news van

and five people milling around the front door. It takes a bit longer than it should to realize they're waiting for him. He's at once anxious and a bit insulted. *One* news van? Not that he should expect a Michael-Cohen-outside-The-Regency-Hotel mob, but this is pretty piddling. On the other hand, his cab driver takes a new view of his passenger when he hears the little group calling out "Arnie! Can you talk a minute?"

"You are a famous man?" the driver asks.

"No. I'm just a guy with luggage in the trunk."

The driver runs out and gets the yellow suitcase. Pepper over-tips him, asks for a receipt, and gets out of the car.

A redheaded woman trailed by a cameraman is from WJ-LA-TV. There's a sportswriter from the Moonie-owned *Washington Times*, a paunchy jock-sniffer in heavy-rimmed bifocals, baggy blazer, and a screamingly obvious toupee. Years ago, Kornheiser started calling the guy Metta Hair Piece. Now Pepper can't recall his real name. Just Metta.

"Hey, man," Pepper says, reaching for some affinity.

"Hey, Arnie," Metta says, recorder extended. "So, are you furious at the reporter who posted your joke on Instagram?"

"I actually don't know who posted it, but no," Pepper says gently. "It's completely my fault."

That's smart: Own it. Another expression that should be banned for life.

"Granted, I won't be opening an Instagram account any time soon..."

Big laughs from the press posse.

Good. Get them on your side.

"So you did make the joke."

"Yes."

"But it's kind of standard sportswriter banter, right?"

"Regardless, I can't stand here and excuse what I said."

Look, up in the sky: It's Mea Culpa Man!

"Have your editors discussed the situation with you?"

"Briefly. Just long enough to set a meeting for tomorrow."

Too honest. No one needs to know that.

Then, with a tinge of embarrassment, Metta says, "What's your response to the locker room video-parlor rumors?"

Pepper's voice and face say, "Excuse me? I don't know what you're talking about"

"Oh *man*," Metta says, pity in his voice.

Jeez, when Metta pities you, something's bad. Rumors?

"Arnie, it seems as if website called Pervo-jock.com has alleged that you have been, for years, taking secret video tapes of naked athletes in locker rooms and holding monthly, all-male viewing parties in a back room of the Old Ebbitt Grill."

"What the hell??? That's insane. I didn't even know The Grill *has* a backroom."

Metta shrugs: "The story went viral this morning on a bunch of mainly anti-gay and anti-mainstream media sites. Now it's making a big dent on Facebook."

Pepper sputters. He feels pulsing in his neck, sure it's a stroke symptom.

"Brett Slocum from TMZ," says a droopy gnome recording video on an Android. "Did you ever conduct a post-game interview with Michael Jordan *while* he was showering?"

Metta shouts, "Shut up, you asshole!" then chops down on Slocum's arm causing the phone to fall, its glass shattering on the cement. Slocum picks up the wrecked phone, threatens a lawsuit, and literally runs away.

"Sorry, Arnie," Metta says.

"Nothing to apologize for, M—man."

The hyper-coiffed redhead and her cameraman step up.

"Carly Hyde, WJLA. Mr. Pepper, several feminist groups, including The American Gynecological & Obstetrical Society, are calling for your dismissal."

"I doubt The American Gynecological & Obstetrical Society would call itself a feminist group."

Dumb. Can't you let anything slide?

"That said, I respect the opinion to which they're certainly entitled."

Too wonky.

"Don't you feel you're just the latest victim of an overzealous age of sexual persecution?"

Pepper is surprised a woman asked this question.

"No, I don't feel that. Do you?"

Challenging her is a mistake.

"Actually, I think there's lots of hypocrites out there. I mean, I came here from the affiliate in Sarasota? Half the reporters down there got their jobs because of their tits."

Pepper almost says, "Even the guys?" but he's saved by the cameraman who lowers his lens. "Uh, Carly. Just a heads up: You and your opinions are on camera."

"Look, I can't comment anymore," Pepper says. "It's been a long day."

A young woman steps forward with her iPhone. Pepper guesses she's about twenty-eight. Short hair like a mink, Jackie Kennedy frames over wide brown eyes, butterscotch skin and no makeup. Thea says makeup is all but invisible now, but she swears she won't use any until she's thirty, at which point she'll reassess.

"Kristen Haynes from DC Metro On-line."

"Oh, you guys do really good work."

Nice. Soften her up. Although it's true, they do serious journalism.

"Thanks, but Mr. Pepper—do you think it's ever appropriate to use women's health in the context of a joke?"

He feels the chill of being on the wrong side of a good question while trying not to be caught gazing at the beautiful symmetry of her collarbones.

"I'm sorry..." he says, starting to turn away.

"Are you sorry for not answering my question, or for alluding to an intimate female medical procedure as a way of humorously but derogatorily depicting a physically timid male athlete as a quote-unquote pussy?"

Pepper turns and over-gazes at her by a full second.

"What's your name again?"

"Kristen Haynes."

You remind me of my late wife.

"Ms. Haynes, you ask very well-constructed questions."

Pepper leaves the elevator at the top floor of his apartment building and labors down the hall, his yellow suitcase in tow. The weight of the day has made him feel like he has early-onset rigor mortis.

Entering his condo, he puts the taxi receipt on the kitchen counter and wonders if the next expense report he files will be his last. *Damn.* The thought of being fired keeps mugging him. Since the *Times* nailed Harvey Weinstein, the sex-related offenses kicking men into career purgatory are well known. Al Franken, once a Democratic juggernaut, forced to resign for being a crummy flirter, while serial harasser Jerry Richardson's punishment is selling the Panthers for two-whatever billion. Cosby pulls the wool over America's eyes for decades and pretty much gets away with it, nailed when he's old and blind and out of the game. Pepper considers the possibility of being fired: a career death sentence for felony joking. He stretches the limits of his own liberalism by trying to file it all under PROGRESS, then crashes into another question: *What would I do for the rest of my life?*

As if to clear the air, he goes around the room opening the windows. His mind wanders at the mundane task; begins to estimate just how long he's got to live...only suddenly he can't remember his age. It's an addled moment that's been happening to him lately. *Keith Richards is seventy-four. Is it possible he's only fourteen years older than me?*

Maybe I should get another dog. It would be nice to have someone around who's aging even faster than me. Or wait a minute. If I got a puppy now, by the time he's eight, I'll be how old...?

Weirdly, Pepper's reflex answer to "How old am I?" is often years above his actual age. Maybe time is racing so fast, his impulse is to aim ahead of it like a quarterback throwing to where he thinks a speedy receiver will be. (*Ugh, sports analogy.*) Or maybe this is a generational syndrome in which Baby Boomers, increasingly drifting off-shore, are turning into ageist pigs against themselves because they were never meant to be so old and baffled and temporary.

Maybe, maybe, maybe...

Theories zoom in and away like freeway headlights but they're all scary. Not scary in a mortality way—mortality is the bum he knows—but in a mad-dash-to-senility way, which feels worse. The fear of being on a need-to-know basis with his own life is so terrifying he won't discuss it with friends for fear of concluding, *Uh-oh. I'm alone on this one.*

That would be really bad.

But he doesn't think he's alone on this one. Age fright feels like a *thing.* Maybe not a thing to where we're talking about the LGBTQAF community, but still a thing. Clues arise from his peers, like when his old college friend Alice Vaughn recently said, "Imagine! Jamie Lee Curtis still fighting Michael Myers at her age!"

"Actually Alice," Pepper didn't say, "Jamie Lee Curtis is *your* age."

Maybe Pepper should worry about his friends more. But then, their inner lives seem less mysterious to him than his own. For the moment, he's willing to consider his problems more important than everyone else's in the world.

Thinking of Alice, he remembers a certain night in 1978. Alice Vaughn covered student government on *The Badger Herald* when Pepper was editor-in-chief. Friday nights at the *Herald* always featured stoned or drunken hours of release. One night, Alice, knocked silly on half a Quaalude, lurched into Pepper's office, gave him a memorably sloppy kiss, whirled around and passed out on his lap in a way that sent her braless left breast flying out of her peasant blouse. As in *Animal House*, Pepper gazed at it ("Look at those gazongas!"), a specimen more breathtaking than any he'd yet encountered. Okay, he did beat himself up later for cheating his fingertips out of a luscious sense memory, but in crunch time, he passed on taking a handful of breast. That's right. College boy Arnie Pepper delicately pulled the blouse over the breast, avoiding skin-on-skin contact.

Too bad Alice has no idea of the escaped tit moment, Pepper thinks. She could be a good reference: "He could have felt me up so easily, Your Honor, and I'd have never known. But he didn't. He was a gentleman, and I see no reason to believe he's not a gentleman to this day."

The memory of Alice reminds him of another apparent symptom of advancing age: his entire sexual history relentlessly replaying in his head. Can any heterosexual man do a thorough review of his sexual past without compiling some semblance of a rap sheet? And even if he can let himself off the hook for various youthful misdemeanors, Pepper envisions others probing into and compiling his unauthorized porno-biography, creating a movie far more interesting than the one he really lived.

On the upside, widower is a sad title. There he could get some dead wife slack. Pepper's sexual sample size significantly dipped after Jane died, his dates arising more out of convenience than desire, his sexual encounters having less to do with love or lust and more to do with resignation: "I guess this is what happens next."

So yes, a truthful investigation into his private life would be disappointing for all. But "truthful" is the problem. It won't be Bob Mueller heading up the The Pepper Probe. It will be web trolls and tabloid hacks conducting sloppy background checks on him, questioning friends, neighbors, and colleagues, following leads to the living rooms of every woman he'd laid a hand on from the day he reached puberty. "Ma'am, do you mind if I record this?" Not at all, they'll say, before unspooling memories at odds with Pepper's, colored by their own years of acid-washed dreams and botched relationships, all dirtied by the values of a ruthless present. Yesterday's innocent sex games, today's peccadilloes. Last century's flirtation, 2018's harassment. Now prosecutable.

Just two months ago, Pepper interviewed Candace Parker, who complimented him on his (only) cashmere sweater. He said, "Thanks. This cashmere feels great. Trust me, Candace, if you think you couldn't keep your hands off me before..."

Candace cracked up because she's crazy cool. But someone else: Boom, another entry to a rap sheet on which God knows what else could be listed. Worse than God knowing, much worse, would be Thea knowing. Even if ninety percent of the charges are drivel...

Pepper's mind snaps back to the present. *Thea. Should I call? Why hasn't she even texted? Did something happen with that Buddhist perv? Or is she really avoiding me? Twenty-five years of diligent fatherhood shot? Maybe she'll call during her meal break. Or maybe she's heard more daddy news today than she can handle.*

With its windows wide open, Pepper's condo feels airier than the city itself, as if the breezy lives of the rich kids at nearby AU cool the whole neighborhood. His condo is decorated with the overstated casualness of a boutique hotel, lamps, chairs, and bookcases all suggest high-end rentals, the one exception a solid glass coffee table with a wedding ring set dead in its middle, looking suspended in space. Mainly to combat his image as a sadly sequestered widower, Pepper has guests over a few times a year. Either no one notices the ring, or no one has the temerity to mention it.

He conjures the memory of a certain night in 2008. A birthday party he threw here for Thea. Twenty-two people. His face grows hot. A Starbucks joke: "A woman barista would be a good wife. She'd already have the coffee-making part down pat." Guests laughed. Maybe some didn't. *Maybe today, hearing the news of his gaff, some of those guests will think: "I'm not surprised."*

Pepper thinks of how, when sexual allegations pop up now,

people reflexively say, "Yeah, I can see him doing that," or "I wouldn't have pegged him that way." No matter if they know the guy or ever met him, Americans exercise their right to an opinion. Where we as a nation went wrong was presuming a right to speak those opinions aloud.

He drifts to the kitchen. A carton of Safeway lemonade stares out from the glass door of his Sub-Zero Pro 48. Why he needed an 800-pound refrigerator is beyond him. The lack of contents inside makes it look huger. *If I lose my job and need cash, I can always sublet my refrigerator.*

Sublet fridge. Even in his hell, there's material to jot down.

He takes the lemonade to his home office. The rare times guests stay over, Pepper gives them his bedroom and sleeps on the convertible sofa in the office where he keeps important, private stuff. People are pathologically nosy, even close friends.

Or especially close friends.

Months after moving into the condo, Pepper's childhood pal from Phoenix, Wally Shockley, stayed over one night before flying to Budapest the next morning "on business." Pepper thought it odd his wealthy friend didn't opt for a hotel, but happily set Wally up on the convertible. After taking a shower, Pepper found his guest rummaging through a desk drawer. Without a trace of guilt, Wally held up tear sheets from the *Times* and *Post* announcing Pepper's Pulitzer Prize. "Hey Pepperoni, you should frame these."

Wally was the only person in the world who still used his childhood nickname and somehow it softened Pepper's sense of violation. While replacing the tear sheets and locking the drawer, he resolved to ban all guests from the office. "Wally, the Pulitzer medal is framed in Thea's room. That's enough for me."

In truth, Pepper quietly viewed a Pulitzer for Sports Writing as an honor roughly equaling valedictorian at a reform school. Memorializing the honor by making his office a museum to himself felt creepy. *I don't need testimonials to my life. I was there.*

While the tear sheets Wally found are still in the drawer, Wally is missing. According to Interpol, Wally went to Budapest, then Uganda before his trail ran cold, his flight facilitated by 200 million dollars embezzled from the Scottsdale retirees he was supposed to be serving. A year or so earlier, with some un-Madoff-like conscience still in his heart, Wally politely declined to take on the portfolio of Pepper's elderly mother. His consideration for his own family was chillier. Before secretly flying to Washington for his layover in Pepper's condo, Wally left a note for his wife and daughters:

Will be late for everything. Start without me. Dad.

Since Wally took flight, Pepper often pictures his friend lying low, blending in, staying off the grid, using a foreign country to live the American Dream of just vanishing.

Pepper's desk looks out over a view of Washington. Two behemoth cranes bookend his sightline. He's been to every decent-sized city in America and knows how real estate development has, or will, wreck them all. Recently, in reporting on the way network TV has coped with the kneeling-during-the-anthem controversy in light of the fact that they have always been in bed with the NFL, Pepper spoke to Jim Rutenberg, a terrific media reporter for the *Times*. Amid Trump's jihad against journalism, *Times* and *Post* reporters have felt a competitive kinship, conferring more than they once did. After agreeing that network play-by-play guys unsuccessfully walk a line between being shills for the NFL and pretend journalists, the conversation turned to New York and how real estate idiots and hedge-fund bigger idiots priced all the cool people out of Manhattan and into Brooklyn. "And soon they'll be bumped out of Brooklyn," Rutenberg said. "In five years, when someone says they live in New York and you ask where in New York, they'll say 'Cincinnati.'"

Pepper is at an age when any news of the world going to shit is vaguely comforting. If not for Thea, the end of the world wouldn't seem such a big deal to him. Melting ice caps, rising oceans, resistant bacteria, hopscotching genocides, a dingbat kid playing with missiles in North Korea...it's all too much for an upper-middle class sportswriter.

Thea? Can a child disown a parent this fast? Then he remembers that the twerp at the airport, Bruce Bader Ginsburg, had mentioned her by name. *He probably saw the photo of us in Wimbledon that made it to my Wikipedia page. Fucking internet. How does that shit get posted?*

Pepper checks Wikipedia to see if the photo is still there. Not that he checks his own Wiki very often, but he can't help noticing an unfamiliar line of text at the very bottom:

"In 2018, Pepper became entangled in the Me Too movement after posting a misogynist tweet alluding to a hysterectomy in relation to a male NBA player's..."

Misogynist tweet! What the fucking hell! Have I been tried and convicted in my absence? This only happened yesterday! Are there trolls that do nothing but update Wiki all day? At least get the facts straight! It wasn't Twitter. I didn't post it. NBA players are all male. Did you ever hear of the WNBA? Look it up on Wikipedia, you brain-dead waste of —

Beside his eight-year-old iMac is a landline he should disconnect, but he can't deal with losing another lifelong link to himself. Stupid. There's the flashing light of a message on the dinosaur. With clingy dread, he fingers the play button.

The ten-second message is from his boss, the *Post's* sports editor, Linda Carlyle. She wants to push their appointment—scheduled for the office tomorrow—back to 1:15. He listens to the message three times but detects no clues about his future.

Stop. Fracking down into Linda's ten-second phone message? Just stop.

When Carlyle, Wharton MBA, had been hired eight years earlier, there were predictable groans around the sports section about corporatization. Pepper wondered when his column would be sponsored by Valvoline. Sports writing legend Tom Boswell, said, "The second she schedules a 'team-building Tuesday,' I'm out of here."

Within a month after her arrival, Pepper started to respect, then like, Carlyle. Her management skills meshed shockingly well with her sports knowledge. Still, it's a mystery to Pepper how this Wellesley Summa Cum Laude, competitive triathlete, serious-but-dryly funny, unmarried-but-living-with-some-guy type of person had gravitated to the infantile world of sports. But it seems to be a trend. He'd recently watched a thoroughly un-air-worthy segment on *60 Minutes* about Harvard kids all wanting to be sitcom writers. *Jesus, what happened to writing speeches for John F. Kennedy? Or aspiring to be W. E. B. Du Bois? Or keeping America straight with the Constitution like that skivvy attention-seeking missile, Dershowitz?* Then again, maybe the trend isn't so new. Conan O'Brien went to Harvard, and you get the feeling he has more to contribute to the world than laughing at pre-cooked jokes burped out by stoner actors plugging their new movies.

And while we're on the subject, how about that Seth Rogen kid...what's the appeal?

He remembers back to that February day in '84, before a Georgetown University basketball game at Madison Square Garden. He was standing at 47th and Sixth, waiting to meet a friend, when two elderly women approached him. Apropos of nothing, the taller one asks, "Excuse me, young man. Do you find Steve Martin funny?" When Pepper indicated he found Martin "hysterical," the woman turned to her friend. "See, Enid? The kids love him."

Now Pepper is Enid, baffled by all that makes young people laugh. He was always one of the funnier people at the *Post*— not an overly competitive category. His dopey joke about creating a scent for Latino baseball players called Bartolo Cologne flew around the *Post* sports section like a Woody Allen line that winds up in Bartlett's. Poor Woody, grouped in with pigs like Cosby and O'Reilly because of the allegations of a nutty actress ex-girlfriend with forty kids, his genius son not talking to him, everyone wondering if Sinatra was the real father. Pepper doesn't buy it. An acquaintance from the Obama administration said Ronan has a wicked sense of humor, but that's dicey, considering that Washington—for all Pepper loves about the town—is a magnet for un-funny-ness, cringe-worthy politicians repeating lame jokes over and over on stump speeches and Sunday news shows. McCain with his sporadic integrity trying to stick it to Trump while down thirty-five points to untreatable cancer, did the same clunky joke on TV a thousand times for years, not to mention his coarse, dumb joke about Chelsea Clinton's appearance. His sidekick, Lindsey Graham, makes endless weak jokes but is somehow seen as Senator Chris Rock. This city either doesn't get humor, or it's just not taken seriously. Or it's taken too seriously, like the fact-driven book Bob Woodward wrote about John Belushi back in 1984. Then again, if anyone deserves a free pass on everything, it's Bob Woodward.

Pepper's longtime, friendship-*lite* with Woodward began when, after he'd read *Wired*, he cornered Woodward in the newsroom one day and peppered him with dozens of questions about Belushi. Woodward had been taking heat on the book's dispassionate tone and seemed gratified by a colleague's interest. They wound up having lunch at the Madison hotel. Ever since, the sportswriter and the world's greatest investigative reporter have played two or three rounds of golf a year for comfortable stakes (much more comfortable for Woodward). By the 90s, it became a running joke that, whenever the match was tight, Pepper would suddenly ask, "So Bob, come on: *Who was Deep Throat?*" Woodward would burst out laughing, which actually loosened him up and improved his golf game. In the summer of 2002, as Woodward, down a stroke, stepped up to a 148-yard Par 3, Pepper said, "This is such a great hole for you to tell me who Deep Throat was." Again, Woodward laughed, took his customary two practice swings, and hit a feathery six-iron that landed ten feet and slightly left of the pin, bounced twice, and curled right into the cup. Woodward yelped, throwing his club in the air. Pepper squealed and bounced over with high-fives.

At which point, Woodward looked at him and said, "Mark Felt."

Pepper said, "Excuse me?"

Woodward gave him a look. "I'm not going to repeat what I just said and you sure as hell will never repeat it," he commanded in his vowel-crushed Chicago accent.

Three years later, former FBI Associate Director Mark Felt revealed himself as Deep Throat. When Pepper saw Woodward after the announcement, there was not even a wink between them. To this day, Pepper has remained silent, never telling anyone about the time Bob Woodward let him in on the biggest secret in history of American journalism.

In Woodward's company, Pepper also remained silent about the Janet Cooke fiasco, the only stain on Woodward's time at the *Post*. Maybe he should have suspected that her gripping piece about an eight-year-old heroin addict was made up. Then again, reporting anything outside utter truth was and is incomprehensible to Bob Woodward. When the story ran in the fall of 1980, Pepper and other younger reporters whispered about not believing a word of it. Sure enough, when the piece won a Pulitzer, it and much of Janet's resume were exposed as false, a paper's worst nightmare, fogging the *Post* newsroom for months. Funny thing is, Woodward (with Bernstein) kind of planted the seed for Cooke's crime against journalism: In the post-Watergate glow, everyone at the paper hunted for the killer story that would make a career. If you were driven or desperate enough to make up a spectacular story, a child heroin addict might be one of the first ideas to come to mind.

Maybe I could feel out Woodward about getting his support in helping me out of this mess? No. That would be overstepping. There is still at least one line in this world not to be crossed.

Against his better instincts, Pepper checks his emails. Hundreds of new messages appeared, a bunch from loyal friends and colleagues all over the country. He feels grateful for them but freaked that this mess has crisscrossed the nation.

His old buddy, Mike Sager, a hardcore, insanely fearless, investigative reporter (who dated Janet Cooke!), writes from San Diego:

Yo. This is all bullshit. Hang in there. If you need to talk, I'm open all night.

Kornheiser weighs in from a beach town in Delaware:

I'm so old I can't judge the blow back from your joke. Hope you survive it. Cheers, Tony.

From Mary Carillo in New York:

Strange times we're in. Be well.

From former *Post* sports colleague and now best-selling author Jane Leavy in DC:

This is a long way from covering the MLB strike of '81, huh?

Pepper's sports section mentor Len Shapiro (another Wisconsin Badger) from somewhere in Virginia horse country:

Don't worry, kid. This will blow over. Be strong.

A surprising one from Jane's best friend, Paula Godfrey, with whom it's too painful for Pepper to keep in close touch:

Sorry about your travails. Know that I still consider you a great guy. If you're ever in Madison...xo

From fellow *Post* columnist Jerry Brewer:

You need to talk, Arnie, I'm here.

From Pepper's kid brother Jimmy, now in his thirty-third year working as a currency trader in Tokyo:

Your joke was fucking funny!!!! (That said, I'm telling everyone your joke was disgraceful.)

From one of the pioneers of women sportswriters, Jackie MacMullan:

I guess sports is officially part of the real world. Take care.

From Mike Wilbon:

This is junk. You could have made the same joke about any NFL owner. Or the entire NCAA. (Matthew says hello.)

From *LA Times* columnist and old friend Chris Erskine:

You're a sports writing icon...Hang tough.

From Lucy Dalglish, dean of the Philip Merrill School of Journalism at the University of Maryland where Pepper teaches a sports journalism seminar:

Guess journalism, like society, never stops evolving. Thinking of you.

Similar support/comfort/bromides have come in from a slew of print guys and a few other TV people: Tim Kurkjian, Tony Reali, Ernie Johnson, Pablo Torre, and Kenny Mayne, Pepper's pick as the only truly funny anchor in the history of SportsCenter. Amazing how all sportscasters evolved into trying to be so funny all the time. Turn to ESPN and there's so much laughter, you'd think Rodney Dangerfield is giving the scores. The egomania really kicks in when the anchors and play-by-play guys get so many laughs in the studio, they start thinking they're *professionally* funny. Joe Buck went miles over his head to host a comedy show on HBO that satisfyingly fizzled in a few laugh-free weeks.

Pepper gazes at an apartment across the street where a man is vaping on his terrace, farcical billows of white smoke rising up as if a new pope was just chosen in a one-bedroom sublet. Out of thin air, a hairball of anxiety floats in Pepper's mind about the emails he's read. First, he realizes the average age of his well-wishers is well into the Lipitor popping sixties, his younger colleagues savvy enough to inoculate themselves from any whiff of sexual scandal. *Love the old dude but no way I'm dropping by the quarantine.*

More haunting is the realization that the emails written by women were more carefully worded, none of them exonerating him, saying he deserves a break, or offering the slightest hint of seeing any humor in his joke. These are the most liberal-minded, thoughtful, iconoclastic women he's ever met, and they expressed friendship but not support, not really. Maybe no one, especially women in sports, wants to risk diving in this kind of swirl. The idea creeps in that he deserves the criticism he's getting. In conversation and in his column, sly humor has distinguished him. But now, after all these years, Pepper questions if he seriously wandered out of bounds. He's never been the kind of successful person with deep-seated insecurities of one day being exposed as a fraud, and yet, that very thought— *I've been found out*—has found him. A life of making sure no one ever thought of him as a bad journalist has been hijacked by the possibility of being a bad human being. Pepper refuses to buy in. *No, no, no, no, no. That's ridiculous.* But an avenging thought trickles in: It all comes down to Thea. If she's shocked or embarrassed or appalled or disillusioned...

I don't want to think about it.

A new email appears from the unfamiliar address JPM81@ wingnet.com. There's nothing on the subject line. Pepper, suddenly daunted by unsolicited opinions, procrastinates by playing the game of trying to figure out who JPM81 is. He flips through the rolodex in his head for someone with the initials JPM and comes up empty. 81? Is that 1981? Is it someone who's 81 years old? Probably not, since eighty-one-year-olds tend to be handcuffed to AOL. The @wingnet.com probably eliminates anyone currently working a job in media. His eyes drift up the list of other emails and stop at Mary Carillo. He knows her from years of covering tennis and admires how she's become a serious journalist on all sports. When they first met, Pepper grilled her on background for insights into the psyche of his favorite athlete to ever cover, John McEnroe. At Wimbledon, his name on the scoreboard was listed as JP McEnroe. JPM. Who happens to live on 81st Street in New York. And who also happens to go back to childhood with Mary Carillo. Pepper theorizes that Mac and Mary were in contact that day, somehow got on the subject of the Instagram scandal, and agreed that Pepper was a good guy deserving of a kind word from afar. Carillo had his email address and gave it to McEnroe. She wrote her email first because women are punctual and conscientious. McEnroe, in his swirling genius, put off the task until it magically popped back into his head hours later. It all makes such sense that Pepper suddenly can't wait to open the email, thinking he might wind up printing it for the giant box of personal memorabilia he never looks through.

Oddly, the first line of McEnroe's email reads:

After all the years of you're [sic] bullshit, blow-hard-y, fag- breathe [sic] columme [sic], it figures Libtard Femi-Nazis would finally kick youre [sic] ass, you cum drunk, jizz gergling [sic] cocksucker.

At this point, Pepper concludes this email is not from John McEnroe.

Youre [sic] days of sucking up to anthum [sic] kneeling overpaid thuggs [sic] are finito. If the snowflakes don't kill you I'll mite [sic] drive up their [sic] to due [sic (*Jesus!*)] it myself, dick wad. Go SKINS!

Pepper awaits a buffet of panic symptoms, but the day has left him fresh out of adrenaline. He reaches half-consciously for his lemonade and misjudges the location of his mouth. Tart and sweet race down his shirt as he reconsiders his principles against owning a gun. He glances at the signed bat Cal Ripken gave him after retiring, wonders if he locked the dead bolt on his door, then regrets not buying the Georgetown condo with twenty-four-hour doormen. He thinks of calling the police. Then the FBI. Then security at the *Post*. Yes: security at the *Post*. If the cops or feds are needed, let the *Post* call them. As he grabs the landline receiver, his cell burps out its gagged-hostage-sounding ring. He grabs it, fumbles it and catches it in midair.

What concentration!!!

"You okay, Arnie?"

"Huh? Yeah, I just fumbled the phone."

"Sure," says Jillian Corbin. "Phones are slippery. We should all carry pine tar rags to ensure a better grip."

"Yeah, I don't know if going to the pine tar would've helped. I just got a sick, threatening hate email. It's too much to go into now, and I really don't want to read it aloud."

"Is it related to the Instagram situation I heard about on the radio?"

Pepper's not surprised his mess has made the radio but still...*ugh*.

"Yes. It's very related."

"You should call the head of security at the *Post*."

"You think so? Good. I thought the same thing."

"Definitely, that's your best move."

"Funny. From the words 'drive up there,' the guy must be from the South—but he's a Redskins fan."

"In his death threat, he mentioned being a 'Skins fan?"

"Well, just after his death threat."

"Southerners do say 'Football is a religion down here.'"

"Right. As if that's a good thing."

"I guess their god is what's-his-name from Alabama."

"Nick Saban."

"Right. Anyway, look, Arnie, odds are he won't drive up here and kill you. The woodwork is so easy to crawl out of now, but most likely, he's some white trash bigfoot who's never driven his Camaro outside the county he lives in."

"Objectively," Pepper says, "I know that. But this *is* my first death threat. Although one guy threatened to gouge my eyes out, because I suggested that the PGA should allow players one Mulligan per tournament."

"Well, that's some pretty inflammatory shit."

"Yeah. I think I'm freaked out now because white trash scares me more than anyone. Taliban, Crips, Bloods, MS13, you name it. I saw *Deliverance*. I'd rather have walked around Southeast the night after the MLK assassination than mix it up with those meth-mouthed crackers down there."

"I agree. They're probably not big on trans people."

"No, I wouldn't think so."

"So otherwise, how are you holding up?"

"Okay. Things could be a lot worse. Actually, things *are* a lot worse, but whatever. Something else weird happened at the airport. All in all, it's been a day."

"Well, that's why I called. I thought you might want to grab dinner, rather than sit around stewing."

"Um..."

The decision-making part of Pepper's brain is on backorder. Jillian, overly familiar with people in fear for their lives, recognizes this. She's just weeks off prosecuting a case featuring an ex-husband, night-vision goggles, and a bayonet. On the upside, there was no Exhibit C.

"Come on. I have to fill out a bunch of subpoenas and listen to a couple of wiretaps. You call security at the *Post*, then we can meet in an hour at Tokyo Gills."

"Tokyo Gills?"

"The sushi place on Connecticut."

"We haven't been there since you told me you started taking estrogen."

"It's my go-to place to not see and be unseen. Besides, there's something else I want to talk to you about."

"Other than the disaster that's suddenly my life?"

"Yeah. Look, I have to get back to the office."

"Where are you now?"

"At one of the few functioning phone booths left in Montgomery County."

"Really? Wow. This is getting interesting. Are you sure you don't want to meet at a parking garage in Virginia?"

"Garages have shitty food. And by the way, bring me a printed copy of the white trash email."

"Okay. And hey...thanks for calling. Really."

"Call the *Post* Security chief."

Pepper hangs up, starts to dial the *Post*, then stops, sensing that this call shouldn't be ad-libbed. Considering his situation, reporting a terroristic threat could easily come off as a sympathy grab or a half-assed attempt at distraction. He's mildly annoyed that the word distraction so easily comes to mind, the language of sports taking over even his inner monologue. Every time some team has to deal with a behavior problem, reporters ask the coach if it's "a distraction." A veteran shooting guard refuses to take the floor in the last two minutes of a blow-out game; an outfielder flips off a fan from the on-deck circle; a free safety beats the crap out of yet another girlfriend. "Is he a distraction for the team?" Coaches ruefully nod. Yes, he's a bit of a distraction. Pepper always wants to ask, "A distraction from what? From playing football? You mean, when the tailback is fleeing for his life from some grotesquely over-muscled linebacker who runs a 4.2 forty, he's thinking, 'Gee, I wonder what Kevin's girlfriend said to set him off...'" Even more maddening: "Is he a distraction in the locker room?" What exactly is going on in a locker room that requires intense focus? Catching all the lyrics of the crap pounding through the Beats by Dre? Deciding which lunch meat to grab off the post-game spread? Not being too obvious about poring over your own numbers on the stat sheet? For God's sake, the whole point of being a professional athlete is to make bazillions of dollars without having to think. Other than rare, thoughtful, athletic geniuses like Kobe or McEnroe, most athletes are Australian shepherds, herding livestock out of pure instinct. If you don't have to think, nothing distracts you. What's so hard to understand about that?

Pepper loved Kobe for the seemingly bizarre reason that he finds team sports a nightmare to cover. There are actually nothing but I's in TEAM, and at least Kobe was upfront about it. Pepper once asked, "Kobe, if you score 55 on 21 of 30 from the floor and the team loses, why do you have to feel bad?"

Kobe laughed and said, "I don't," then slapped Pepper on the back and said, "Always a pleasure, Pep-man."

Refocusing, he considers how to avoid having his call to the *Post* security chief sound like he's planting mitigating evidence or fishing for sympathy.

After a murmured rehearsal, he calls the *Post* operator. Brenda Williams, a former DC detective with bullet fragments still lodged in her hip, will be gone from her office, but she's among the expanding group of employees required to be reachable at all times. The *Post* operator tells him to hold, and, within seconds, Williams is on the line.

"Mr. Pepper. Are you holding up okay?"

From those seven words, Pepper assumes she knows about his shitstorm.

"I'm fine. Thanks, Brenda," he says, too jauntily. "How are you, Brenda?"

Stop saying "Brenda" like you're her hunky boyfriend.

"I'm wonderful. How can I help you, sir?"

"Well, it's probably nothing, but I got kind of a whacko email full of implied racist stuff, blatant misogyny, and ending with a fairly standard death threat. You know, the whole shebang. Like I said, I'm sure it's nothing, but it's protocol to report stuff like this, so I thought, you know, better safe than sorry."

Despite his closing cliché, Pepper feels like he's hit on the right tone: a veteran reporter who's seen it all but adheres to being a dutiful employee of a great American newspaper.

"Can you read me the email?"

A shiver. He doesn't want to read it again. The email's precise words are lost to him now, comfortably replaced in his head by a more vague, manageable version of the horror.

"Uh, Brenda, actually I could forward it to you. Is that okay? I'm just thinking that if I read it aloud, I'll add some intonation that could be, you know, misleading in some way."

Nice pull!

Brenda chuckles. "Are your acting skills that good?"

Pepper feels like an obfuscating child.

"I'm just kidding. Sure, Mr. Pepper. Just send it along. Although, I enjoy your writing so much, I'd probably find it engrossing to hear your intonations, misleading or otherwise."

"Oh, thanks. But believe me, I'm better on the page."

Pepper cringes. *Believe me.* Trump's verbal tic every time he's about to lie.

"I'll read it and, if need be, investigate the sender."

"Oh, thanks, Brenda. I'm sure it's nothing. Of course, if I'm found hanging over my balcony with twenty bullet holes in me from an AR-15, you'll know I was wrong about that."

Dummy.

Brenda pauses. "You're too funny. Have a nice evening and please call again with any questions or concerns."

How is it a security chief speaks more economically than a sixty-one-year old columnist? It doesn't matter. Pepper can't see Brenda calling Carlyle and saying, "He sounded kind of full of it over the phone."

Dinner is fifty minutes away and killing the time feels impossible. TV news or sports is out of the question, although a few minutes of Fox would be infuriating enough to distract him. After the Ailes-O'Reilly blow-ups, Thea said, "When I had that summer internship at Fox News, nobody hit on me the whole time. I should start a Twitter movement called "#WhatAboutMe?" Pepper smiles at how witty his daughter can be, how her bosses at NPR love her, and then refocuses on killing fifty minutes.

"Fifty Minutes" would be a good name for a sitcom about a therapist. I should call CBS.

A life around sports warps all sense of time. Two-hour baseball games are lightning fast. Two seconds in an NBA game is "plenty of time." Sometimes you look at a game clock, and it seems like it takes a minute for one second to click by. Then the games end, and life returns to the rush of making America great. Run to locker rooms, grope around for a few slightly unscripted quotes, hit the press room, beat up on an innocent laptop with stream-of-consciousness writing, and hope it achieves some cogency before deadline. Although, the whole concept of deadlines has changed. The online edition of the *Post* knows no down time. If, after the final edition closes, Bryce Harper mentions that it might be fun to live in New York, it's back to work. Or not, depending on who you are. Usually, the beat guys deal with that stuff without the luxury of thinking, *It's just sports*, and going home to sleep.

It's different for the incredible *Post* reporters covering Trump's mess. Phil Bump, Roz Helderman, Ashley Parker, Robert Costa, Carol Leonnig, Phil Rucker, Shane Harris. Pepper wonders how they do it, filing multiple stories a day while conducting months-long investigations, while appearing on MSNBC, while tweeting, while staying up all night reading the big dope's tweets. They are REPORTERS, and Pepper's proud to work in the same building. His love for newspapers has only grown during the White House assaults on "the failing *New York Times*" and "the Amazon *Post*." He finds it possible that Jeff Bezos is a total douche but buying the *Post* and building a new headquarters forgives all sins of the Amazon mogul. Pepper misses the old newsroom on 15th Street, but knows the new, super hi-tech newsroom is critical to the paper's future. The survival of the *Post* means everything to Pepper. It sickens him that words like "fuck" and "pussy" found find their way into print, no less the front page, but journalism is still a holy profession. He admires and envies today's young reporters, especially war correspondents, living in hell holes, interviewing crazed soldiers, sleepless, dressed in tragedy-casual clothes, having desperate love affairs with other correspondents who might be blown up by an IED the next morning. He sometimes wishes he'd shaken the playpen of sports and done hard news. He still dreams of becoming the oldest wunderkind in the history of foreign correspondence but knows why he does what he does and why they do what they do. We're cut out for what we're cut out for. All in all, he thinks, in my default arena, I've done damn good work.

Funny how Trump reporters are more stylish and fit since they began popping up on TV so much. When chatting up

Helderman or Costa in the rare moments they come up for air, Pepper feels like the jocular senior vice president of the Baby Boom, jabbing them about their telegenic advancements.

"Have you determined what your good side is?"

"What's your philosophy on bronzer?"

They laugh and get back to work. Pepper imagines them back at their desks thinking, "It's good to have sportswriters around. They lighten the mood in the newsroom."

When Pepper regularly appeared on ESPN, a make-up woman suggested Preparation H to reduce eye puffiness. *How do they come up with these remedies?* Still, he'd have let his face be airbrushed with a blowtorch just to sit beside Jim Murray or Bob Lipsyte, sportswriting legends who made him feel like he could contribute to society.

Most sportswriters now ask such stupid questions, Pepper can understand why the athletes give pat answers. Or mocking answers. Or no answers, like Kobe often did with his legendary death stare. Half the time, sportswriters don't even ask questions anymore, instead reciting stats and bogus hearsay, then waiting for comment: After your three fumbles, some say the team should disembowel you and trade your harvested organs for a draft pick?

Or they do ask a question so unanswerable: Do you feel your missed free throws led to the burning down of Rupp Arena?

It's amazing there are no mass shootings in press rooms.

Pepper developed a practice of asking outrageous questions of athletes when first meeting them, his way of standing out. Best example: NBA draft night, 2009, when he asked Blake Griffin: "Your father is black, and your mother is white. Did you ever worry that the white half of you would hurt your chances of having an NBA career?"

Griffin, a comedy savant, deadpanned: "I used to cry myself to sleep, asking, 'Why? Why do I have to be half-white? Why can't I just be guaranteed to play in the NBA?'"

Ten seasons later, Griffin and Pepper talk all the time.

TV interviewers are not only inept, they're easily intimidated— most notably by Popovich, of whom they repeatedly ask the kind of vapid, in-game questions that made them terrified of him in the first place.

Strange how ESPN looks down on sportswriters and yet, the hosts and guests on every other show they air are veteran sportswriters. Kornheiser, Wilbon, Ryan, MacMullan, me. Stranger yet, who told Tom Shales he should do an oral history book on ESPN similar to the one he wrote about Saturday Night Live? *Arnie Pepper, ladies and gentlemen. When I heard the book would be titled* Those Guys Have All The Fun, *I gagged at how it confirmed ESPN's self-delusions but hell, it was a great read and Shales, the all-time greatest TV critic, treated me to an exorbitant dinner at Marcel's.*

Remember back in 2010? That panel on sports journalism with Shales and Sally Jenkins at the Newseum when I proposed a women's news channel called PMS-NBC. Big laughs. Were some attendees offended, their affront drowned out by loud men? Don't recall Sally laughing. I make that joke now, I wind up at a Taco Bell with Mario Batali.

The aroma of a neighbor barbecuing on a terrace reminds Pepper of the last distinct odor of his day, "estrogen spray." Instead of wondering if he's contracted a new form of artisanal carcinoma, he decides to shower. It's an activity, a time-killer.

He washes his timid, graying hair with strawberry Suave shampoo, another sense memory of his college days. Among the million shampoos selling at champagne prices, Suave is dirt cheap. His $172,000 a year is unexceptional in a time when money is so twisted, but it's a lot to him, wealth having never been part of his plans. He misses the days when had to watch his pennies, his nostalgic yearning bottomless. What's the deal with that? It's not like life has sucked since Madison. Other than one catastrophic personal crisis, it's been pretty great. No reason to be like most Americans, pining for the past despite knowing the old days were as unruly as the frenzied now. Facebook has its Throwback Thursday, as if one day's backward glance is different than any other, people posting old photos as proof they used to be whatever they're not today. What's the—

Stop using the expression, 'What's the deal with that?'

The second he's out of the shower, the phone rings. He groans, then thinks it could be Thea and sloshes to the phone.

"Arnie, it's Bruce Bader Ginsburg!"

Jesus.

"Just calling to make sure you found my little sign on the back of your sport jacket."

"How—"

"How about the smell from the estrogen mist?"

"How did you get my number?"

"Come on, Arnie. There's no hiding behind an unlisted number anymore. Time to ditch the landline, dude."

"Look *Bruce*, I don't know who the fuck you are, but one day you're going grow up and regret the hell out of whatever you're up to now, because it will have ruined your life."

"If it casts me in a better light," Bruce says mildly, "I argued against adding the sterilization powder. Seeing as you're sixty-one and have a daughter, it seemed like overkill. But the other guys wouldn't hear of it."

"*Other* guys? My *daughter*?"

Pepper feels guilty about the order in which his questions came out.

"Listen, asshole—"

"I'm not an asshole, Arnie. We've been through this."

"Okay, then how about this? I may not look like Liam Neeson, but if you go near my daughter—"

"Oh, no, no, no. We wouldn't dream of it. She's a woman. Our mission is to defend all women against misogynist predators like, say, you."

"Predators? I made a bad joke. I didn't *prey* on anyone."

"Misogynistic jokes are gateway signs to predation."

"Jesus. Did you recite that straight from the Yale Undergraduate Guide to Safe Spaces?"

"Don't try getting me to reveal where I go to college, Arnie. Besides, bad-ass RMFs are at colleges nationwide."

"RNFs...?"

"Not N. M. RMFs. Radical. Masculine. Feminists. Wow, Arnie. For a newspaper man, you're seriously ill-informed."

Pepper wants to break the kid's collar bone. *Is there an app for that?* "Look, I don't care where you go to college or if attacking me at an airport was part of a summer internship. I care about how wrong you are. Do you ever read my column?"

"Sure. Long-time reader, first-time caller."

Pepper looks out the window to see if the world is still there.

"Actually, I'm a big Serena fan and always read stuff you write about her. Although, truth? Usually I bail after reading a few graphs because my mind wanders. I'm a little spectrum-y, so don't take it personally."

"How should I take it?" Pepper says, "As a group?"

"Ha! Another good one. Such a witty guy. Again, off the record."

"No, actually it's on the record."

For this, the kid has no snap answer. "Pardon?"

"If you want something off the record, you say so before your statement, not after. Everything you've said to me, at the airport and on this call, is on the record. I can write a column about our encounter—and this call—relating everything you've said and done along with a full description of you."

"But, but you never identified yourself as a reporter."

Pepper's laugh is purposefully taunting. "*You* identified me as a reporter. Jesus, you know, if you were a little smarter, you would realize just how dumb you are. In fact, the French have a saying that's perfect for you. *'Il ne faut pas péter de plus haute de son cul.'*"

Another useful bit of French favored by Jane. He pauses to give the moment weight, then: "Loosely translated, it means, 'You shouldn't fart above your asshole.'"

"I don't get it."

"Of course not. Maybe if you just sit down, take your Adderall or Ritalin or whatever else can't make a dent in your damage, you'll figure it out."

A hollow moment passes, then: "Fuck you, Arnie!"

"Really, Justice Ginsburg? Fuck you, Arnie? That's your best comeback?"

"No, you'll get my best next time I see you. And it won't be estrogen mist. It'll be Novichok. How do you like that?"

Click.

Pepper, feeling both satisfaction and dread, reviews notes he made during the conversation with Bruce Bader Ginsburg.

"...off the record." "...identify yourself as a reporter." "I bail after a few *graphs*."

Maybe the kid's a journalism major. Then again, maybe he saw the *Post* or *Spotlight* and picked up some jargon. Pepper has no theory for the Novichok reference. Odd the kid would know of a Russian nerve agent that made sparse dents in the news cycles. College students with the standard 25,000 apps on their phones rarely keep up with any current events, much less international news. A weasel like "Bruce?" *Half his life's probably taken up with Tinder alone. Lazy pieces of shit, these kids, can't even put in the work to seduce a girl. Let the goddamn phone say sweet nothings to her, let the camera give her meaningful gazes, let the Cloud hold her hand, let Pandora figure out how the hell to unhook her bra and rip open the condom he doesn't want to use but has to because we demented Baby Boomers created our own unbearable STD. Let tech do all the prep work. Then call in Bruce from the bullpen to prematurely close the deal. Jesus, human contact is on the road to Chapter 11 and we're all buying in. Thank God I'm not young.*

That time in 2011 I scored a ticket to the White House Correspondents' Dinner. Thea was in Arizona with her grandmother. An AP reporter (what was her name?) gravitated to me because she found political reporters "crushingly dull." We got a little loaded. She asked if I can help get her a job at the Post. *I nodded and said, "I can't guarantee anything, but, you know..." A half-hour later, upstairs at The Washington Hilton, she took off her bra and groggily said, "My grandmother fucked Omar Bradley at the Hay-Adams." I said, "Wow, that was before pussy was even popular." She laughed, a little, we closed the deal, then I immediately said I had to go because I have a daughter at home. She said, "You told me she was with her grandmother in Arizona." Remarkably guilt-free: "Did I? Oh." I bolted anyway and didn't return her calls. Before that night, I hadn't had sex in three years. Not the highlight of the memoir I'll never write, but still: Has the concept of "consenting adults" lost all its power of acquittal?*

Pepper gazes out the window at the cranes now blending into the dusk, their blinking red lights all that's saving some traffic helicopter from mid-air disaster. For years, he's been seeing signs hinting at the end of the world. Now, as Director of National Intelligence Dan Coats recently said, the signs are flashing red. Pepper comes up with an idea for a new international competition: The End-Of-The-World Cup.

After jotting it down in his notebook, he thinks of a day earlier in the summer. Pepper had been fairly up front in his lack of interest in The World Cup, yawning at the TVs in Chatter, the sports bar owned by his old friend Tony Kornheiser with Maury Povich. It's not that Pepper doubted soccer's beauty, strategies, or athleticism. He just lacked the head space for getting into a sport in which the hand is a vestigial organ. For decades, he promised to bone up on soccer the day it delivered on its eternal promise to take over America. The national interest in World Cup 2018 was closer to palpable than ever before, but for Pepper, not close enough. Still, one Saturday morning in June, he flipped around and came across a game between [some country] and Sweden. The "match" itself didn't captivate him, and, apparently, the same held true for the director of the FOX Sports telecast. In seemingly every break in the action, no matter how brief, there was a cut to another heart-stoppingly beautiful Swedish girl in the crowd. A ball would dribble out of bounds (is that the term?) and during the eight steps it took for a winger (?) to reach it, the screen filled with another drop-dead specimen of blonde perfection. It felt like Fox assigned maybe three camera operators to follow the actual game and twenty-five others to case out Swedish hair flowing into golden cleavage. You'd think Roger Ailes's horny corpse was calling the shots from a coffin squawk box he had installed with his $40 million payout. Admittedly, Pepper found himself rooting for breaks in the (soccer) action, but at the same time, he was appalled by the blatancy of it all. He thought of knocking out a column about it, a rip job on Fox Sports and its thinly disguised telecast of "Soccer Girls Gone Wild." He realizes now it would have been, by definition, a pro-feminist column, one that could have bolstered his non-sexist credentials. He regrets having chosen instead to write a column about how Bill Belichick is Mitch McConnell with three fewer chins.

Pepper changes out of all the clothes he'd worn during this monstrous, crummy day. In safe L.L.Bean attire, he allows himself an assessment of looking good at his advanced age. His face has no deep creases, his jawline still sharp. A pre-cancerous growth removed from his nose left barely a scar. *I should start a support group for Survivors of Totally Curable Cancers.* At five-ten-ish, 175-ish, he has no—or no discernable—pot belly, despite spending much of his life surrounded by free food. Sometimes, when he's with a group of sportswriters, he worries about the structural engineering of the press box.

He should go to the gym in the morning but knows he won't. It pays to know yourself. It might also pay to surprise yourself on occasion, but that ship sailed in the '90s. To be exact, it was '96, the year so much in his life capsized, the year he took his only leave of absence from the *Post*, a month-long bereavement sabbatical timed specifically to miss the Atlanta Olympics. Looking back, he thinks he could've written some good pieces about Richard Jewell, the rent-a-cop who found the bomb in Olympic Park and should have been a hero but wound up a suspect, his life ransacked first by the FBI, then canceled by diabetes, eleven years later.

On the other hand, maybe Pepper couldn't have written good pieces about Jewell or anything else during that black-clouded time. He made the right move taking Thea on a trip to Cambodia and Vietnam. Exotic and far away were the only preferences he asked of a random travel agent in a storefront on K Street. "This is the best vacation of my life!" three-year-old Thea said during their second day in Saigon. Years later, while studying the Vietnam War, she was reprimanded by her teacher for a joke she made in class: "I went on a vacation to Vietnam with my dad, and I don't know what all those Vietnam veterans were whining about. I had a great time!" Pepper thought it was in the top eight most hysterical, albeit dark, jokes he'd ever heard and stopped by the school to reprimand the teacher for inhibiting his daughter's sense of humor.

It was another joke her mother would have loved. Jane's Santa Monica surfer girl youth immunized her to shock. In college, where her long-legged, dark-eyed, streaked hair-LA-ness clashed with all things Wisconsin, she found everything funny. Once, she told Pepper about her swimming scholarship and her endless hours in the Olympic-size pool. Pepper said he could only swim laps in a Special Olympics-size pool, a line Jane repeated to everyone, including her coach, who sternly told her he had a Down syndrome child. Jane was still telling that story in the mental clinic.

If I made that Special Olympics joke now, I'd be taken to a black ops site for enhanced interrogation.

As he leaves his bedroom, a sheet of paper flies under his door, settling into the edge of a foyer throw rug. As he steps toward it his landline rings. The besieged feeling of this whole day re-fills his veins as he reverses field into his bedroom and grabs the phone.

"You pissed me off, and I'm going to fuck you up, Arnie.

We'll see who's farting above his asshole."

Click.

He flashes to the Russian Novichok attack on that guy and his daughter in England. Unsure he'd survive like they did, he imagines federal agents in Ray Bans saying, "Whatever you do every day, Mr. Pepper, stop doing it." Bye to the Starbucks baristas always telling him to "have a good one," and to the guys he shoots baskets with at Northwest Sport & Health. Bye to his route to work that's so automatic he arrives not remembering a second of the drive. Maybe even bye to this part of town. Or this city altogether.

Pepper nixes the idea of calling back Brenda at *Post* security and recounting the airport episode and how it's mushroomed into him being a target for a Russian nerve agent, again fearing it may come off as a sympathy grab. On the other hand, there's been talk at the *Post* of hiring bodyguards to protect reporters covering Trump's psychotic rallies.

A month or so ago, he was chatting with Eugene Robinson, who'd just written (another) brilliant column about Trump's "base." Pepper casually said, "It's like Trump's full-time job is being the keynote speaker at Idiot Conventions." When Robinson burst out laughing, Pepper said, "Feel free to use that line in a column." Robinson said, "I'd love to use that line in a column, but I'd also love to continue walking in public without having to wear a flak jacket."

Soon, Pepper thinks, reporter's notebooks are going to come with health warnings, like a pack of Marlboro Lights. As it is, the *Post* was more fun when it was filled with cigarette smoke. Why are people so hell-bent on living forever?

He remembers the sheet that slid under his door and reluctantly goes for it.

Dear Neighbors,

Herb and I are happy to tell you that he is successfully recovering from heart surgery. His mitral valve was repaired, and the maze procedure was performed to eliminate the atrial fibrillation which the mitral valve prolapse had caused in the atrial chamber.

Lillian Drexler

Pepper puts the paper on the kitchen counter next to the Do Not Resuscitate Form. *Who are Herb and Lillian Drexler?*

His interactions with neighbors are rare and perfunctory. He's oddly comfortable being in the elevator with them and not acknowledging their existence, like he's living in New York without all its grinding hassles. One divorcee roughly his age lives three doors down and shares his un-neighborly attitude. Occasionally, against their wills, they find themselves amid some tenant dispute and conspiratorially exchange eye-rolls. Thea bugged him to ask the woman out, but he said, "What if the date goes badly? For as long as we both live here, I'll have to avoid her, creeping around the halls like a cat burglar."

"Daddy," Thea had said, "people have evolved to the point of being able to be civil after a bad date."

"Thea, I don't even know her name."

"Ask her. Maybe you can just be friends. You could use some women friends."

"My best friend is a woman."

"Who was born a man. You know I love Jillian to death, but her brain didn't undergo a transgender procedure."

"Actually, I bet Jillian has put more thought into what it is to be a woman than anyone you know."

After the killer laugh she inherited from her mother, Thea conceded, "That's a good point. Nevertheless, strike up a convo with the woman in your building."

Convo. Soon we'll ban all words over two syllables.

The thought of not having heard from Thea since her text eats at him all over again. *What is going on?* He always avoids calling her at work, wanting her NPR colleagues to view her as an adult. Amazing, he thinks. Even self-serious, more-enlightened-than-thou NPR had its sexual harassment scandal. In all shapes and sizes, white men are the biggest problem in America. That famous eighty-four-year-old architect, the opera director, the attorney general in New York, even the girl-empowering guy who made up Buffy—overruled by their own base impulses. Thea's bosses seem decent, giving her more and more responsibility, like in October, when they sent her to Puerto Rico to help with Hurricane Maria coverage. The assignment came through so fast, she begged Pepper to take in Cronkite, her lab-cattle dog mix, for a week. Naturally, that was the one time a mouse broke in through a hole under the kitchen sink. At three in the morning, Cronkite barked like he'd found his mission on Earth.

The next morning an elderly man knocked on Pepper's door. "Your dog woke me up last night."

Sleepless himself, Pepper said, "Well, if the dog ever wakes you up again, you know what you should do? Go back to sleep."

The zinger staggered the old man, his face looking like a collapsed lung. Then a voice from down the hall screeched, "Herb, you idiot! What the hell are you doing out there?"

Ten months later, Pepper regrets the moment, wondering why he couldn't just be nice, apologize, and give his assurance that the dog was only visiting. "See, there was a mouse and..."

Now he realizes the old man was Herb Drexler, the very Herb Drexler lying in an ICU, wired and intubated and blissfully unaware of the detail into which his wife delved in order to inform the prick with the dog of all that happened in some DC operating room.

Pepper has side-by-side parking spots in the condo's underground garage, a perk of owning a three-bedroom unit. He alternates between the two spots so neither is spotlessly clean, no need to rub his tiny privilege in neighbors' faces. He drives out in his 2013 Subaru Forester and circles in front of the building to check if the puny media contingent assigned to him is still out there. He wishes he still had his Prius, purely for its noiselessness. He'd read that gangs prefer the Prius in drive-by shootings for that very reason. Bet those painstaking Toyota engineers never saw that coming. Tough shit, Tokyo. Welcome to the world of unintended consequences.

If you're convicted of murdering someone who drives a Prius, do you get both the gas chamber and the electric chair?

He writes down "Prius—gas chamber" on his notepad, sees the press pool is gone and pulls onto Wisconsin before taking side roads connecting to Calvert Street. The drive is a breeze in a town that's become a traffic nightmare. Last year on a major Jewish holiday, Pepper drove all over town interviewing people about national anthem kneelers. The traffic flow was so smooth, he called Mayor Bowser—who always takes his calls —and suggested a new law in which one ethnic group per day was banned from driving. She laughed and said, "I'll get right on it, Arnie."

As he's driving, he remembers a *Post* Christmas party in 1986, when that woman who covered city hall noted that the wine bottle she was cradling looked "kinda like a penis." *I laughed and asked her, "What wine goes best with pussy?" She blushed in embarrassment. Or horror? Whatever. (Probably) unrelated, she left the paper a few months later. Doubt she still knows anyone at the* Post *to report me to. But as Jillian said, the woodwork is so easy to crawl out of. It's possible I get too much of a kick out of the word "pussy."*

He finds a parking spot on Connecticut two blocks from the restaurant. He exits the air-conditioned car and the humidity smacks him again. A line comes to mind: "The air is dead as yesterday." He opts against jotting it down, suspecting he'd heard someone else say it, maybe Richard Pryor or Stephen King? Anytime, especially now, is no time to start plagiarizing, a much more fireable offense than what he's facing today.

Damn. Fireable.

He considers the prospect of losing the joy he's always felt when someone asks, "What do you do for a living?" Nine-ty-eight percent of Americans dread that question. He rarely reveals his job unprompted, but by throwing out words like *interview* and *deadline*, he's a black belt at begging the question. The question now chilling him: "If I can't say, 'I write for *The Washington Post*,' what am I?"

I don't want to think about it.

He walks, trying to identify one store still existing from even ten years ago. Too much change, he thinks. *Give me one year with no births, no deaths, no scientific advances. Just a year to let me breathe. These kids with their new inventions, new economics, new rules, coming and going at sickening speeds, as if the past was so primitive, so inconvenient, so conscience-free. We Boomers thought the same thing, and we were wrong about everything. These kids don't want to learn anything from us. And speaking of kids: Jesus Christ, why hasn't Thea called?*

Tokyo Gills immediately reneges on its promise of being a place to not see anyone you know. As Pepper arrives, two men walk out, one an unidentifiable, somewhat more robust version of Stephen Hawking, the other tan and instantly identifiable as Les Moonves, the chairman of CBS and a big presence at major sports events. Pepper has interviewed him several times about the future of sports television, most notably the exorbitant fees networks shell out for broadcast rights.

The Hawking guy says, "Thanks for your time, Les,"

Moonves says "My pleasure, Phil."

Phil turns, looks at Pepper for a long second, and walks off.

Pepper, a smidge too jocularly, says, "Mr. Moonves, what's a media mogul like you doing in a place like this on a day he can be golfing in Ireland?"

Moonves rolls his eyes. "Board meeting in New York this morning, dinner with a tedious FCC lawyer tonight. It never ends, Arnie."

Pepper is moderately surprised Moonves remembers his name. He can take it as (a) a compliment, (b) a long-cultivated bit of executive charm, or (c) a sign this zillionaire has heard about HysterectomyGate.

Pepper nods and says, "'It never ends' is becoming the theme song of our lives."

"That's for sure," Moonves says with an exhale.

"That CBS-Viacom war you got going sounds pretty nasty."

Off no response, Pepper senses he's hit a no-fly zone and flips the subject: "I guess we all have our wars."

Moonves quietly says, "Mm, I heard you're in a bit of a jam."

Pepper shakes his head. "Unbelievable, huh?"

"Not really. It's a sick country. Sometimes..."

Moonves looks up to the night sky.

"Not to be a journalist—but, 'sometimes' what?"

"Sometimes I don't know why I don't move to Australia."

"Well, New Zealand's been good for Matt Lauer."

From the way Moonves stiffens, Pepper guesses Lauer might be a friend of Les' and quickly backtracks.

"The times I met Matt, he seemed like a good guy. And really smart..."

Moonves shuffles and says, "I don't know him that well."

"Why would you? He worked for an inferior network."

Moonves' light chuckle emboldens Pepper to muse further. "Can't blame Lauer for fleeing to another hemisphere after what came out about him. Guy's a major network star, married to a model, but still needs to lock women in his office and bang them over his desk? I mean, Les, what makes a guy act like that? Especially with women who work for him."

Pepper fails to notice the CBS chairman's face emptying of all human experience, and just continues.

"Same with Charlie Rose trying to seduce employees by flashing his Johnson while showing videos of his old interviews. Creepy. And O'Reilly—"

A motorcycle zooms by. Pepper waits for it to pass. "At least those guys are celebrities. You can almost see how they get so warped. But these horny executives like Ailes and Weinstein?

Old guys hitting on young women who find them totally repulsive?

"Yeah, look Arnie—"

"I mean, not to throw around bogus feminism, but we are a pretty fucked up gender, you know, Les?"

A vibe sends Pepper back-peddling again. "Hell, what am I asking you for? Julie's such a great girl." Pepper has never met Moonves' wife. He's only sixty-percent sure her name is Julie.

Moonves says, "You know, it doesn't matter anymore, even if you do have a paddle on shit's creek."

It sounds like a line Moonves co-opted from one of his sitcoms. Pepper fakes a laugh and says, "Can I steal that line?"

"It's yours, buddy," he says, starting to walk. "Hope things work out okay for you."

"Yeah, thanks. Whatever 'okay' means."

Moonves stops: "It means keeping your job."

Pepper's response feels involuntary.

"Actually no, Les. It's not enough to just keep my job. I want my name back, the good name I had yesterday. In fact, what I really want is to go back in time *one day*. Most guys my age would want to go back forty years to when they were thin and full of false hope. All I want to buy back is twenty-four hours. To be the same poached white guy I am today with the same reputation I had yesterday. Same Arnie, different day."

Moonves buttons and unbuttons his sport jacket.

Pepper slumps. "Sad thing is, right now, I barely remember yesterday's me."

Tokyo Gills is narrow and clean, tables lining a brick wall opposite a sleek sushi bar. A petite hostess leads him to the second table from the end. Of all the diners, only a slim, red-haired, forty-five-ish woman reading *Harper's* glances up at Pepper, then does a double take. There's no escaping the see-and-be-seen of this tiny, tiny town.

The last table is occupied by a couple, possibly grad students.

The guy is reading *The Best and the Brightest* by Halberstam, the woman *Anti-Intellectualism in American Life* by Hofstadter. The table on the other side of Pepper's is empty. He debates which chair to take, facing in or out, then wonders how many decisions a human brain can make before crashing like the old Raytheon system that, in 1980, ushered the *Post* into the computer age. He opts for the aisle seat, based on a vague recollection of a column by Miss Manners about how the woman should always face out in a restaurant.

Jillian enters and walks to the back like Michael Corleone, not looking at anyone but not looking away. She's in gray yoga pants, a lavender long-sleeve top, and three strings of turquoise beads around her neck that accentuated the blue eyes that once attracted so many Wisconsin girls when Jillian was Jerry. It was a running joke how girls befriended Arnie as a way to get closer to Jerry. Against strict Tri Delt rules, Jane told him that her sorority sisters voted Jerry "most wanted campus penis." Back then, Jane's leaking to Pepper of the sacred sorority vote made him think he might have a shot with her, until his investigative reporting revealed that she only dated jocks: a backup Badger quarterback, a six-five Badger swingman, a Badger pole vaulter.

Pepper made it to the quarterfinals of the intramural one-on-one tournament.

He had loose, off-hand/hands-off ties to Jane for all four years, then never saw her again until a life-exploding chance meeting on Massachusetts Avenue a decade later.

"Nice beads."

Jillian smiles. "Thanks. I overpaid for them in Florence last month and then kept forgetting to wear them. Off your compliment, now I'm going to wear them constantly."

"I feel that way about my boxers from The Gap."

After ignoring a beeping text, Jillian says, "So Arnie, what were you talking to Les Moonves about?"

"Huh?"

"I saw you talking to him, so I told my Uber driver to circle around the block."

"We just talked about my shit storm. Why?"

"He's the head of a network and I have to tell you something I don't want coming back to me."

"What?"

She glances at the grad students at the next table. "I'll tell you later. Speaking of your shit storm, you told me something happened at National."

Pepper recounts the estrogen episode for Jillian, who nods. "We've heard about these kids. It's a loosely strung together 'movement.' Hell, everything's a movement now. Anyway, there have been over 200 attacks nationwide, by college guys calling themselves Radical Masculine Feminists."

"Yeah. He mentioned the RMFs."

"They didn't really think the acronym part through. Besides, it's not like Al Qaeda with a central command and organized sleeper cells."

"I wonder how you become a member of Al Qaeda. Do they have rush parties?"

"Good question. As for RMFs, my theory is that they're just kids who want to get laid."

"Isn't that why any guy claims to be a feminist?"

"Yes, but you didn't hear that from me. And don't worry about the estrogen mist. The FBI determined it to be water, vinegar and something to make it smell bad. I forgot the name of it because, well, I'm old and can't remember anything. Last week in court, I couldn't come up with the word 'injunction.'"

"Do you have to say 'injunction' a lot?"

"No, but it's nice to know your terminology."

We're all aging at a breakneck pace, Pepper thinks, but that's a calamity for another time. "So RMFs assumed that estrogen smells bad. Kind of a latent misogyny, isn't it?"

"No, it's overt misogyny. Actually, some RMFs have upped their game. In Grosse Pointe, a preschool mogul accused of harassing a female employee got doused with pig blood. I saw photos. Guy looked like a Brooks Brothers version of *Carrie*. Eventually, they'll spray acid and blind some horny prick, and their 'movement' will get shut down."

As a waiter takes their orders, Pepper feels eyes on him and glances at the woman who'd recognized him earlier. She turns away. Pepper says, "Did you check out my hate email from the homicidal Redskins fan?"

Jillian drops her shoulders.

"That bad?"

"Well, I only got as far as tracking down the sender and reading up on one piece of his past before getting a call from the Governor's office."

"And..."

"Well, in high school, after being thrown off the varsity football team, he abducted the offensive line coach, tied him up in a basement, and waterboarded him with Gatorade."

If there's a human reaction to this, Pepper has no access. Jillian answers Pepper's silence, saying, "I know."

"Okay," Pepper says. "That was high school. Everyone's a little nutty in high school."

"Imagine the odds of you, a cosmopolitan writer for the *Washington Post*, ever having contact with a person who performs in-home waterboarding."

Pepper puts his elbows on the table and says, "So Jillian, you think I'm in trouble? My job?"

"Tough call. You made a joke in a time where humor is malignant. The fact that it was funny is beside the point. I mean, the guy *is* the softest player in the NBA. He's six-eleven and pulls like, two rebounds a month. Shaq said the guy's allergic to paint. Anyway, I guess the tough part of your joke was your use of the word 'hysterectomy.'"

"Funny thing is, I almost said endometriosis, but I didn't think guys would know what it is, and it would hurt the joke."

"You were right. Hysterectomy is much funnier than endometriosis."

"But I guess the funniness of the joke is irrelevant."

"Actually, no. Look at Roseanne. Her joke was tasteless, but just as damaging was the fact that it *wasn't* funny."

"You should represent me. 'Your Honor, you can't deny the joke was funny.'"

"That would be great. We could both lose our jobs."

"Lose our jobs" zings through Pepper's nervous system.

"Amazing. I've done forty years of conscientious reporting on women in sports. The only way I could be more empathetic to women is to go on the pill."

Jillian spit-takes a spray of sake. "Don't use that line as part of your defense."

Pepper shrugs but has a rebellious thought of making the same joke to his editor tomorrow, just doubling down on his fraudulent misogyny as a reverse-psychological way of showing how absurd this all is.

Doubling down. A term used constantly on MSNBC. When did everyone start playing blackjack?

Jillian starts to say something, but Pepper stops her. "One second." He writes down in his notebook: *College student who's a reverse psychology major.*

"Good to see you're still jotting down your little notes."

"May as well stay optimistic. Hey: You got a little blotch of sake on your..." Not knowing whether to say "blouse" or "shirt" or "top," Pepper just points.

Jillian rolls her eyes, stands up and sidles between tables. "I need to use the bathroom anyway."

Pepper turns and catches the redhead staring at him again. She quickly looks away, and Pepper wades into a dark thought that maybe she saw the Instagram post. *Is this the way it's going to be? Because of one joke, there will be women all over the place who look at me like I'm OJ? That I'm the guy who should be in prison asking Cosby, "So, what was Lisa Bonet like?" And the thing is, even if they're not seeing me that way, I'll think they are. Can it be that, for the rest of my* life, I'll never catch a woman looking at me and be able to delude myself into thinking she finds me attractive? *Oh wow, she's checking me out!* Has that eternally sweet thought flown out of my head for good? And I'm sitting here obsessing over keeping my job. What a joke. Job or no job, the stench is attached. There's some psycho-sociological term I heard on NPR for this...Oh yeah: The Affective Wake. Like I need specific terminology for why there's yellow police tape around my life. Holy cow! My lawyer, my dentist, my insurance rep, even my tech guy: they're all women! Will they drop me as a client/patient? Does Charlie Rose even see his dentist anymore? Maybe now he just says, "Screw my teeth. They're not worth it." Charlie Rose. Really now, as if I should ever be mentioned in the same sentence as him for any reason other than having twice been a guest on his show. As if, unlike him, the blowback from my little joke should inevitably wind up in the first paragraph of my obituary. Not that I give a shit about my obituary. This whole thing about a personal legacy is so moronic. Sports people always cite Willie Mays as having "tarnished his legacy" by playing one season for the Mets, as if anyone hears the name Willie Mays and thinks "retired too late." It's totally—

Hey, speaking of retiring on top. My piece about female athletes taking time off for motherhood? I interviewed Annika Sorenstam and, two years later, she credited me with helping her feel it was okay to have a kid and retire while still being capable of winning on the Tour.

Anyway, look at LeBron. Dopes talk about his record in the NBA finals as "tarnishing his legacy." He got to the finals eight times in a row. Five with horseshit teams. And that's aside from his true legacy, which has a lot more to do with Trayvon Martin than how many triple doubles he—

And by the way, my contribution to Annika's maternity retirement paved the way for Lorena Ochoa to choose motherhood over being number one in the world.

If having a great legacy meant you were magically returned to being twenty-two years old, that would be something. But Mandela, Gandhi, Einstein, Linus Pauling, Mr. Rogers...all dead. Same for Babe Ruth, Ali, Curt Flood and thousands of other sports immortals. And even the athletes still breathing...it's so tedious hearing arguments about who should *and shouldn't be "enshrined" in The Hall of Fame. Five years after you retire, you're so desperate for attention that you pray for the chance to make some mawkish speech about your past in front of a bust that, if you're lucky, is vaguely identifiable as you? Believe me, Rodin isn't sculpting those things. You also get a blazer, less ugly than the green one they give you for winning the Masters but still unwearable in public. And it's not for nothing they stuck all these Halls of Fame in dipshit cities. Even sadder, after you're enshrined, the debates about your legacy pick right up again. Wait, what was I...? Oh, my obit and how I'm stuck with the stain of one joke forever. This is what happens in a society that takes 240 years to notice social sicknesses, then launches the indictments without a thought of grading them on a curve. You're infected, period. Live with Krazy-Glued-on aftermath.*

Did I not recently write that hiring Kara Lawson as TV analyst was "the only smart move the Wizards have made since drafting Earl Monroe?" Yes. I did. That was me.

Pepper cops another glance at the woman. She looks away again. Jillian returns and, right on cue, says, "Who's the woman who keeps looking at you?"

"You saw that too, huh?"

Jillian shrugs. "It's what I do."

"No idea, but she recognized me when I came in."

"Probably some typically demented Skins fan who reads your column. I mean, come on, you're famous."

"Unfortunately, more famous than I was yesterday."

Jillian looks at the grad students at the next table, now under headphones while reading. She notes the guy's finger tapping lightly in rhythm and deems it safe to talk.

"Arnie?" she says, leaning in. "I have something that may help you out at the *Post*. Then again, it may not..."

"What is it?"

"A scoop. A story that may make your editors a little less, you know, vaginally focused."

"You got a sports scoop at the prosecutor's office?"

"It's not sports."

"Oh."

"I heard from an immaculately reliable source that there was a lunch for summer interns at the White House today. In attendance was a horde of Ivy League Young Republicans *and* several very senior administration officials."

"Little outside my purview, but go on."

"So, a conversation starts up at the lunch about use of the term Radical Islamic Terrorism."

"The term Mattis told Trump to not say."

"Exactly! See? This story is right in your purview."

"Hey, I write for the goddamn *Washington Post*."

"There you go. So anyway, some kid who got a Trump Administration internship despite having a heart, stands up and criticizes a fellow intern for depicting all Muslims as terrorists and actually says Islam is a beautiful religion."

"Uh-huh..."

Jillian pauses for effect then says, "At which point, a senior administration official says to the kid: 'You're right. Islam is a beautiful religion and it's not fair to let 75 million bad apples spoil the whole bunch.'"

Pepper wants to laugh but says, "Holy shit."

"Yeah."

"I'm guessing your source didn't give you a name of the senior official."

"No."

"I should call Phil Rucker."

"Yes, you should. But not first."

Jillian slides a card with a name and phone number.

"This is my source. Now your source. She's a White House official. Call her for confirmation and any other questions you may have. She's expecting to hear from you."

"Really? Why would she want to talk to me?"

"That's the really weird part. She knows I know you, and she reads your column all the time. Big fan." Jillian pauses. Then, "Strange how more women are into sports, huh?"

Pepper shrugs, knowing there's no right answer.

"Anyway," Jillian says, "she saw your Instagram mess and called me, ostensibly to ask after you. Then we talked some more and she sounded down, so I asked if she was okay and she told me 'something sickening' happened at a White House lunch. I ultimately dragged it out of her about the Muslim thing. I sensed she wanted the story to get out so I told her she should leak it to a journalist, and I was shocked when she said, 'How about Arnie Pepper?' She felt that since you're in sports, talking to you would feel less like leaking."

That rationalization feels iffy to Pepper, but he pulls out his cell. Jillian stops him and hands him a different phone. "Use this. There can't be any documentable connection between you, me, and her. This is a prepaid phone. They call it a burner."

"Yeah, I know what a burner is. I saw *The Wire*. David Simon is a friend. Well, an acquaintance. I met him once."

Pepper glances to his right, and the woman turns away yet again. His paranoia about her switches channels.

"Maybe I'll make the call outside."

Jillian nods and Pepper walks out the door. From a vestibule of a closed store, he calls the number on the index card. A woman answers, and, after hearing Pepper identify himself, talks as if she's gotten a call from her kid brother.

"Oh hi! How are you?"

"I'm on a burner phone outside a sushi joint. And you?"

"Nervous. But kind of excited in a newly liberated way."

"Hm. So what led to your liberation?"

She says she was at the intern luncheon and in a dark mood. "Or pretty much my mood every day in this White House. The whole crew laughing and eating like nothing was wrong was pissing me off, yet again. I was on the periphery of the Islam discussion and felt a tinge of hope when the kid spoke about it being a beautiful religion. Then this...*person*...gets up, and he or she makes the '75 million bad apples' joke. I knew these people were evil in a general sense but hearing it so blatantly—in front of kids!—well, I just snapped."

Pepper refrains from asking her the identity of the official. *Bring her along slowly.*

"When he or she made the 'bad apple' comment, about how many people heard it?"

"Maybe fifteen."

"What was their reaction like?"

"I'd say the kid who defended Islam and I were the only two people who didn't laugh hysterically."

She wants to name the speaker. Don't rush her.

"Boy," he says, "maybe we should rethink that whole idea that the children are our future."

Now she does laugh. "Yeah. Whitney Houston's rolling over in her grave."

"Did anyone record the moment the joke was made?"

"I don't know. But that's the right question to ask."

Pepper gets a warm tingle, like a cub reporter getting a compliment from an editor.

Go for the gold.

"The person who made the joke. Is he or she, by any chance, bald?"

Another laugh. "Nicely done. That was a really good try."

"You know, I'm a sportswriter, so I'll probably have to eventually pass this story onto someone in National."

"Yeah, I kind of figured. Look, I wouldn't have said anything about this if I didn't happen to call Jillian about your little scandal and then let her drag the latest Trump poop out of me. This is my first leak, believe it or not. It's crummy logic but leaking to you feels like a safe gateway drug into leaking to Ashley Parker or Peter Baker."

"Baker? You don't want to leak to the *Times*."

"I shouldn't leak at all. Oh well, it's just a job in a presidential administration. I can always leave it off my resume."

"Funny, I've been thinking a lot about my resume today."

"Yeah, I hope that all works out okay for you. I'm a nutty

Steelers fan. And even though your column is understandably Redskins-centric, I enjoy it. At least you seem to know that the Redskins are a horseshit franchise."

"Off the record? I love it when the Skins lose."

"Ha. I knew I could trust you."

There's a moment of dead air. Pepper, the journalist, won't hang up first.

"Hey, Mr. Sportswriter..."

"Still here."

"Very bald."

Click.

Pepper immediately calls Phil Rucker, confident he's chosen the right editor. Rucker is calm, analytical and shockingly uncynical for a hardened newspaper man. His mood-inside-the-White-House pieces, often written with Ashley Parker, are stunningly precise and insanely well-sourced. Since appearing regularly on MSNBC, Rucker's grown a beard. Done to convey gravitas? Probably not. More likely, swimming in the Trump Zone, he doesn't want to waste time shaving.

Rucker listens to Pepper run down the story and is careful in his enthusiasm.

"Hm. Sounds a lot like when Kelly Sadler said that thing about McCain."

"'It doesn't matter, he's dying anyway.'"

"Good memory, Arnie. Word for word."

"I got lucky."

"Look, this can be a good story, and we need to nail it down fast. I'll have to hand you and the reporting over to Ashley Parker, you know, seeing as—"

"I'm a sportswriter. I get it. Don't worry."

Rucker laughs. "I appreciate you taking the bite out of a potentially awkward moment. That said, here's another awkward thing: You would have to tell me or Ashley who your source is."

"I'll tell you right now."

When Pepper reveals the source's name, Rucker drops to a whisper. "Seriously? She's the only human in that White House who has never leaked anything! We've been tag-teaming her since the inauguration, trying to coax her into talking."

"Hey, glad to help."

"In that case, let me ask you one more question. How did you come to meet her or get her to talk or whatever?"

"Phil, that is a question to which I cannot respond. I mean, that's why I'm calling on a burner phone. Purely to protect that connection."

"Fair enough. Hold on. I'll connect you with Ashley."

Ashley Parker has been at the *Post* a couple of years, after first being a DC correspondent for the *Times*. Pepper knows her only to say hello. Most of the hard news people he does know are sports fans who seek him out. With nothing to back up his reasoning, he assumes Ashley is above giving a shit about why the Nats can't score any runs for Max Scherzer. She's become a polished MSNBC contributor as well, her face a bit more expressive than most but a voice for whom other panelists lean in.

"Hi Arnie. Ashley Parker. Rumor has it you have a story."

He repeats everything he told Rucker. Parker says, "I'm shocked you got her as a source. The woman's a sphinx. I mean, if you've broken the ice with her to the point where she's a regular source for us? I'll lose all respect for her, but still, it would be huge."

Pepper hangs up feeling high off his moment of meaningful journalism. Usually he humbles himself after breaking good stories by thinking: It's only sports. Still, there's no denying he's had more than his share of impressive scoops. He was first to report at least three of the Redskins' 35,000 coach firings. Breaking the story of Gilbert Arenas bringing an arsenal of hand guns into the locker room was a pretty big deal. Way back in the '80s, he got advance word that California Supreme Court Chief Justice Rose Bird would be coming right to the edge of accusing the NFL of colluding with the city of Oakland to keep the team in town. After that story, Ben Bradlee cruised past the sports section, barked out, "Hell of a scoop, Pepper!" and disappeared.

Jesus, Pepper thinks, you feel like every second of your life is recorded somewhere. Why can't that moment be floating around YouTube?

He turns to go back to Tokyo Gills when a guy who looks like the mug shot version of Nick Nolte walks up, pulling along some hypoallergenic poodle mix. "Hey Arnie: How funny would it be if the Redskins changed their name to the Washington Dead Cherokees? Ha-ha!"

Pepper looks empathetically at the dog. *Welcome to another episode of "God, I Hope Your Master Never Had Kids..."*

Reentering Tokyo Gills, a lingering buzz of bravado kicks in as he sees the redheaded woman getting up to leave.

"Do we know each other? I saw you looking my way..."

Pepper is now certain she's aware of his scandal and, oddly, he wants her to call him out as a sexist monster. Pointed responses line up in his head, ready for launch.

"I'm sorry for staring," she says. "You wouldn't remember, but we had a nice little chat in Rio."

Weapons loaded. Pepper has no target.

"The Olympics?"

"Yes. We chatted in the gymnastics venue. I didn't have a great time in Rio. Really, I don't even like sports much."

"Yeah, me neither."

The woman endearingly giggles.

"The Olympics was a dopey bucket list thing for me. Within three days, I got pick-pocketed on the street and groped by a concierge. So I crossed those dreams off the list. By the way, I'm Danielle. Marino."

"Your name is Dan Marino?"

"I know. I should've kept my maiden name."

"What was it? Rather?"

"What? Oh! Dan Rather! I get it."

Danielle laughs and lightly touches his arm, adding to the tingle of his calls with the White House source and *Post* reporters. Pepper feels like someone else.

"It was actually Klinger."

"Did our conversation happen before or after you were pick-pocketed and groped?"

"After. I'm sure I struck you as kind of a woe-is-me, emotional mess, but you were really nice. So, belated thanks."

Pepper remembers Jillian at the table and looks over. Jillian encouragingly makes a writing motion, the international "Waiter, can I get the check?" signal. Uncharacteristically quick on the uptake, Pepper knows Jillian is actually telling him, *Get her number.*

Pepper slowly shakes his head.

"Is something wrong?"

He looks at her and says, "I'm just considering the irony of a woman telling me what a nice guy I am on the very day I've become a feminist pariah."

"Why did you become a feminist pariah?"

"Long story."

"Okay..." Danielle says. "Are you here on a date?"

"Oh. Um, no. She's one of my oldest friends. From college. I mean, my best buddy. See, back then, she was, you know, a guy."

Pepper feels a pang of disloyalty in revealing this to a stranger. Danielle glances at Jillian then back to Pepper. "So you're a feminist pariah whose best friend is trans?"

"When you put it like that, it does sound a little incongruous. Come on, you should meet her."

They walk to the table where Jillian's bemused look is highly appropriate. The students under headphones are gone so Pepper takes a vacated seat and motions Danielle into his. She takes a close look at Jillian.

"Wait a minute. You're the Attorney General of Maryland, aren't you?"

The Montgomery County prosecutor smiles.

"Close enough."

Pepper, having seen alcoholism ravage lives and marriages in the newsroom, never exceeds one drink. As Jillian and Danielle reload their sake glasses, he sips 7-Up and recaps his day of "inadvertent misogyny." Danielle sporadically interjects with "Wow" or "Jeez" and one "Oh, for heaven's sake."

When Pepper wraps up, he awaits Danielle's verdict, but she abstains, choosing instead to tell a story.

"I have a cousin who lives on Long Island, a chiropractor who, coincidentally, is also named Arnie. He's in his fifties, twice divorced and still dating in bulk. So he goes out with a divorcee who tells him her nine-year-old daughter started menstruating. Arnie says, 'I guess New York needs to lower the age of consent.'"

Pepper and Jillian both laugh then apologize for laughing. Danielle says, "I reacted the same way. I knew it was offensive, but, Jesus, it was so funny."

Pepper asks, "How did your cousin's date respond?"

"She freaked, calling him a misogynist dirt bag. My cousin's like, 'Oh, lighten up. It was a joke.' She says it wasn't funny. He says, 'No, it was tasteless but definitely funny.' They argue about whether it was funny, so get this: Arnie suggests they hire an arbitrator to decide if the joke was funny. The loser pays the arbitrator's fee plus that night's dinner. And she agrees to it! Yada, yada, yada, they find an arbitrator on LinkedIn, he hears the joke, and rules that it's not funny. Arnie later finds out that the arbitrator's kid brother was molested in church but it's too late to appeal—he's already shelled out $450. But there's a kicker to the story: Arnie goes to a diabetes charity auction, bids on, and wins a lunch with Adam Sandler. Over lunch, he tells the story of his date and Sandler pays him $5,000 for the rights to the story because he's producing a movie about a guy who's a total asshole."

Pepper says, "Please tell me your cousin married the girl."

"Oh God, no. She has a restraining order against him."

Jillian says, "Understandable." Pepper reluctantly agrees.

Danielle shakes her head. "There must be a moral to this story, but who can make sense of all this rigmarole?"

Rigmarole. The word warms Pepper's head.

Danielle and Jillian go off on a tangent conversation from which Pepper momentarily zones out. As if he's hit the mute button, he watches the two women talk and gesture and laugh. He is blown away by Jillian's adaption to talking so naturally, so woman-to-woman. When he brings back the audio, Pepper hears Jillian say, "I know, I know: Even the saleswomen in that place seem like gay men!"

Danielle giggles and says, "Exactly! Could they be more intimidatingly snotty?"

Pepper's cell rings. He looks down. It's Thea. He feels a jolt of either joy or dread, then motions to Jillian and Danielle he's going to take the call and walks a few feet away.

"Hi, honey. Are you okay?"

"Actually, Daddy, I was calling to ask you the same question."

"I'm fine. Why?"

"Why? You got spray-attacked at the airport by one of those guy feminist Nazis. Have you been examined? Remember those deadly Russian gases they used in the UK?"

Pepper is relieved to hear her specific concern is about his health. At least she doesn't think she was raised by a monster.

"No, no, honey. It was *nothing.* Just vinegar and water and something smelly. I'm fine. How did you hear about it?"

"Oh my god. You don't know?"

"Know what."

"You're all over the web. You've gone viral. The guy who sprayed you posted a video on Instagram."

"Viral? *Jesus.* I saw the phone peeking out from his pocket."

"It's gotten like a zillion views. I mean, who was this guy?

You can't see him in the video. You hear him talking a little..."

"It was just some loony kid. Nothing to worry about."

"Okay, if you say so. But I guess you've had some day, huh?"

"So...you know the *whole* story?" he asks tentatively. *Please tell me I raised a girl who doesn't drink Kool-Aid.*

"Yeah. Pretty crazy."

"Crazy? That's your take on my little hysterectomy scandal?" He sighs deeply. "After not hearing from you, I was worried that you were...disappointed in me."

"Daddy, I kind of know you well enough to give you the benefit of the no doubt."

A wave of humane relief flows through Pepper, the kind of warm and gentle lessening promised by a thousand antacid commercials. Only now does he realize his shoulders have been hunched up for hours, half a day in which his muscles have been in the protection racket against his lethal fear of losing his daughter's respect, admiration and love—everything—of having his life reduced to regret.

"Thanks, honey. That's all that...the rest is...Well, it'll all work out."

"I'm sure it will."

"Speaking of which, I was more worried about you and the Buddhist freak. I take it you worked it out?"

"Yeah, well, 'worked out' is one way of looking at it...Anyway, I'll tell you about it when I see you."

Pepper sees Danielle glance his way. "Look, honey, I'm at Tokyo Gills with a couple of friends."

"Jillian?"

"Uh-huh."

"Who else?"

"Broiling hot weather, raw fish: What could go wrong?"

"Oh, you can't talk? Is the other person a woman? I mean, a woman who was born a woman?"

"As far as I know."

"A woman you might ask *out*?"

"Possibly."

"Yay!"

"Hey, how about meeting me for breakfast tomorrow? I have the morning free."

"Count me in."

"Great."

"Love you, Daddy."

"Love you, too, sweetie."

Pepper hangs up and returns to the table.

"Thea says there's viral video of the kid spraying me."

Jillian expertly summons the video on her phone. Pepper is gripped by the look of utter terror on his face from the moment he'd been misted. This is another new phenomenon, a human being having the chance to see himself in a moment of primal terror. It's been staggering enough for Pepper to regularly see the agonized faces of athletes in brutal, super slow motion the moment it sinks in that they've snapped an Achilles tendon or blown a game, botched a season, shattered a team, crushed a fan base. Now, seeing the animal instinct of his own horror in his own eyes is almost unbearable.

"Don't worry, Arnie," Jillian says. "The video's only been seen by...?" She looks at the phone. "Oh. 1.8 million people."

Pepper sullenly says, "Now it's 1.8 million and three."

Danielle chimes in, "That sounds like a lot of people, but, worldwide, 1.8 million isn't that much. Not really."

Pepper appreciates the cold comfort, but only momentarily. "Did I mention that—also according to anti-social media—I'm alleged to be the emcee for monthly screenings of locker room videos of naked athletes at the Old Grill?"

After Jillian pointedly pays the Tokyo Gills check in cash, she and Pepper walk Danielle to her car, two blocks in the opposite direction from Pepper's, her Virginia cell number now among his contacts. As she unlocks a black Range Rover, Pepper sees a slew of folders on the passenger seat and says, "With my usual intense charm, I never asked what you do."

"I'm an archivist at the Library of Congress. In essence, a librarian."

"Nice car for a librarian."

"My husband left me money. He died on 9/11."

"Oh my god. Was he in the Pentagon?"

"No, on the New Jersey Turnpike. He flipped over a guard-rail with a blood-alcohol level of 2.1. But it did happen on 9/11."

She drives off, taking a look back that reminds Pepper of Travis Bickle dropping off Betsy at the end of *Taxi Driver*.

Jillian nods approvingly. "I like her."

"Yeah, she's got something going on. Whatever that means. Come on, I'll give you a lift home."

"No, no, Arnie. I'll just get an Uber."

"Look, I'm kind of wired. The drive will do me good."

"Aaaight."

Pepper shoots her a look. Jillian shrugs and says, "I like how black guys say 'aaaight' to their public defenders, as if they're trying to lighten up all the formality they hear in the courtroom."

"The halls of justice are kind of constipated."

"Yeah, every time I enter a courtroom I think, 'Smells like geriatric spirit.'"

They walk on Connecticut Avenue, Pepper dialing back his normal stride so Jillian can keep up. She's mentioned that gender reassignment took some toll on her body, and that she's mildly disappointed by still having her previous gender's less elastic muscles.

Pepper thinks of how young women joggers in his neighborhood run like Jerry Rice, perfect form, athletic. Something about them flying along, their pony tails bobbing, god-knows-what streaming through their ear buds, strikes him as incredibly beautiful. It's how he felt watching Marion Jones sprint in the Sydney Olympics, which made it doubly painful for

Pepper to break the story about her urine sample coming up dirty. If ever there was an athlete he wanted to cover up for, it was Marion. Her adorably warm smile...who'd have thought she was pumping herself with Erythropoietin? When she was asked to give back her medals, Pepper wanted to tell her to keep them, let the IOC worry about the official records. The older Pepper gets, the more he reminds himself not to give life advice to athletes he covers. *It's not your job.* Once, after a long interview, a one-and-done NBA lottery pick asked Pepper if he should marry his high school sweetheart. Pepper said, "Do you love her?" The kid said, "Yeah, I guess. Whatever." Three years later, the kid, averaging 1.8 points in six minutes of playing time per game, was arrested for abusing his wife with a jump rope.

Years after Sydney, Pepper bumped into Marion at DFW. Despite knowing he'd been the guy who first reported the pop in her career bubble, she greeted him with her sweet kid smile. Special athletes appreciate people doing their jobs the right way, even if they themselves are cheaters.

Should've been easier on Tonya Harding. The movie redeemed her some, but still. Actually, I wasn't a fan of Nancy Kerrigan. Pretty girl, but a vinaigrette facial expression. Tonya, knee whacking aside, was more fun to talk to.

Nearing Pepper's car, Jillian says, "So, my ex-wife wants to fix me up with a woman she met at SoulCycle."

Pepper's mind trips. "So, this woman is a lesbian?"

"I guess."

"Are you a lesbian?"

"I like women. Let everyone else pin labels on me. I'm already trans. How many LGBTQ categories can I fill? There should be rules on this somewhere."

"There should be rules on a lot of things but, in a way, that's where our lives fall apart. Baby Boomers broke all the rules with flower power and love-ins but now we want the rules back, like we got gypped."

"Don't say gypped. It's seen as racist. Y'know, gypsies."

"Oh, help me, Rhonda."

"I know."

"The human mouth should come with a disclaimer. 'May cause suicidal thoughts in oversensitive listeners...'"

"Those disclaimers are written by asshole lawyers like me and even I can't get through two sentences of them. I mean, the legalisms that went along with gender reassignment? It was crazy. The doctors didn't understand the lawyers, the lawyers didn't understand the doctors, and I didn't understand what either of them were saying."

"You didn't understand what the doctor was saying?"

"Well, some of it. The crucial stuff. But let's face it, at the time I was still a guy, and what guy really has a grasp on stuff like the vulva or cervix? He's throwing around these terms, and I'm nodding like a dope."

"But you're up on all that stuff now."

"I guess. Pretty much. I don't know..."

"Overall... still happy you jumped genders?"

"Oh yeah. It's great. It's like being reincarnated without, you know, dying."

Whereas now, anyone with an adult kid knows plenty of trans people, Pepper has a longer history with them. At the 1984 Volvo at Madison Square Garden, he noticed he wasn't seeing McEnroe's scowl clearly. After the match, he mentioned it to Arthur Ashe, the single most exemplary human being to ever walk the face of the Earth.

How the damn hell does anyone but a vicious, malignant, psychotic God let Arthur Ashe get AIDS from a transfusion?

Arthur recommended Pepper see Dr. Renée Richards. Pepper had interviewed Richards a few times when she coached Martina and knew she'd returned to ophthalmology, a field in which she'd been prominent as Dr. Richard Raskind. By dropping Arthur's name, Pepper got a quick appointment and a prescription for "cheaters" from the woman he still considers a friend and the best doctor he's ever had.

A roaring white Porsche tears up Connecticut, doing the forty in two seconds just to stop at a red light. Jillian sighs, "Imagine the devotion to cliché it takes to be a middle-aged man driving a Porsche in 2018."

The Porsche roars again before steaming off.

"Maybe NBA players are onto something, the way they go through life under noise-cancelling headphones."

On cue, they hear a voice behind them.

"Heel, Pumpkin. Heel, you little shit."

It's the Nick Nolte-looking dog walker again. Pepper hopes he's being paranoid, but—*Who walks a dog this long?*

"I'm baaaack," the guy says in a kid's voice, apparently confusing Schwarzenegger with the poor little actress who died after *Poltergeist*.

Now Pepper notices sickly reds and blues of faded tattoos inching over the lowest button of the guy's JCPenney polo. His hand gripping the leash has more ink, letters above each knuckle. Pepper can't make them out and doesn't want to. The population of demented people is soaring, but at least these days, the nuts give you clues. Although, if he dated more, Pepper has had the thought that a girl with multiple tattoos might be a good idea. At least he'd know going in that he's with someone who's willing to make a huge mistake.

"Arnie," the guy says, "you got a mention on the news. What's it mean when they say, 'The *Post* is looking into the situation?' It's not like they need a CSI unit to figure out that you fucked up big time."

Being out in public—ever—is starting feel like a mistake.

"Walking your dog and saying ignorant things to strangers—Is that your job?"

"My job's none of your business, Arnie, but you can be sure it's better than writing suck-up articles about billionaire blacks who wag their dicks at white girls all day but won't stand up for the anthem."

Pepper turns to Jillian. "What does dick wagging and the anthem have to do with each other?"

"Yeah, I missed that connection, too."

"Can you believe people like this guy exist here? On Connecticut Avenue? In Washington, DC?"

Jillian picks up on the third-person invisible. "Dopes like him have always been here. It's just now, they're free to go public with their stupidity and believe the misconception that they have something to live for. What I don't get is why he gives a shit about that crappy anthem. Francis Scott Key? Biggest one-hit wonder of all time."

Pepper laughs. "Hey, if I get to write any more columns, can I steal that line?"

"It's all yours."

Pepper whispers to the dog walker. "Don't tell anyone I steal my friends' lines for my column."

"I won't have to, *Arnie*. You're not going to write any more columns. Your dick's in a ringer. First, your limp dick liberal bosses will say they feel a 'moral obligation' to 'take appropriate action.' Then, when the shit dies down, they'll chop your dick off for good."

Pepper has no rebuttal. *This is the way things go down these days. The #Me-Too routine is so pat, even this cretin knows the steps.*

Jillian says, "You like saying 'dick,' don't you?"

With unfathomable depravity, the guy says, "Yeahhh!"

As punctuation, his dog craps on the sidewalk.

Jillian quietly says, "I'm a prosecutor. Pick up after your dog, or I'll have fifty federal agents here in two minutes."

The guy pulls out an orange *Washington Times* home delivery bag, picks up the glob, and is about to tie it closed. "Don't tie it," Jillian says. "Give me the open bag of shit."

The creep shakes his head, hands Jillian the bag, and says, "Enjoy your retirement, Arnie." He walks away.

Jillian mashes the burner phone against a brick wall, drops

it in the bag of dog shit, and tosses it into an overflowing trash basket.

"I like learning tricks from guys I prosecute."

Driving along River Road, Pepper and Jillian talk about the dog walker, agreeing how weird it is that so many people summarize their lives with credos etched into their skin by some Hell's Angel with a needle. Imagine the profitability of the tattoo removal business, Jillian says. Pepper comes up with the ad-ready name of Dr. Tataway. Jillian names his partner Dr. Inkoff. Pepper tells Jillian about Paul McKay, a moderately inked up new kid who works in the sports section. McKay graduated summa from Sarah Lawrence and sent his resume to the *Post*. A deputy editor from the Sarah Lawrence class of '81 asked the kid to mail in a writing sample.

McKay sent a copy of *The Great Gatsby*.

And was hired immediately.

Jillian snorts. "The squeaky wheel gets the grease."

"Yeah, I never really got that expression. I mean, if the wheel doesn't squeak, it doesn't need grease. So who's the big winner and loser there?"

"Boy, you're really going deep now, aren't you?"

Pepper laughs, enjoying a kind of conversation he doesn't get in press boxes. Most sportswriters spend their lives arguing about who's better between Manny Machado and Honus Wagner, as if anyone ever wins these arguments. There's insanity in comparing players of different generations, anyway. If tennis never sold out by letting everyone use gigantic racquets, McEnroe might still be Number One in the world. Hell, Mickey Mantle would have hit 800 homers if he had access to Advil, not to mention the cream and the clear and whatever other PEDs are still eluding drug testers, worldwide. In baseball, fans only objected to PEDs because they warped the record books, but Pepper feels it's just better baseball through science, not much different than Tommy John surgery. *Thea once asked what would happen if a doctor got a pitcher on his operating table and accidentally performed Elton John Surgery. She really is funny. The girl's going to be a star.*

In 1998, when McGwire and Sosa's pop-ups were sailing thirty rows into the left field seats, no one in MLB talked aloud about juicing. The league loved it. Once busted, they went with the "bad influence on kids" excuse for cracking down. As if baseball players would think, "I'm hitting .210 in July but I won't take PEDs because children are our future." Baseball refers to "the Steroid Era" as if it's history, as if loads of major leaguers wouldn't still risk a dope-fueled month of ten homers and thirty RBIs in exchange for a sixty-game suspension, back zits, increased hat size, and the corrupting of some testicle-shrunken kid in Tulsa.

The Olympics should be different, but aren't—at least since '92, when amateur athletics lost its last wisps of idealism. No one in Barcelona acknowledged it except for one kill-joy sports columnist for the *Washington Post*, who got world-wide vitriol for slamming The Dream Team as the ultimate sellout of American ideals. Our college kids lost Olympic gold in Seoul '88 to a bunch of Soviet professionals by *six points*, so we opted to get into the gutter with the enemy and send our NBA monsters to Barcelona just so everyone knows the baddest basketball players in the world are American—the pathetic sign of our shame the inclusion of one amateur, Christian Laettner, a warped version of affirmative action benefiting a kid who had never faced discrimination in his life. Pepper compared the Dream Team to our ginned-up wars against Panama and Grenada. We sent Bird, Magic, and Jordan in for the overkill and, just as the foray into Grenada was like an attack on a Holiday Inn, our hoop bombers shelled tiny countries without breaking a sweat. The blowback on Pepper for ripping the Dream Team was swift, vicious, and, as usual in the case of sports fans, incoherent. Then again, it wasn't just fans. The press, IOC, and USOC all rained rebukes down on a reporter whose only mistake in Barcelona was bringing his wife. *Damn.* Ultimately, *one* person that summer had the independence and guts to sidle up to Pepper and say, "Everything you wrote in that column is true. Someday all these clowns will realize you were the only guy who got it right." That man was the truth-addicted American treasure, Charles Barkley. Even though Chuck got it partly wrong—the clowns never realized anything and we still merrily send NBA players to the Olympics to beat up on kids from Swaziland—the gratitude Pepper felt from Barkley's comments is the second strongest memory he has from Barcelona 1992.

"Hey," Jillian says out of nowhere. "You know what word is really getting on my nerves lately? *Narrative.*"

"That's so weird. Just recently, Thea told me that 'Narrative is the intelligent-sounding word for people who've never read a book.'"

"Exactly. By the way, how's she doing?"

"Great. They love her at NPR. Although she did a story today about a Buddhist guy who teaches inner-city kids to meditate? So while she's interviewing him, she happens to mention the Dalai Lama—and the guy suddenly goes full Mussolini on her, ranting about how the Dalai Lama is an asshole who just wants to fuck all his Hollywood actress followers."

"Well, that's a unique take on a Nobel Peace Prize winner. Not very Zen, but unique."

Driving along Democracy Boulevard, Pepper crosses the DC line into Maryland. His window cracked, the thick trees smell sweaty, crickets chirp like it's a chore, the humidity sucking the joy from stuff that comes naturally. Imagine the AC bills around here, Pepper thinks. Not to mention the water usage, sprinkler systems doing CPR on every lawn, and the price of irrigating the vaunted local golf clubs—Avenel, Congressional, Burning Tree—and the lush private school campuses like Georgetown Prep or Holton Arms. *Jesus, can this country afford any more rich people?*

"So how did Thea handle the crazy Buddha?"

"Apparently just fine. But I still haven't heard the end of the story. I'm seeing her for breakfast tomorrow."

"She can handle herself."

"Like an idiot, I told her to flee the interview. But God bless her, she just dug in her heels."

"The way people just gravitate to Thea must give her a certain confidence. How she speaks and looks you in the eye and her face...Ah, what do I know? Even after seven years as a woman, being a beautiful woman is as mystifying to me as when I was a guy."

"Oh, come on, you're a hottie."

"Aw, that's so sweet. Want to pull over and make out?"

"Thank you. You're the first woman to ever ask me that."

"I keep thinking about how Fran Lebowitz said that Bruce Jenner was the only person to ever *want* to be a sixty-five-year-old woman."

"She's really funny. Fran Lebowitz, I mean."

"If she'd said that in 2010, I may have dropped the whole sexual reassignment idea altogether."

"Or maybe you could've just gone for a minimally invasive sex change operation."

"Huh. Interesting concept."

"I like how it's called sexual reassignment. As if a guy's boss says, 'Look Johnson, your work as a male has fallen off so we've decided to reassign you to female. But don't look at it as a demotion. You pick up your productivity over there, we'll re-reassign you ASAP.'"

"Re-reassignment. Yikes."

A moment of thoughtfulness clouds the car before Pepper says, "Can I ask you a totally retarded question?"

"Yes. But don't say *retarded.*"

"If someone on the street happens to call out to a guy named Jerry, do you still turn around?"

"That's not a mentally-challenged question. It happened within the last year and yes, I did turn around. It kind of bummed me out, actually. But fifty-whatever years of being Jerry doesn't just vanish."

"Hm. And every time a new #MeToo scandal pops up in the news, are you more offended than you would have been as a guy?"

"It kind of depends on when I took my last estrogen pill. I'd like to think I'm equally offended in both formats, but hell, the world's changed even more than I have. Besides, I've prosecuted so many deviant acts by so many epically warped people, I barely know what offends me anymore."

"Yeah. The sheer hell of other people is too much."

"Funny, one thing that does offend me now is the term 'tranny.' And even then, I'm not offended in a bigotry sense. It's more, like, auditory. *Tranny* sounds so jovial, like calling someone a foodie. As if my sex change arose out of a hobby I got a little too into."

"When do you ever hear anyone say tranny?"

"In May, I interviewed a grad from Emory Law. His qualifications were strong, he had a hunger for public service. So I tell him about the job, the late nights, the dangers, then ask him if he has any questions. He thinks for a second and says, 'Why did you decide to become a tranny?'"

"Get out."

"Word for word."

"What did you say?"

"What could I say? I told him to 'get the fuck out of my office, and I hope you get stabbed to death on an unemployment line.'"

"That's a reasonable response. Have you hired any trans lawyers?"

"Not yet. Just haven't gotten the right applicant. But I am intent on hiring and championing women, trans or not. Look, you and I have known each other so long, we talk pretty much the same way we always have. And I love that, the continuity of it. I don't want a *total* break from who I was. But with most other people in the world, I'm trying to be seen and heard for what I am, a living, thinking, talking woman."

"Well, I think that's great."

"Thanks. And thank you. Transitioning at my age was tricky, but you never made me feel weird. My own kids...it's strange. Sons are usually affected by a trans father worse than daughters, but Josh has been great. It's Liza who never misses a chance to stick it to me. She had a break-up recently and wouldn't talk to me about it beyond saying, 'What would you know about women's problems?'"

Pepper puts a hand on her shoulder. "That's awful. I swear, these millennials are great until they disagree with you on anything. Then they're monsters."

"Not your Thea. She's an exception to all the rules."

"Thanks. I take no credit. Funny thing is, if I wimp out and just go along with her opinions, she calls me out on it. She *wants* me to disagree with her."

"Wow. I'm at the point where, if Liza says Eric Trump reminds her of Cicero, I agree just to avoid her wrath. You know I love her like crazy, but she ain't easy."

"Maybe you should fix her up on a date with the lawyer who called you a tranny."

"I wouldn't even do that to him. Actually, I feel a little bad about how I reacted to him. He's probably a good kid who just needed a little boning up on etiquette. I could have done a good thing by just giving him a break."

"Giving people a break has become un-American."

Pepper, realizing his words seem self-serving, quickly adds, "And honestly, I'm not alluding to my situation, just in general."

Jillian says, "You *should* be alluding to your situation. It's fucking ridiculous."

Pepper shrugs, looks at his dashboard clock, thinks of turning on some music, rejects the idea, drums his fingers on the steering wheel, checks his rearview, cracks his window, drops the thermostat three degrees, sniffs for no physiological reason, and stops at a red light.

"I mean," he begins, "in just one of these cases, can't someone just be outright forgiven? I'm not talking Weinstein or Steve Wynn or Cosby or Lauer or Dominique Strauss-Kahn or Roy Moore or even Clarence Thomas. But just some guy, the typical, generic American male who confuses what he thinks he's entitled to with what he knows he doesn't deserve. Ugh. Look, I know what I'm about to say is really bad and stop me if I start devolving into a Neanderthal... But here goes: Let's say some guy so nondescript that you couldn't even describe him if you were staring at him, suddenly finds himself in his brown shoes pulling down a million a year in a corner office he never dreamed of having and suddenly he can't help wondering what the point is of all his success if he can't attract one nice girl. They're all over his office with skirts and ponytails and bracelets piled up on their impossibly thin wrists, so finally he takes his shot with one of them. But of course, he's a pathetic flirter and doesn't know how to segue from discussing gross profits to discussing dating, so he fumbles around with some spastic small talk when, somehow, the words 'your tits' slip out."

Pepper feels his scenario getting away from him, absconding to heinously impolitic places, but he can't stop.

"Is that it? Does that *have* to be it? His life as he's barely known it *must* be over? All that diligence and overachieving is wiped out in two words? I just can't believe there's not one higher-up in all of America who's willing to dash off a memo saying, 'Mr. Swanson acted inappropriately with a woman under his charge, and we never have and never will tolerate that kind of behavior. But that said, I feel he's done superb work and has apologized profusely to the woman in question, expressing the kind of remorse that indicates a full grasp of the anguish he's inflicted on her. So, after much deliberation, I've decided to let him remain in his position under the umbrella of double secret probation. I sincerely hope I'm not making a tragic mistake and if I am, his termination will be merciless and swift. But for now, I'm willing to try the unprecedented option of forgiveness.'"

The big hypothetical feels done, but—

"How about that, Jillian? How about someone in this world being FORGIVEN FOR BEING A TYPICALLY DEFECTIVE, NEEDY, LOVE-STRUCK PUTZ?"

Jillian browses for a response, but Pepper gets an eighth wind.

"But hell, what chance does a Joe Blow-like-that guy have in a society that ruins a big-deal guy like Al Franken for next to nothing? And he was ruined by liberals! His own people! People like us! It's like he was attacked by some kind of left-wing autoimmune disease."

Jillian silently computes how long he's been a Franken fan, while her friend loads up another harangue.

"Now, every slob on the street's been deputized in the hunt for social felons. Funny, the one group that has an easy route to forgiveness is athletes," Pepper says, again hating how he always winds up back at sports. "They screw up and all they have to do to atone is say, 'It is what it is.'"

"'Yes, on my Criminal Justice 101 paper, I copied word-for-word the writings of Lawrence Tribe so I could have more time in the weight room. *It is what it is.*'"

"Or, if it's really egregious, they say, 'I made a bad decision.'"

"'I'd like to apologize to my Brigham Young teammates. I take full responsibility for driving the getaway car my friends used after paralyzing a teller at the Wells Fargo branch in Provo during an armed robbery. I made a bad decision.'"

"'Oh! You just made a bad decision? Why didn't you say so?

Tell you what: visit a double amputee at a veteran's hospital, autograph a pair of compression shorts for him, tell him your yards-after-a-catch stats, and it'll be like nothing ever happened.'"

Jillian, unsure if it's her turn to speak, runs her fingers through her hair, still taken with its increased thickness.

"On the other hand," Pepper says, "get this: "Last April 20, a local TV news station in Colorado did a story about the 19th anniversary of Columbine. Twenty-whatever minutes later, the sports guy reports on the NBA play-off win for New Orleans over Portland and accidentally says, 'Nicola Mirotic and Anthony Davis *Columbined* for fifty-eight points.'"

Oy, Jillian says to herself.

"Before he could get back on set to apologize, he got so many death threats he ultimately moved his wife and twin sons to Canada."

Jillian finally speaks: "To err is human; to forgive, sub-human."

"Oooo, good one," Pepper says. "And thanks for treating me to a diatribe."

"Not at all. I enjoyed it. It was like a Lawrence Diatribe."

"Wow. You're on fire."

His cell rings. He hits speakerphone.

"Mr. Pepper, it's Kristen Haynes, *DC Metro Online.*"

Pepper glances at Jillian who rolls her eyes.

"What can I do for you, Kristen?"

"Sorry for calling so late, but I heard from a source, that you were already terminated by the *Post.*"

"Kristen." For some reason, Pepper likes saying *Kristen.* "I promise I've been told no such thing. Tomorrow, I have a pow-wow with my editor about my future."

"Okay. Thank you. I appreciate you for responding."

"It's only because you're a good reporter. I can tell."

"Well," Kristen says with a laugh, "if you find me so deserving, you have my number should you feel the urge to call a reporter right after your meeting."

"Don't sit around and stare at your phone."

"I understand. And by the way, don't say 'powwow.'"

"Right. In a city obsessed with the Redskins, I don't want to offend native Americans."

It feels like a moment for the call to end but something in the ether feels unfinished.

"Anything else I can help you with, Kristen?"

In a lowered voice. "Well, I hate to bring this up, but I also got a call from a former AP reporter who claims she had sex with you after a White House Correspondents' Dinner."

The sneak attack has Pepper again on defense, inquisitor as target. A private life he barely deals with is again fair game for the world. He avoids glancing at Jillian, who never asks about his relationships after Jane.

"I'm guessing you intentionally buried your lede."

Kristen is brushed back by Pepper's tone. "She claims you promised her a job at the *Post* but didn't follow through."

"No, I didn't promise her a job. I said I'd look into it. Anyway, is this a revelation? A widower and a single woman in a hotel after a notoriously liquor-infested banquet? Look, I didn't know her or her work. Clearly, I shouldn't have said I'd help her get a job. But that doesn't mean our rendezvous was transactional. Crazy at it sounds, women do occasionally find me attractive. Granted, most of them are in desperate need of Lasik surgery..."

His joke eases Kristen's voice. "Actually, when I spoke to the woman, I heard clinking of ice in the background. She sounded a bit...wasted. I'm sorry for bringing it up."

"Don't be sorry. Confirming information is your job."

"Yeah. I've actually heard you say that before."

"Pardon?"

"I was in the J-school at Maryland. You guest lectured."

"Your tuition dollars at work."

Kristen laughs. "Off the record, I hope things work out for you."

"Well, the worst that can happen is I get fired, and it'll be the end of a totally insignificant era," he says.

When Pepper hangs up, Jillian says: "Boy, you were awfully nice to her. I'd have told her to stick it. At least when I got vetted, it was by trained investigators, not some kid from an online rag. But I guess you know the journalism game."

"No. Not this side of the game. And by the way, that online rag does good work. They're a serious outfit."

"I know. I read it. Well, I read it when they write something about me. Otherwise..." Jillian breaks into a slightly evil smile.

"What?"

"You know what would be an interesting experiment? If you call this Kristin back and ask her to drop the whole story in exchange for you going down on her."

Pepper accidentally honks his horn.

"Really, Arnie. Test her commitment to journalism. If she's offended, you can tell her you were just kidding."

Pepper reboots his lungs enough to say, "Hey, I thought *I* was the thought criminal, here."

"Yeah. It doesn't seem fair. I am a total trans chauvinist pig."

"Trans chauvinist pig. I like that. I'd write it down but where it would fit in a sports column?"

"You never know."

"Actually, the reason I was nice to Kristen was because she reminds me of Jane."

Anytime Pepper mentions Jane, all levity goes *pfft*. Jillian glides past the moment, saying, "I can't believe you, of all people, are getting calls from reporters at night."

"The last thing you want as a reporter is to be the story."

Jillian nods. "Lately, it feels like 'the last thing we want' is all we get. What kind of society is this where you're watching every sentence out of your mouth, when every time you meet someone new you start out from a place of suspicion? We're at a point where the bar is so low, parents have to teach their kids to hate everyone peacefully. The whole use of the word tolerance...It's like, 'I have no respect for your beliefs, but I'll tolerate you.' I think that's why so many people now try to dictate what you should think of them, preventing others from ever getting to know them based on human perception. Everyone thinks they have their own brand—which is, by the way, another bullshit word that's taken over the world. Personally, I don't know what to do with all this warped, self-deluded garbage everyone's trying to sell about themselves. Just ordinary small talk feels like work. Hell, I don't even trust fun anymore. I'm so far behind the curve, all social interaction makes me feel like suddenly I'm the fucking idiot in the room. Which is weird, because I've spent my life sure I'm the intelligent person in the room. But even if I am, what's the point? Most people nowadays look at being smart as just another gimmick."

Jillian cracks her window. "Wow, that was pretty incoherent."

"In places, yeah."

Maybe we weren't meant to live long enough to realize we're idiots.

Pepper wants to jot down the thought, but cruising from Democracy Boulevard to Democracy Lane, he hesitates as the streets narrow and darken. Still, whenever he puts off jotting down a thought lately, it escapes his head, lost forever. As his right hand twitches off the wheel toward his notepad, the world goes into slow motion. In an oncoming Jetta he sees only the top of a blonde head. Pepper has always believed he's the Wayne Gretzky of driving, seeing everything before him in decelerated time, sensing all movements before they happen. The Jetta is doing a classic cell phone drift across the middle line. He instantly opts to attack the gas pedal as he sees the blonde head snap up behind the wheel. It's the right move a millisecond too late.

The Jetta smacks his rear left door, coughs out its airbag, spins, and finally stops after bonking up against the brick retaining wall of a front yard outside a sleepy Tudor home. Pepper expertly eases off the gas and smoothly brakes, stopping his Subaru two feet from the trunk of an American Sweetgum.

The universe takes a hushed vacation before Jillian says, "So Arnie, aren't you glad you offered me a lift home?"

"I made a bad decision."

"If you didn't speed up," Jillian says, "we'd be head-on accordion meat. Ballsy move."

"Well, coming from you..."

They incongruously laugh. Pepper mindlessly checks his pulse and says, "Jesus, this day just won't let go."

"On the upside, how often have you had a day that you'll remember forever?"

"I can't recall."

"We should check on the girl," Jillian says.

"Oh, you saw it was a girl, too?"

"No. But who else drives a white Jetta?"

As they get out into the dead air, the girl is squeezing past a dutiful air bag and out the door, which she leaves open before taking a few steps on liquid legs, both hands holding a cell phone like it's a baby duck. She avoids looking at the metallic guts spilling out from the back and front of (most likely) THE BEST BIRTHDAY GIFT EVER! (Emoji) (emoji) emoji) (emoji)...

"Oh my God!" she rasps. "I am SO sorry."

The girl starts sobbing. Thea, miraculously, has never cracked up a car, but Pepper paternally comforts the girl like a seasoned veteran.

"It's okay," he says, "it's okay. You're fine. Accidents happen to the best of us. Nobody's hurt is all that matters."

He wants to give her a hug but America's too perilous for that, especially with this girl. He sees her as sweet Loretta Martin in her low-neck sweater. Except it's a low-neck tank top, white and explicit. *Sorry, Sir Paul.*

"I wasn't even texting or on the phone," she says, already copping a plea. "I dropped a piece of paper with the address I was going to and reached down, and I guess the wheel turned."

"It happens," Pepper says. "Think of it as a life lesson in which you got off cheap."

"What do we do now?"

"We exchange information and—"

She looks up at him. He doesn't want to alarm her by saying they should call the police.

"And that's it. We exchange information and go safely back to the comfort of our homes."

"Oh. Okay, my papers are in the car. I think. I already called my dad. He's on the way."

She looks down as she walks back to her wreckage.

Jillian whispers, "Arnie, you know her story is going to completely change when her father gets here, don't you?"

"Really?"

"Trust me."

Pepper's phone rings. It's Ashley Parker. He marvels at how the world goes on outside his own wreckage.

"Hi, Ashley."

"Hi, Arnie. You sound awake."

"Yeah, I'm at the scene of the car accident I just had."

"Car accident? Are you okay?"

"I'm fine. It's nothing. Fender bender. What's up?"

"Okayyyyy...I was just calling to say I spoke to your source. She corroborated most of the story but held off on a few details I'll have to track down myself.

"You think she'll be a source in the future?"

"I'm cautiously optimistic. She sounds pretty fed up. No offense, but I asked her why she spoke to a sportswriter first. She said she's a sports nut and talking to you was too exciting for her to pass up. So kudos to you."

"Thanks. It had been a pretty kudos-less day for me."

Parker lets his comment drift for a moment.

"Yeah, about that," she begins. "To be honest, I thought your hysterectomy joke was fairly revolting. Maybe more offensive than the 75 million bad apples joke."

Pepper feels instantly ill but says nothing.

"I'm very pregnant right now, but I don't think that unfairly prejudices me. Comparing a hysterectomy to say, a pulled hamstring—well, it takes callousness to a new level."

Pepper is momentarily stunned.

"But," Ashley says, her voice brightening, "since you handed me a pretty good story and a potentially great source, I'm willing to take it on faith that you're a fantastic human being who made a mistake."

"I appreciate that."

"It will be weird getting a co-byline with a sportswriter."

Sensing a chance to show his journalism chops, Pepper says, "No, Ashley. I don't think my name should be on the story. White House people must know the source is a sports fan so my by-line could throw suspicion her way. And even without that, people will find it a little hinky seeing a sportswriter's name over a piece about White House intrigue."

"Okay, good," Parker says. "I thought the same thing but didn't want to presume."

Pepper hangs up and relates the conversation to Jillian.

"She was ready to give you a byline even though she didn't think it would be a good idea?"

"Reporters like Ashley are lousy with integrity."

The upside of an auto accident in suburbia is the inevitability of some nosy neighbor sparing you the drag of calling the police. A Montgomery County Squad Car pulls up, twirling lights on but sirens off, the Ambien-induced sleep of the Potomac elite protected. Officers Conrad Hamilton and Angela Suarez come over and instantly recognize Jillian.

"Damn, Angela," Hamilton says. "The prosecutor beat us to the scene of the crime."

"That's why Ms. Corbin makes the big bucks," Suarez says, with a laugh. Cops assigned to overbred suburbs are generally happy people.

"Good evening, officers," Jillian says with the tinge of an inside joke.

"So, what do we have here?"

Before Pepper can speak, Jillian says, "Rich girl on a learner's permit, on her way to see rich boyfriend, drops directions in the car, reaches down, swerves into oncoming traffic."

Hamilton looks back at the skid marks on the road and nods. "Exactly how I'd have read it." Suarez goes to the Jetta where the girl is rummaging through the glove compartment. "Are you okay, miss?"

"Oh, yes. Thank you, ma'am. I mean, officer. I'm just looking—oh! Is this the registration?"

Suarez shines a flashlight at a paper and says, "That's it... Emily," then angles the beam to a note with an address on the driver's side floor. "Is that where you were headed?"

Emily looks down. "Yes. My friend Diane—her family just moved from Quince Orchard. Her parents went out, and she got kind of freaked being alone in the house, so I was just going to keep her company."

Suarez wants to say, "Kind of dressed up to see a girlfriend..." but hours of sensitivity training kick in.

"Maybe you should call Diane to let her know?"

"Oh my God! You're right."

Emily barely looks at her phone and it's dialing. "D? Oh my God! I got in an accident. I'm so sorry...Don't be scared! Are the doors locked? The alarm on?"

Returning to Pepper and Jillian, Suarez says, "Amazingly enough, she apparently was just going to a girlfriend's house to keep her company." She looks at Jillian, "Counselor Corbin, I can call a squad car if you'd like a ride home."

Jillian politely declines. While Suarez goes back to Emily, Hamilton ducks into the air-conditioned squad car. Watching him, Jillian says, "Funny, Hamilton looks like Channing Tatum, but somehow he's not at all good-looking."

Pepper burps out, "Kind of like that girl in Madison who

looked like an unattractive Olivia Newton-John."

"I remember her. Seth Meacham called her 'Olivia New-ton-John the hard way.'"

"Meacham was such an asshole."

"Why? Just because he had that life-size poster in his room of that Manson girl who took a shot at Gerald Ford?"

"Squeaky Fromme."

"Right."

"Oh, for the days when girls attempted assassinations. Don't quote me on that."

"You never said it. Anyway, one slow day at the office, I Googled Meacham. He died of AIDS in 1993."

Pepper is always thrown by news of peers dying of natural causes. His mother calls in the bulletins from back in Arizona. Gary Frost from high school, pancreatic cancer. Robbie Hench from his Cub Scout troop, a massive coronary on the golf course. This whole aging business won't back off, always jumping into your lap.

As Pepper shoos away images of Seth Meacham wasting away, a Bentley SUV bolts out of the darkness and stops with a screech. A man in black jeans, shiny black loafers, and an olive polo, jumps out and beelines to Emily, who hangs up on Diane at super speed. Hamilton comes back to Pepper and Jillian as Emily's father officiously leads her into his Bentley and shuts its doors.

"Here comes the revisionist history," Jillian says.

Pepper says, "Jesus, a Bentley SUV. I mean, if that isn't the all-time let-them-eat-cake car, I don't know what is."

Jillian nods and walks over to chat with Suarez.

With a lull in the action, Hamilton walks over to Pepper and says, "Hey, Mr. Pepper, I hope you don't mind me saying, I'm a big fan and I'm sorry about all the grief you're getting for your hysterectomy joke—which I thought was totally funny."

Montgomery County PD thinks I'm funny. Maybe I can get a Netflix special. "Thanks. Appreciate it."

Hamilton shakes his head. "All this PC crap going around

these days. You know, my buddies and me? Once a month, we go on what we call a 'Freedom Drive.' We just drive around spouting all the stuff we grew up on: 'pussy,' 'fags,' 'dikes,' 'chinks,' 'camel jockeys,' 'spics.' You name it, we fucking say it all just to feel American again, you know? It's such a high, like a catheter."

"Catharsis."

"Right. See, that's why you're a writer and I'm a cop. Anyway, you ever want in, call me at the station house. We'll take my Tahoe out and fucking rip it up for a few hours."

"I'll keep it in mind," Pepper says, quarter-heartedly.

"You got a Super Bowl prediction?" Hamilton asks.

"Put your money on the Patriots winning the dullest game ever."

It's nearly five minutes before Emily's father leads her out of the car, waves the police over, and starts manipulating as if she's Charlie McCarthy on his lap.

Hamilton and Suarez return to Pepper, who asks, "So, did she say I threw eight bottles of Jack Daniel's down a sewer right after the collision?"

"No sir," Suarez says. "That would have been a more believable story."

Over the next fifteen minutes, information is exchanged, and tow trucks arrive. Pepper tests his car and turns one truck away, the Subaru's damage purely cosmetic. The police leave. The incident feels over. But before Emily gets into the Bentley, her father motions to her to go over to Pepper. She follows his orders, looks down and says, "My father wanted me to thank you for handling this in a gracious manner."

"Of course, Emily. Take care and be good to yourself."

Pepper's kindness quakes her lower lip. "I'm really sorry," she says, straying off-message. "Please don't hate me."

She falls into Pepper for a hug. He keeps his hands visibly off her as her father leans out his window, agitated, sensing a deviation from his instructions.

Pepper wants to say, "Oh, Emily. Who can possibly hate you?" but he refrains, again deferring to the age of take-everything-the-wrong-way. Instead, he gently backs off her and says, "Emily, I have a daughter. I know a nice girl when I see one."

"Thank you. That's really nice of you."

The conversation should end here, but Pepper can't help himself: "In fact, Emily, the only thing I feel bad about is that your father made you lie to the police."

He expects the girl to tear up again, even hopes for it.

Instead, she ices up. "My father," she says, "is a monster."

Pepper drives Jillian the remaining few miles home, wondering what it takes for a girl to call her father a monster. *Thea wouldn't come within 10,000 miles of saying anything like that.*

In truth, he's aware of the conscious effort Thea makes to assure him he's everything in the world to her, every "Daddy" a drop of reassurance, every big decision she makes diligently done with his consultation. She was accepted to Cornell, Duke, Wisconsin, UVA, and Georgetown, where she wanted to go to stay close to him. Pepper urged her to have the full experience of living in a dorm in a college town, so they settled on UVA. Two hours away. Beautiful school. Pepper had warm memories of just starting at the *Post* and covering Ralph Sampson's first college game. He drove Thea down to Charlottesville for her freshman year, choking up the closer they got. On entering her dorm room, she dug into her suitcase, pulled out a gray *Washington Post* T-shirt, and pulled it over the white long sleeve tee she'd already had on. When her roommates arrived—funky Esme Asher from New York and pudgy, curly-haired Denise O'Dowd from Dayton—it took no time for Thea to say, "Oh, if you're wondering about the shirt, my dad is journalist for the *Washington Post.*" Pepper knew they barely noticed the shirt. They were wondering about this beautiful, cocoa-skinned girl with her chalky-white father and no mother to be seen.

Six years later, when Pepper helped move Thea into her first apartment on New Hampshire Avenue in Washington, DC, they wound up sitting on boxes in front of a brand-new Toshiba LED watching tiki torches march through her beloved Charlottesville. Thea puffed out her cheeks and sighed, just as her mother used to do. "I feel like America's becoming a prison and we're all in the general population."

"White supremacists chanting 'Jews will not replace us' is so sick. Why would Jews want to replace them? It would mean taking a huge pay cut."

"I have to tell Denise that line," Thea said, beating back a laugh. "Did I tell you she's studying to be a rabbi?"

"Rabbi Denise O'Dowd?"

"Actually, she's soon to be Denise Blum. She's the Ivanka Trump of my friends. Although when Jared goes to jail, Ivanka will probably run back to Christianity."

As Pepper drives on roads with vintage street lamps casting anemic light, Jillian says, "I think I'll run a little check on Emily's father tomorrow morning."

Prosecutors love getting the goods on assholes.

"What do you hope to find?"

"No idea. But when a girl calls her father a monster, there's usually a reason."

"Let me know if you come up with anything really juicy."

Jillian says, "Could you imagine how you'd feel if Thea referred to you as a monster?"

"Actually, I was just thinking about that."

"She reveres you."

"She should. She raised me."

Jillian nods, then quietly asks, "Does she ever ask about her mother? Or the circumstances of her existence on Earth?"

Pepper marvels at how a near-death experience induces a heightened intimacy among people, shedding the daily trifling of life in favor of more primal subjects.

"No, not really. It's my fault. I should have prompted her to discuss everything when she was ten or twelve or a teenager, but I kept thinking, or rationalizing, that she seemed so well-adjusted that she'd ask when she's ready. Now she's twenty-five, and it feels too late. I mean, she's such a together girl. But I can't help thinking that she's constantly observing herself, wondering what unforeseeable genetic personality trait will come out next. She's got a limited well of hereditary information to draw on. A mother she barely remembers, a biological father she never knew and has absolutely no chance of ever knowing."

Jillian waves her hand and says, "Yeah, but she's a practical girl. I always felt like she realized her situation, instinctively knew where to look for guidance, and kind of imprinted on you, like a baby lion who winds up being raised by a gorilla in some wildlife preserve. Well, bad example, but you know what I mean. I'm just saying, she's a lot like you. You are her father."

"Well, I appreciate that. Even the gorilla part. The weird thing is, you know how you always hear about adoptive parents getting so upset when their kids want to find their birth parents? I feel sad that Thea can't search for her birth father. Even if she wanted to, what's she going to do? Track down every black athlete from the '92 Olympics and ask if they had a one-off fling with an American white woman during the games?"

"Pretty amazing that both her biological parents were athletes and yet she chose to go into journalism. Your profession. You sure as hell did something right."

"Yeah, I'm pretty happy about that. Although, somehow, at eight years old—eight!—she kind of sensed that the world of sports was a sandbox."

"Still, my kids would have rather been embalmers in a funeral parlor than go into law."

Pepper pulls into the gravel driveway of Jillian's home. During the '90s, she—he, at the time—worked in private practice at Wilmer Hale (long before Robert Mueller worked there.) The sexier cases that distinguished the firm—Enron, Beatrice (*A Civil Action*)—didn't come his way, but his expert handling of radiantly dull litigations earned him enough loot to buy a Craftsman home in Potomac, a change of gender, and a shiny new divorce.

"Embalmers probably make more money than anyone at NPR. Speaking of money," Pepper says, "chez tu, amigo."

Pepper expects a mini-yuck from his mixed tongue announcement, but Jillian instead says, "You know, Arnie, I've tried to imagine that moment in GW Hospital when you first laid eyes on Thea. And If I'm overstepping here…"

Pepper cuts the engine.

"No. It's fine. I've told you more than anyone else about Jane and Thea and everything, and I still feel bad I haven't told you more."

Jillian says nothing, her courtroom experience telling her when a defendant should be left to confess.

"From the second the doctor told Jane she was pregnant, everything got so bizarre, although I didn't really acknowledge the bizarreness. For seven-plus months, I was so euphoric about the prospect of having a kid that I pretty much ignored the fact that Jane had stopped laughing, stopped being so energetic, stopped being herself—or what I thought herself was. When we got the sonogram photo, she stared at it so long she looked like an eyewitness trying to ID suspects in police mug shots."

"You know, I'm not supposed to say 'suspects' anymore."

"What do you mean?"

"They're called 'community members' now."

"I can't even…"

"Go ahead with your story."

"The first time the baby kicked, we were in bed watching *Airplane!* I hadn't seen it since it first came out. While I laughed my ass off, Jane would say in a monotone, 'That's funny.' Midway through the movie, Jane told me the baby kicked, and then she buried her head in her pillow. So much seemed weird, but I attributed everything to hormones. Then, in the delivery room, I'm doing all the bullshit coaching that deludes guys into thinking we have a role in what the doctors spent a dozen years learning how to do. I'm calling out 'push!' and 'breathe!', fully knowing I could be yelling, 'twenty-second time-out!' and it wouldn't matter.

"Finally, the doctor says, 'Almost here! Keep pushing!' A minute later, Thea's head comes out, and, god knows why, I notice the tops of her ears are the darker than her forehead, like mahogany. All dazzled and ignorant, I think: 'I guess all babies come out like that. Who knew?' But then I see the OB-GYN and nurses looking at me, like they're caught in a private moment of horror in which they don't belong. When Thea fully emerges, Jane takes one look at her, glances at me for a nanosecond, and closes her eyes. The OB-GYN pats the little brown-eared, gooey girl on the butt, she cries, the umbilical cord is cut, Thea's cleaned up, ushered back to us, and, in all that time, Jane never opens her eyes. But my eyes were wide-open, and I didn't see any of me in that little face. As much as I didn't want to, I started counting backward nine months.

"I don't know why I hadn't done the math before. Clearly, Thea was been conceived around the time of the Olympics in Barcelona. Jane was with me, but I didn't really see her very much. My schedule was so manic. And I was getting a ton of heat for slamming the Dream Team. The point is, Jane had a lot of time to fend for herself over the two weeks we were there. And clearly she did just that."

"Jesus," Jillian says. "I never get over how life can change in one second. Hell, three lives."

"Yeah. And then a few minutes later, it changed again. I held the baby and I was just mesmerized. Every slob in the world thinks his baby is the most beautiful in the world but... wow! I didn't care about the math. It didn't matter."

"I remember. She was breathtaking. She still is."

"Anyway, we took the baby home. We didn't discuss the parentage. We didn't discuss the fact that these two white people had just had a mixed-race baby. We acted like nothing out of the ordinary had taken place. It was like weirdest Tennessee Williams scene ever."

"How long was it before you finally talked about it?"

"Well, Thea was born in late April, and Jane and I finally talked about it...never."

"What?"

"We. Never. Talked. About. It. How sick is that?"

"Wow..."

"It's like our marriage turned into cold fusion. Does that analogy make any sense?"

"If you're a scientist."

"What I'm trying to say is that every couple, even one that seems perfect, has its own set of weird, ad-libbed bylaws."

"Hey, look who you're talking to. I bought clothes for my wife in my size."

"You're a special case. Maybe it's the only way marriages survive. The bylaw I had with Jane came down to ocean-deep denial. I mean, now it's mind-blowing how tightly I held on to useful fictions about my situation, but I bought in, whole hog. I can't imagine what went through Jane's head. Or mine! I do remember we were having a lot of sex at the time. Three times a day, minimum. She'd put Thea down for a nap and off we'd go. I mean, what new parents have sex all the time? It was crazy, like instead of make-up sex, we were having anesthesia sex.

"The moment that really stays with me was Thea's second birthday party. I was on the ground in Rock Creek Park surrounded by toddlers but really just watching Thea eat ice cream. I mean, the sheer joy in her face was almost too, like, rhapsodic to bear. At some point I just kind of looked up and saw Jane...loved me."

Jillian delicately says, "Maybe that's what killed her. A lethal cocktail of love, brain chemistry and guilt."

Pepper absorbs Jillian's guess. In over two decades of solitary review, retheorizing and reimagining the cold case file of his wife's death, he'd never considered this angle. Amazing. Talking to other people can sometimes be helpful.

"By the way," he says, "for the record, despite all the antidepressants I never knew she was taking, Jane was a really good mother."

"For most women, that would be enough to..."

Pepper has a thought that raw moments like this should at least cue up an uncontrollable attack of soul sickness. But no, his brain just cooks thoughts into English and ships them to his voice, like ordering lunch. No matter how fraught, life feels like a non-event.

After a moment of contemplation, Jillian says, "If you never discussed anything with Jane, how do you know she had a one-night stand with a black athlete in Barcelona?"

"She let slip a few drug-induced details while she was hospitalized—she called it the 'bin.' She described it as being something like Erica Jong's zipless fuck. No names, no talking. I don't even know if he spoke English. She also left me a note, but there wasn't much more in there..."

"At the time, I thought it best not to ask you what it said."

"I'm sure I appreciated that."

"Here's a truly vile question. The note...Where do you keep something like that? In a bank vault?"

Pepper chortles. "It's in a drawer under the *Post* and *Times* tear sheets from when I won the Pulitzer."

A spitefully high-wattage motion-detector light flares. Pepper looks around like an escapee in a prison yard. Jillian shakes her head and says, "It's probably a cat. The security system the county set up for me—it's nuts. Just because I bust some murderers and junkies. I also got a 9mm Glock and shooting lessons as a gift from some cops I know."

"Jeez."

Pepper flashes to a night he'd interviewed a hoops prodigy from Archbishop Carroll. As he walked to his car, a drive-by shooting went down half a block away. The blasts, like the street was in Dolby Surround Sound...

Jillian opens the car door. "Great night, huh?"

"All kidding aside? It *was* a pretty great night."

Jillian gives Pepper a hug. "Hang in there, buddy."

"Hey, one last confession? I thought the Muslim joke about the 75 million bad apples was funny."

"Me too. Any reasonable Imam would laugh at that. Shit, ten years ago, you could have sold that joke to what's-his-name with the chin on *The Tonight Show*."

"Jay Leno."

"Right."

Pepper is no rush to get home. He drives past the scene of the accident, seeing no trace of tail light glass or white German metal. Upon awakening tomorrow morning, all will be pristine for the fortunate sons and daughters of Democracy Lane.

And by the way, say hello to the first reporter to write about the sexism faced by Laila Ali and how she had every right to pursue any sport she wants, no matter how primitive and brutal, no matter how pathetically the dopes at HBO and Showtime keep boxing on life-support, pretending there's beauty in poor people vying to inflict the most permanent brain damage.

Back over the DC line, he passes a furniture store hyping its fifth semi-annual sale of the year. Ownership has changed hands countless times since he bought all new furniture for Thea's room as part of his over-gifting on her sixth birthday.

The general facts surrounding Pepper and Thea were hazily known in DC area sports circles. When he took her to work with him, his subjects went out of their way to heap affection on her. Juan Dixon, the leader of Maryland's 2002 NCAA championship team, played with a four-year-old Thea after practice one day. A note fell out of her pocket with her name, phone number, and "In case I am lost, my daddy is white" written on it. He quietly stuffed it back in her pocket and later told Pepper, "I really admire what an awesome dad you are." In 2002, Derek Jeter saw Pepper with Thea and offered his wisdom on biracial children, "If you ever need it, Mr. Pepper." Black athletes, so many with complex family backgrounds, innately trusted Pepper, in part because of his role as a single parent. It got to the point where he considered limiting her appearances at practice facilities just to avoid looking like he was using her as a way to get players talking. That problem was solved when the eight-year-old Thea woke him up in the middle of the night with a confession that had clearly been eating away at her: "Daddy, would you still love me if I told you that I don't really like sports?"

"More, Thea," he said, "I'd love you more."

"Why?"

"Because it means that you already know that there are more important things in the world."

"But writing about sports is your job."

"But what if my job was cleaning doodoo out of the cages at the National Zoo? Would you feel bad about telling me you don't like animal doodoo?"

Thea thought it over. "No," she said. "But I do like the zoo. And my friends' parents all call it 'poop.'"

"I prefer doodoo. And I'm a highly respected writer."

"Actually, I *do* like the writing part of your job. Why did you pick sports, Daddy? You don't even seem to like sports very much."

Pepper sat Thea down and told her how the '72 Olympics led him to become sportswriter; how he had watched ABC's coverage every night, wanting to know more; how he'd gone to his local library during the day to read the *New York Times* articles about the endless controversies and tragedies of the Twentieth Olympiad in Munich. Rickie DeMont losing his swimming gold for taking asthma medication, the U.S. basketball team getting ripped off by biased referees; Eddie Hart and Rey Robinson missing their one hundred meter heats due to a disorganized coach; black runners Vince Matthews and Wayne Collett denounced for chatting and fidgeting on the victory stand; pole vaulter Bob Seagren having his pole banned—not to mention the small matter of the massacre of eleven Israeli athletes. And then IOC Pig/President Avery Brundage comparing the tragedy to the ban of Rhodesian athletes and bellowing, "The games must go on."

Thea listened to Pepper's half-hour litany, thought a moment, and said, "Yeah, I guess that could make sports kind of interesting. Although most sports stuff is boring-er than that."

Thea's conscious drift from her father's area of expertise ultimately inspired Pepper's six-part look into the relationships of sports stars and their parents. Lengthy interviews with open, eloquent people like Bernard King, Keith Hernandez, Tony Gwynn, Jennifer Capriati, Andre Agassi, Shaq, Isaiah, Jalen Rose, the Williams sisters, and a slew of others, produced gripping, sometimes tortured, recollections. The series was a way for Pepper to get across the aspects of being a professional athlete that obsessed him and that fans overlooked. As early as 1978, he watched McEnroe's outbursts with a strange empathy. If you're the most gifted human being to ever pick up a tennis racquet, how can you not rage against the imperfections of some hyper-polite British umpire sitting courtside in a lifeguard tower? During a 2001 interview, Pepper found himself staring at the hands of Kobe Bryant. Those hands, along with the body to which they are attached, have more God-given basketball talent than anyone in the history of the sport. What is it like to grow up as that person?

His series probed deeply into what it's like to raise an athletic child prodigy, to be dealt a joker full of jealousy, fear, and dangerous projection. On publication, Pepper expected a six-day string of letters from brain-dead fans along the lines of: "Oh, those poor guys who play games for all that money. Boo-hoo."

But the response was nothing like that. The series actually made some contact with the angrily repressed humanity of readers. The letters to the editor were sensible, even compassionate. The calls he got as a studio guest on sports radio—the media equivalent of drunken bar talk—were respectful and gratifying.

Then again, this brief bout of civil discourse did little to diminish Pepper's disdain for sports fans. Aside from the spotty presence of rational parents who don't force their toddlers to root for the home team and do let them think that ballparks are simply gigantic restaurants, and the even rarer people who simply appreciate the beauty of supreme athleticism, sports fans are, on a good day in Pepper's weary eyes, putrefying savages. Without knowing quite when the habit began, he enters venues peering into the stands like a Secret Service agent doing advance work on a Presidential speech. Who's the maniac who'll throw beer on some kid in the penalty box? Which freak shelled out a grand to a scalper so he can be heard calling the strong safety a nigger? And yet, TV's play-by-play drones describe every city as having our nation's most knowledgeable, loyal fan base. Raider Nation, Clipper Nation, Brewer Nation—all nations under God, insatiable, with bloodlust and venom for all. Arnie Pepper is perpetually scared shitless of the whole lot of them. But he still trudges to the press box and, like last January in Durham, becomes appalled all over again at hearing some semi-literate sportswriter who's chewed enough of his twelfth hot dog to say, "Hands down, Duke has the greatest college basketball fans ever." Trust fund monsters whose parents can shell out three hundred grand to a school that gives students carte blanche to chant personal insults at a kid who managed to get an athletic scholarship out of poverty. That's your greatest college basketball fans. The wantonly false sense of entitlement American fans assume—purely on the basis of paying for a ticket—is grotesque, the epitome of confusing liberty and license. The arena should be safe, the team should show some effort toward putting a decent product on court, and that's it, the only entitlements fans have a right to expect. You want to let them tailgate outside and gulp unlimited beer inside? Good luck. You want to show a guy with his mistress on the Kiss Cam five minutes after he's lost a week's salary betting on the coin toss at an in-stadium gambling kiosk? Knock yourself out. Someday soon, civil fans will vanish from the stands, realizing the "stadium experience" can't touch the "living room experience." Even historically fanatical fans will reassess the NFL's Super Supporter Package and start dropping out. Just wait for the inevitable Sunday when the Redskins don't sell out for the first time since the Carter Administration. It'll happen soon. Just because a fan is brainless enough to wear a hognose to games doesn't mean he can't identify a raw deal.

The parent-athlete series won Pepper a Pulitzer Prize. There was champagne in the newsroom, a hug from Donnie Graham, the rejection of a pay raise Pepper never requested, and later, Thea saying she was "super proud" of her dad—before mentioning that, according to her research, Nobel Prize winners get "like, a million dollars."

Pepper's meandering route has him back on Connecticut Avenue. At a red light, a youngish guy crosses the street with a guitar, probably coming off a gig at the kind of club that barely existed in Pepper's early years here. Still calling DC a company town rings false. Flocks of kids are moving in with artsier leanings, comedy clubs are everywhere, above and below ground, packing in audiences nightly, according to what Pepper reads in the style section. He smiles, remembering a conversation a year or so ago in which he asked Thea, "When did you kids get all this music and comedy talent?"

"In the future," Thea said.

She really is witty. And quick. Thank God she's not upset about my hysterectomy peccadillo.

When Thea confessed her ambivalence about sports, Pepper started taking her to museums and theater and tons of movies. He'd been a sporadic filmgoer before then but found himself loving it. Few people first become movie buffs in their forties, but he saw an upside: the first time he saw certain seminal films, he actually understood them. The downside was his discernment in choosing appropriate movies for Thea. Fourteen wasn't the age to see *Taxi Driver*. Thirteen was a little young for *Apocalypse Now* and *Five Easy Pieces*. And the best parenting tip ever? When your eleven-year-old daughter's nanny is eight months pregnant, save *Rosemary's Baby* for another time.

After that, if you happen to be a widower, avoid *Love Story*. It's no good when your daughter hears you sniffling in a theater *before* the leukemia sets in. *Jesus, around the eyes, Ali Mac-Graw looks a little like Jane.* Aside from that, Pepper and Thea had starkly different takeaways from the unbearably lovely Jennifer Cavilleri. When Pepper told Thea he'd be working more hours while writing his book, she asked if he would miss her debate club matches. Pepper assured her, "Nothing will change, Thea. I never went to your debate club matches." To which she laughed and said, "I guess love means never having to say you're not sorry." Pepper's takeaway was a quiet comfort in Oliver Barrett's leftover existence, the feeling that he'd lost the love of his life and hence was afforded the luxury of wallowing, of leaving the game, of embracing an imperviousness to loneliness. At the time he took Thea to see *Love Story*, he'd been seeing a woman for a few months. He abruptly broke up with her for no stated reason. She suggested he see a therapist, and that was that. He never saw her again nor a therapist ever. He did wonder if Ali MacGraw had any idea how many relationships she'd wrecked.

Still, movies touched off many of the conversations a widower and his daughter should have, the kind that would have been way too awkward for Pepper to bring up on his own. As it is, when they watched *Juno* in a hotel room in Hilton Head, he had to bluff his way through a seminar on ovulation.

That ditz at the hotel in Dallas in '86, the one who believed me when I told her I was a screenwriter and wrote both ET and Tootsie in the same year, causing her to grab my crotch at the hotel bar—was that criminally deceitful? Giving her a fake phone number that started with "555" and my home address as "10050 Cielo Drive," the address of the Manson Murders... Jesus, that was pretty bad.

He hits another red light at 18th, near the Metro station where, in 1980, his first year at the *Post*, Pepper seemed to cross paths with Ted Koppel three times a week, always saying, "Hey Ted, what day is Iran holding us hostage today?" Koppel always smiled and called out a number. Good guy, a TV journalist print people respected. Pepper never told his colleagues that he was happy the hostage situation led Carter to (wrongly) boycott the Moscow Games, Russia a place never on his bucket list.

Bucket list. Another of ten thousand witless American idioms. They pop up in the culture, Hollywood names a movie after them, you can't get rid of them. The bucket lists themselves— jumping out of a plane, seeing a game at Fenway, eating six meals a day in Italy, owning a Ferrari, a racehorse, a vineyard, seeing a high school bully from forty years ago and punching him in the face—show the poverty of ambition people have these days. And then they pass their empty dreams down to their kids, like the parents of that poor dying kid in Indiana finagling the Make-A-Wish Foundation into getting him floor seats to a game at Madison Square Garden, "the mecca of basketball." As Sarah Silverman said, they should call it The Make Another Wish Foundation. But no one told the innocent, cursed Hoosier he'd be sitting with a pack of money-grubbing tools from Wall Street, all talking on the phone the whole game, tucking in their ties in case some sweat from the league's worst run franchise flies into their direction. The kid and his beeping life support system flew in from Muncie, a real mecca of basketball, so he could sit in on a board meeting of people who go out of their way to contribute nothing to society, his only thrill having someone point out to him a few celebrities he's never heard of. Instead of seeing Spike Lee's terrific movies, the kid got to see a major talent at his worst, as a Knicks fan.

Sushi and rumination mix in Pepper's digestive system, a

case of battery acid reflux floating up to his throat. He's at a point in life where digestion requires planning, but who could've planned for this day? As much as he doesn't want to, he needs to get home to his bed and what he assumes to be one of the world's largest private collections of Pepcid. He wonders how he'll feel at this time tomorrow. It might be nice to not really care but then, he knows it would it would be awful to not really care. *Who could shrug off the end of a sterling career and just move on? What kind of life is being lived without caring about a major change?* His thoughts drift to some totally lost time zone in which, at this very moment, his fugitive friend Wally is sneaking through another day, definitely caring if Interpol throws him against a wall, slaps on cuffs, and delivers him to an American Embassy. Pepper can't believe he has to remind himself that even though nobody is out to snatch his freedom, his daily life matters. His job matters. *We're talking about* THE WASHINGTON POST, *people.*

Pepper's meandering drive lands him in Foggy Bottom. It takes some a priori knowledge of DC to detect that a college resides here—GW is an odd, citified campus where the academic buildings are camouflaged as regular downtown buildings. A few blocks away is the State Department, or what's left of it after Tillerson gutted the joint. Among the trillion rumors floating around Trump Town is the juicy tidbit that the Russians chose the Exxon planet-killer for the job. It's all too much to grasp, but Pepper tries to keep up. *The truth is, everyone at the* Post *knows Trump has been a big boon for the paper's circulation. When you get right down to it, Trump's whole mess of a circus is a lot more entertaining than if Hillary had won. Of course, who wants their government to be entertaining? Does the China tariff mean they'll have to change the name of the 99 cent store to $5?*

Late night in the nation's capital erases all signs of coast-to-coast chaos. The snoring city now looks incredibly beautiful, its hosed-down sidewalks glimmering outside walls that have seen so much. *Really,* Pepper thinks, *if you know where to look, this is a town anyone would be proud to show off to visiting dignitaries. They wouldn't need to see the rest of the country. They'd just assume, by extension, the USA is a lovely, generous place.* Pepper sits behind the wheel in momentary awe, considering how, even now, when the country feels palpably wrecked, millions of Americans are doing amazing things every day. *For every worthy cause, some group is raising money and awareness, consulting with experts, trying to make things better.* Like his friend Alice Vaughn, who annually solicits Pepper for donations to fight epilepsy—her son having been disabled for life by neonatal seizures. *We Americans suffer for a minute and get to work.* Twelve years ago, on a visit to Evanston, Il., Pepper witnessed the breathtaking effort Alice and her husband, Christian, put into injecting every possible joy into their boy's life. "We're making huge progress, Arnie," Alice said. Pepper nodded and asked directions to the restroom, where he took a moment to compose himself, to remind himself how, as he flies from game to game, the homes far below each contain miraculous beauty.

Now, driving wherever the lights take him, he vows to do more than his part to encourage America's "better angels," as the yearning historians on TV seem to say fifty times a day over the last two years. To diversify and increase his charitable donations.

How rich do you have to be to give it all away?

A tactless dump truck heaves garbage over Pepper's reflections. He'd like to retrace the thought sequence but knows it's run its course. Having been through a day in which the world's traumas have been overshadowed by his own, Pepper turns on NPR.

Sometimes, listening to the iconic station, he hears a piece Thea told him she'd worked on and he practically memorizes it, thrilled to talk to her about it later. At the moment, there's an interview in progress with the author of a book about America's plans for nuclear holocaust, how the government has stored up billions of dollars in cash to reboot the economy after the incineration. The cash, sealed in a city-sized, underground shelter, is nearly all two-dollar bills because the treasury realized no one in pre-nuclear winter America wanted to use them. *Boy,* Pepper thinks, *these bureaucrats put everything to use. Then again, what's the point? Why get the economy up and running again? With no major cities left, we're going to unwrap two-dollar bills and throw them into rebuilding twenty-five NFL-ready stadiums with retractable roofs and corporate boxes? Who even wants to live after a nuclear war? All those post-apocalyptic sci-fi movies where the bomb or some Martians blow up the White House, the Sears Tower, and the Hollywood Sign, end on a hot guy with a hotter wife and their wisecracking kids managing to come out unscathed, freeing the audience to skip out of the theater on the breeze of another happy ending. Then again, after 9/11, all the pundits were saying America would never be the same, but aside from a new tower and TSA agents, it's exactly the same. All that talk of American resilience translated into a long rebound into sleepwalking through freedom, no one looking for suspicious packages in trains, classrooms, or packed arenas, everyone circling back to believing whatever it is, it can't happen here. Maybe the whole human survival instinct has been bred out, the long-underrated path of least resistance took over when we weren't looking. All that incomprehensible theorizing about a collective unconscious—there must be something to it. Has science fleshed that out yet, or did America's big brains decide there was no money in it? Arm angles and fly ball trajectories and lean muscle mass and twitch speed, that's where the 5,000-square-foot indoor gym money is. You want the fast track to a Nobel? Build a better Tim Tebow.*

Ugh. Again, back to sports.

It's not a total accident when Pepper turns onto 15th Street and cruises toward the Old Ebbitt Grill, Washington's oldest saloon, one of the prime expense account joints in town. Slowing down, he sees two police cars outside restaurant, whirling lights flashing silently. Four cops casually stand around, semi-vigilant at best. Pepper reaches for his press credentials and eases up to the cops.

"Arnie Pepper from the *Post*," he says, flashing his press

card. "Good evening, officers. Just driving by. Everything okay at the Grill?"

One officer steps forward to the window of his car. His name is Bui. Pepper wonders what type of Asian he is. "It's quiet now but we're maintaining a presence due to an incident a couple of hours ago. One of your buddies from the *Post*—Franklin—was here before."

The name is unfamiliar to Pepper, but that's not unusual. There are hundreds, each one as self-important as the next. *He must be from Metro.*

"What was the incident?" Pepper asks.

"Someone threw a suspected pipe bomb at the place."

"Did it detonate?"

"No. The pipe didn't contain a bomb."

"What was in it?"

"A pile of gay porn magazines and a few photos of Kevin Spacey from *Entertainment Weekly*."

"I'd say you're bullshitting me," Pepper laughs, "but who could make up something like that?"

"Apparently some of the employees have received death threats from internet nuts buying into the baloney about a sex ring working out of the place."

"Wow, your job gets crazier and crazier. *I guess he hasn't heard that it was me running the scandalous screenings.* I feel for you guys."

"Well, thanks, Mr. Pepper. But didn't I see online that *you* have something to do with whatever is allegedly going on here?"

Pepper sputters, taken aback.

"Don't feel bad about your involvement in this on my account," the officer grins crookedly. "I'm getting overtime pay. And by the way, I thought your hysterectomy joke was *hilarious*. But my partner"—he motions toward the cop behind him—"thinks you're a dick. His eldest sister had a hysterectomy last month so..."

"Mm. Well, thanks, officer. I don't want to take up any

more of your time."

As Pepper shifts into drive, Bui says, "You think the Wizards have a shot at ever signing Durant?"

"Don't bet your overtime money on it."

Stepping on the gas, Pepper winces at the smallness of this city, how tiny a public profile you need to be famous everywhere. *DC is like a sorority house. There is no escaping recognition or gossip or admiration or hate.*

I don't want to think about it.

He clicks his thoughts to the safe zone of sports, focusing on Officer Bui's question about Kevin Durant. *Durant is from the DC area, so fans assume he wants to play here. Truth is, smart star athletes want to get as far away from their hometowns as possible, away from family, old friends, and all other childhood leeches. Okay, LeBron wanted to play in Cleveland near his hometown of Akron, to "bring a title to The Land." Well, he brought a title and then beat a hasty retreat to LA, less for basketball than sun and show business if you ask me. Meanwhile, clinging to its one championship in a thousand years, Cleveland is back to being Cleveland. No better, maybe worse.*

For the last mile of Wisconsin Avenue leading to his condo, Pepper seeks out a rerun of Howard Stern on Sirius. He loves everything about Stern: his voice, his incorrigibility, his bad-kid-in-high-school-makes-good fearlessness. It's perfect thought dispersal listening until Stern discusses Harvey Weinstein. He says something about Bill Cosby at least having the decency to drug his victims.

Yesterday, I'd have cracked up from that line. Yesterday...

At the top of the ramp leading into the condo's garage, Pepper waves his key card, then eases down and backs into his parking spot, hiding the dent in his rear quarter panel and fender. Of his two parking spots, he opts for the one not in the shadow of a massive Escalade. He turns left, twists his body to look out the back window, and backs neatly into the spot.

Before he cuts the engine, he notices the time, 1:31. Then he pushes the door open, swings out his left leg and—

A movement below the Escalade catches Pepper's eye. He hears a human cough—panic sends his body stampeding back to his seat. His returning left foot lands on the brake pedal. In the red light, he makes out a body on the concrete floor, near the front wheel well of the large SUV. He takes his foot off the brake. The darkness ups his terror. He flicks on his high beams. It is Bruce Bader Ginsburg.

Pepper's first instinct is to honk his horn or hit the panic button on his remote key. Instead, he slams the driver's door shut and locks it.

His second instinct is to drive away, but he fumbles his keys to the floor. Leaning down, he bangs his head against the steering wheel.

"Please Mr. Pepper, Sir! Please! I just came to talk!"

The word "sir" slightly dials down Pepper's panic. The window is open a crack. "How the hell did you get in here?" he barks.

It feels like the wrong question, but it jumped out first.

Still seated on the garage floor, Bruce raises his hands over his head, palms forward, as if surrendering to a SWAT team. "Okay, okay. See, I was just, you know, upstairs at the front door before and I buzzed your apartment, and no one answered and I was about to leave but this really old lady came out of the elevator and opened the door. She looked kind of hysterical, you know, in a bad way? So I, like, asked her if she was okay and she said she had to get a taxi to the hospital, that her husband was in some kind of, like, coma or whatever. So I go, 'Look ma'am, it's super late and it's going to be hard to get a taxi and you don't want to stand out there' so I got her an Uber. It was here in, like, two seconds."

Pepper grunts and puts his right thumb against the underside of his left wrist. He estimates 108 heartbeats a minute.

"Anyway, I kind of wedged a magazine under the door to keep it open and went in. I rang your doorbell and, like, knocked. Then I decided to wait for you down here."

Bader Ginsburg appears to have been photo-reduced back into a child, sitting there with his legs straight out, like Lily Tomlin's bratty kid in the big chair from *Laugh In*. The smirking menace from the airport and the phone calls has been benched, subbed out for a frail loser.

"How long have you been sitting here?"

A hairline shrug. "Two hours..."

Dreading the kid's answer, Pepper asks, "Why?"

From a fallen head come the words: "My girlfriend broke up with me."

Jesus. What, now I have to switch on some empathy? It seems unfair.

Pepper rechecks his pulse. Back under three digits. He gets fully out of his car, closes the door, and sits on the hood. His heartburn calls out in a soft burp.

"Bless you," says Bader Ginsburg.

So now life's tiny civilities have resurfaced in a garage on Wisconsin Avenue?

"She saw the Instagram video of me spraying you at the airport and broke up with me. I told her I did it for her, that I was standing up for all women. But she said women don't need me standing up for them, especially in a moment when there are no women around. Then she called me an asshole."

"Maybe," Pepper lies, "she'll feel more forgiving tomorrow."

"If you saw the look she gave me before she walked away—"

Pepper sifts through his thin library of wisdom regarding relationships.

"A woman in Milwaukee once told me break-ups never last if they happen because of just one mistake."

"Was she your girlfriend?"

"Actually, she was a prostitute," Pepper says, not fully committed to pity. "I was interviewing her for my student newspaper."

"Don't say prostitute."

"Excuse me?"

"You're not supposed to call them prostitutes anymore.

They're 'sex workers.'"

"Oh, for God's sake," Pepper says with too much disgust before quickly backtracking. "Sorry."

"It's okay. All that vocabulary drives Mia crazy too. That's my girlfriend's name—Mia."

Pepper wants to say that Mia sounds awesome but thinks better.

"Also, my name isn't Bruce Bader Ginsburg."

"No shit, Bruce, really?"

With a weak laugh: "My name is Jackson Whitney."

"Jackson's a cooler name than Bruce."

"My parents named me after Jackson Pollock. Pretty ironical after how I sprayed you today, huh?"

Ironical? Isn't ironic enough?

Jackson shakes his head and says, "Maybe the video was just the excuse Mia needed. Like she was thinking of breaking up with me anyway. I just didn't see it coming."

Pepper rides more annoying waves of pity and says, "Hey, the more you're in love, the less perceptive you are and the more signs you miss."

This note of human kindness sends Jackson to the edge of tears. "I'm such an idiot..."

Pepper slides down from the hood and sits of the floor, across from the kid. "No. Your heart was in the right place. Granted, the right place was a little perverse in your case but... Okay. Look. The point is, we're guys. We're all idiots."

"I'll never find another girl like Mia."

"Sure you will. We all do eventually. I mean, not me. But everyone else..."

Amid thick breaths, Jackson asks, "Your Wikipedia page didn't mention your marital status. Are you married?"

"No."

"But you have a daughter, so I guess you were married."

"Yes."

"Did your wife dump you?"

"No, I'm a widower."

"Oh, I'm sorry. Did your wife have cancer or something?"

"Clinical depression. She swallowed a fistful of pills in the mental health clinic where she was 'resting,' as the professionals put it."

Sitting there, Pepper realizes that he has told these facts to only three other human beings—his mother, Jane's mother and Jillian. Then, for the next twenty-one years, not a peep. Now, perhaps riding the momentum of tonight's talk with Jillian, he's recapping the darkest story of his life to a nobody, a jilted fetus on the cement floor of a parking garage. And he doesn't want to stop.

"If the professionals were more professional, they might have figured out how she obtained the pills nineteen days into her stay. No one knows. The doctors, staff, my wife's friends, her family—everyone had theories. Her father still calls me with new thoughts. Poor Harvey. His daughter's death is like his own Kennedy assassination. I started to look into it a few months after she died, like who visited her and snuck her the pills, but that lasted less than a day. I just couldn't do it. And what was the point anyway?"

"Getting closure?"

"Bruce—I mean, Jackson—closure is bullshit, a media term, not a reality. Reality was, my wife wanted to be dead. I fell in love with and married someone who wanted to be dead. Although, before she wanted to be dead, she was a great girl."

Pepper looks at Jackson half expecting to hear, "Don't say girl" but instead: "What was her name?"

"Jane."

"What was she like?"

"What's the difference what she was like?"

Jackson just looks up, sad but wide-eyed.

"I don't know," Pepper says, "kind of delicately joyous, I guess. Big personality, high-strung, adventurous, independent, secretive. You knew she was in the room. She was always first onboard with every new trend: aerobics, punk rock, veganism, belly button rings, Prozac, rollerblading. Very athletic. Got into college on a swimming scholarship but separated her shoulder skiing on her first spring break. She seemed to accept it with a smile and her kooky laugh, but I think, to compensate, she exclusively dated athletes. Although now that I say it, it sounds like a stupid theory. Or an excuse for never asking her out. I mean, I had a crush on her from freshman year—"

"Don't say freshman."

"Oh, God."

"Freshman is a gender-based word. They're called 'first years.'"

"Excuse me while I blow my brains out."

"Sorry."

"You kids are amazing at coming up with solutions to non-existent problems."

"Yeah, I guess. Anyway, how did you wind up marrying her?"

"How is that relevant?"

"I want to know."

"Jesus. Okay: I bumped into Jane years later outside the Haitian Embassy. She got her master's in French—in France—and was working as an interpreter at some AIDS-related forum. I hadn't seen her since college, and it was nuts I saw her that day. On any other Tuesday in my career, I'd have been at work. But that one day I was walking my dog mid-morning after a Monday Night Football game in Baltimore went really late, and boom! There she was, in a black suit, looking tall and healthy and unlike anyone else in the history of Massachusetts Avenue. Well, anyway, we got married in Martinique eight months later because they speak French there. The next three and a half years were pretty fantastic."

"Then what happened?"

"My wife gave birth. Leave it at that."

"I saw a picture of Thea. She's really pretty."

"Thanks."

"So Jane was African American."

"White as the driven snow."

"Oh. I guess I should have assumed that from the swimming scholarship."

"Because black people can't swim?"

"Oh my God. That was a horrible thing to say. Sorry."

"No problem. Look—"

"So, wait. Does that mean your wife cheated on you with an African American?"

Pepper feels a slowing in his urge to spill his guts.

"Jackson, really, how is that your business?"

"It's not. I'm just curious."

"Yeah, I noticed. Look, he could've been an African European or an African Asian or just African. But not African American. Let's leave it at that."

"Are you still in love with her?"

"Look—"

"That's my last question. Promise."

How do stupid kids ask such smart questions?

"I don't know if I'm still in love with my late wife or just in love with the idea of her, what she represents. It's not like a divorce where your ex-wife is still walking the planet, occasionally popping back in your life long enough to remind both you of everything wrong with each other. It's like how NBA fans look back at Karl Malone and only remember—well, actually forget that. Damn. What I'm saying is, my feelings about Jane are a muddle. I do know I'd like to talk to her. I have some things to say to her. Maybe it would clear up my all-over-the-place feelings. I've probably over-idealized her over the years. But what can I say? Overdosing makes the heart grow fonder."

Jackson scrunches his face, not nearly up for a suicide joke. *A humorless generation, Pepper thinks, all of them cramped by moveable crap like right and wrong. If the world doesn't end first, they'll all live past a hundred, doctors propping them up on a thousand meds purely so they can keep on scowling.* The image of Jackson one day hunched over his titanium hips with the same hopelessly offended face, grumbling at his half-deaf third wife, snaps Pepper fully out of his confessional mode. Flipping the conversation, he says, "So tell me: Why did you come to talk to me tonight instead of, say, your parents?"

Jackson's face hardens in imitation of his apparently lock-jawed father. "Jackson, your mother and I will be vacationing on the Tuscan Peninsula this summer."

Another resented father. Pepper has had enough of Daddy Issue Turnpike for one night. "Look," he says, "I need to sleep."

Pepper gets none of the expected resistance. Jackson simply looks down and says, "I know. I'm sorry for imposing. I really appreciate you talking to me. I don't deserve it after what I did to you. And by the way, there's no such thing as estrogen mist."

"So I've heard."

Jackson pulls himself to his feet and starts moping his way to the garage door, his sadness turned physical.

Poor kid.

"Hey, Jackson..." Pepper says, against his better instincts.

The kid turns his weighted head.

"...Don't get too comfortable in your grief."

In a moment of implausible clarity, Jackson looks away from Pepper and says, "Funny. I was just kind of thinking that about you. Like maybe you haven't, like, moved on from your wife's death."

Pepper gets under his blanket, lies on his back, and looks up, finding himself in a position he's pondered in the cases of hundreds of other people: lying in darkness at the end of a life-changing day. Tiger Woods' first night alone in rehab. Jared Fogle recalling his last meatball sub while staring at the ceiling of a federal prison. OJ closing his eyes after knifing his wife's head off. Ted Kennedy after Chappaquiddick.

A wildly obvious conclusion drops from the ceiling: *I'm overrating my situation. I may lose my job. But I won't die, go homeless, gain 200 pounds in lock-up, or become a worldwide pariah. I won't be buried in legal fees, deported, disowned by my mother, or excommunicated from atheism. People won't walk out of restaurants at the sight of me. At least they probably won't. And if they do, fine. Faster service for me.*

Pepper rarely sinks this deeply into himself. It amazes him how the smallest amount of public attention remodels your own bubble, how media focus is a viral form of terminal narcissism, deluding you into thinking you actually matter to the outside world, that your self-absorption is shared by others, that your "profile" is part of the public's daily consciousness. But you see it everywhere. If Andy Warhol could see the caliber of people who quote his line about "fifteen minutes of fame," he'd lace his Campbell's Soup with strychnine. So many nobodies get their brief whiff of notoriety, then spend their lives desperately trying to get it back long after being forgotten. As a last resort, the dream of a media tour leads to an idea for a book title and then to the pesky chore of actually writing a memoir. This ass-backward way to write a book isn't even the tail wagging the dog. It's the tail wagging another dog's tail wagging the dog.

Pepper tells himself, in many uncertain terms, that maybe all this will turn out just fine. *Who knows? Maybe, in this random universe where nothing is meant to be, all this happened so I'd move on to something better. Maybe getting fired will lead to writing another book. Not a profit-free collection of my best columns, but a bestseller not about sports. Or maybe all this happened so I'd be freed up to travel somewhere and meet a nicer, less judgmental God. Or, even better, maybe all these recent events were engineered so I could meet Danielle. Because of a hysterectomy joke, I got a woman's number! Or maybe the universe wanted to take my friendship with Jillian to a new level. She's even smarter and funnier as a woman. Holy cow. Could this shit storm be full of possibility? Really, when you get right down to it, how do you know that what happens to you isn't good?*

Before his new logic begins to rot into rationalization, Pepper turns on his side and sleeps.

The not unpredictable dream, as much as Pepper can piece it together, has him playing one-on-one against Diana Taurasi at an arena in Munich before a crowd of 3.2 million fans, all women.

It's just under a sell-out and Pepper worries he's let the promoters down. The game is to twenty-one, winner's out. In no time, Pepper goes up 12-0 and Taurasi calls for a twenty-second timeout. The PA announcer announces to the crowd that, "Life is a game of runs," and is roundly booed. Pepper is interviewed at mid-court by Doris Burke, who says, "Arnie, you're six for six from the floor and your three assists is a new record for a game of one-on-one. What about that sexist joke you made?" Pepper shrugs and says, "I made a bad decision. It is what it is." Pepper goes to sit on a park bench on the opposite side of the court from Taurasi, who reclines on a chaise longue surrounded by coach Lisa Leslie and assistant coaches Sue Bird, Martina Navratilova, Rosa Parks, and Angela Merkel. On the Jumbotron, he sees Leslie pointing at him and hears Merkel yelling, "Diana! He's ALT! Get physical with him!" Two-and-a-half minutes into the twenty-second time-out, Thea comes over to Pepper and says, "Daddy, take it easy on Diana. You don't want to beat the best women's basketball player ever in a blow-out." Pepper nods. "You're right. Sorry. I'll back off, honey." Thea says, "Don't say cunt." Pepper says, "I didn't say that word. I'd never." The buzzer sounds. On the first possession after the time-out, Pepper purposely dribbles the ball off his foot but it caroms off Taurasi's shoulder and into the basket. 14-0. Over the PA system, Thea says, "Daddy, what did we just talk about?" Next possession, he aims a three-pointer clear over the backboard, but it hits a newly installed scoreboard, banks off the front rim, back rim, and drops through. 17-0. Pepper argues with referee Ruth Bader Ginsburg that the scoreboard is out of bounds and his basket shouldn't count. RBG disagrees and slaps Pepper with a technical foul, automatically adding two points to his score. 19-0. Pepper turns to his bench and sees Thea defiantly putting her arm around Jane, who's wearing a Barcelona '92 jacket. He takes the ball out at the top of the key, throws it up in the air, turns around, and bicycle kicks it. Swish. 21-0. Game. The entire stadium instantly clears out except for three female Swedish soccer fans, who simply say, "Good game" and Sarah Huckabee Sanders, who says, "I love hysterectomy jokes." Sanders is promptly replaced by Jason Robards as Ben Bradlee who pats Pepper on the shoulder and says, "You fucked up, kid. When is someone going to go on the record in this goddamn story?"

The Next Day

At 6:10, Pepper's ancient clock radio broadcasts the urgent voices of WTOP Radio. News, sports, and weather. He wants no part of all three but is too tired to argue.

He hears the name "Trea Turner," who either hit a game-winning double, stole three bases, or made a game-losing error. Pepper is too foggy to focus, slipping in and out of half-sleep. Only a screeching ad for an auto parts store jolts him to full consciousness. He flicks off the radio and thinks about a recent column he'd written about Turner after the Nationals shortstop was in pregame tears, owning up to and apologizing for tweets from his college years at NC State featuring both racist and homophobic slurs, with some added shots at the mentally disabled.

Turner was the third MLB player in July to have offensive posts from his feckless past come back to haunt him. When Josh Hader took the mound in Milwaukee just days after a trove of his racist posts turned up, much of the Brewers' crowd gave him a standing ovation. Jesus. If he'd murdered a few black guys, he'd have probably gotten the key to the city.

Pepper had interviewed Turner a few times about trivial baseball stuff—as opposed to interviewing the lead-off hitter about the pros and cons of third world debt relief—and had the general impression of a nice, friendly, fun-loving kid who runs really fast. When it came time to write about Turner's Tweets, Pepper had felt stuck. What can you say about an instance encompassing so much of what's disastrous about America? A middle-class kid from a nice family in a neighborhood of Florida where he was surrounded by aged liberal Jews spends three years in college and yet somehow the flesh-eating plague of Twitter entices his thumbs into bashing gays and Down syndrome kids. Pepper remembers when he was fourteen, his father telling him "Don't pick on the fags. Deciding to live like that? They have it tough enough." His father died of a massive coronary in '88, too soon to see gays trying to get married and fight in our unwinnable wars. If he'd held on to see all that, Pepper imagines him saying, "Marriage? The military? I don't get the appeal, but if that's what they want, fine." Now we've got America's youth throwing around all their ignorant enlightenment. Hopeless, Pepper had thought, when he sat down to write the column about Turner. How could he, a fairly intelligent, two-legged mammal, write 1,500 words of cogent wisdom about how viciously deranged we are?

He wound up writing a column devoted to reminding everyone that when we talk about professional athletes, we are talking about children, forgivable children, who drop a pass or miss a shot and call their moms in Wichita in the middle of the night, crying their eyes out. And yet, we grow up admiring athletes as gods and never get over it. Including himself in this syndrome, he wrote about how, in the middle of locker room interviews, it's dawned on him that he is thirty years older than his subjects and still looking up to them! He comes up shy of the crucial thought: I know so much more about your life than you do. You're a kid! In fact, he wrote, most professional athletes are less than kids. While they were practicing crossover dribbles and curveballs, everyone else in their high schools was socializing and taking baby steps toward being an adult. In America, the blessing of ungodly physical talent is a gift that does stop giving. It stops giving over and over, limiting the experiences and futures of adolescent wunderkinds again and again. Pepper wrote of hearing about a recent NBA first round draft pick getting home from a road trip to find no working utilities in his condo. Turns out he had no idea he had to pay for water, gas, and electric. Children. In 2010, after two-thirds of the world's tackiness came together to stage The Decision, LeBron got worldwide criticism for handling the situation with a lack of class. Put aside the fact that a bunch of parasitic agents in Hollywood plotted out the whole debacle, not to mention the presumption that anyone can define what the hell qualifies as class. Why would anyone assume a twenty-six-year-old kid from Akron should live up to any pseudo-sophisticated Caucasian conception of propriety? We're talking LeBron James, not Gwyneth Paltrow. A basketball prodigy who never gave college a thought, not Barack Obama. A child born to a sixteen-year-old mother, not Prince Harry. The fact that LeBron has grown into a man of conscience is incredibly gratifying, but irrelevant to the point at hand. The greatest athletes in the world are, by and large, children, and the psychological transference of fans upon their idols goes a long way to keeping them children.

All in all, Pepper looks back at that column as an admirable miss, passionate and correct but not altogether cogent. Oh, well.

He sips from a water bottle on his night table, his throat perpetually dry from a combination of air conditioning and a disorder he calls *Washington Post* Nasal Drip. He swivels out of bed, moves toward the bathroom, robotically performs his morning hygiene, and then throws on his clothes from last night for the walk to his Starbucks on Wisconsin. As he reaches the living room, he thinks he should at least change his shirt when he gets back. He'll be out and about later and, on the trillion-to-one shot he bumps into Danielle, he wouldn't want her to get the right impression that he's someone who would wear the same get-up two days in a row. The long-lost thought of there being a specific woman he'd rather not disgust gives him a nervously pleasant buzz. It's a good day to have a thought oasis.

The moment he steps out of his front door, he sees Mrs. Drexler in a baby blue terrycloth bathrobe, walking slowly with her back to him. When she reaches the end of the hall, she turns around and walks back with her head down. Pepper is reminded of something he read about Rose Kennedy. Upon hearing of Bobby's death, she walked down the street bouncing a tennis ball. *Amazing how you can read something that sticks in your head forever. Probably why there's no bandwidth left to learn anything new, like French or piano or the guardrails of humor.*

Guardrails. Another term beaten to a pulp by TV pundits.

"Good morning, Mrs. Drexler."

She doesn't look up, giving Pepper the sense that she's put off by having her trance interrupted.

"I had a thought for your husband when I woke up," he lies.

"He's not doing well," she says, continuing to walk with her head down.

"I'm sorry. If I can help in anyway..."

Finally she looks up.

"That's kind of you. Especially since, from what I hear, you have your own problems."

There's a reason that clichés like "misery loves company" attain cliché status, Pepper thinks, but he wants no part of this poor woman's commiseration, especially the tinge of judgment he senses in her voice. He volleys back with partially blocked resentment.

"Mrs. Drexler, my problems are nothing."

The elevator door opens, providing a rescue. Pepper rides down, marveling at how the jousting match of human contact never takes a time-out. *Fifty thousand sporting events, fifty-two weeks a year, and there's really only one game in America: "My Life Is Better Than Yours." This elderly woman up to her eyeballs in her life partner's mortality still finds the wherewithal to comment on my travails? How does the human nervous system make room for that? Hell, she was in the hospital all day and on a vigil all night. How did she even hear about my situation? Maybe she saw something about it on a hospital TV while the doctors were monkeying around with her husband's mitral valve. They have a million TVs in those going-out-of-business wards, anything to get loved ones' minds off the inevitable. Then again, maybe she wasn't even referring to my current situation. Maybe she was just commenting on my life in general. A participant in even the shittiest marriage will look down on an unmarried man living alone.*

For Pepper, this is a depressing thought, leading him to assume that lots of people beyond Mr. Drexler will now look down on him as a man living alone and dealing with the sexual chaos of 2018. He can't help reasoning that people—readers, colleagues, neighbors, friends—are probably theorizing about what perversions and vices might be going on in that spacious condo of his, their radars dialed up for clues, their memories flipping back for missed signs. *No matter how safe, antiseptic, and run-of-the-mill my life really is, their imaginations won't buy into a solo private life without extra-strength decadence. These days, perversion is run-of-the-mill and a vile and freaky secret identity is assumed—a question of what, not if. Maybe, they're thinking, the nuts are right this time about what I've got going on at the Old Ebbitt Grill. Or maybe they think I'm on a first-name basis with an international buffet of Russian hookers (sex workers) or that I've got a safe room crammed with enough leather to dress the Hell's Angels or that I'm just the one pedophile who liked sports too much to go into the priesthood. After all, the guy made a hysterectomy joke. There must be something pretty damn repugnant going on there.*

For once, he wishes someone else was in the elevator, someone to distract him from himself.

He gets off on the ground floor and goes to the mailboxes, his slot thick with junk. He recycles everything but two bills and an emaciated copy of *Time* magazine, flimsy as a menu. The cover blends the faces of Trump and Putin, the resulting visage even more horrifying than theirs are individually. *Thirty years ago, a* Time *cover like this would have shocked the nation. Now, nothing. How did Americans get so hard to shock but so easy to offend?*

Pepper recalls a recent magazine piece predicting that global warming will put all major American cities underwater by 2032. He'd showed it to Thea who said that, due to climate change, some of her friends don't see the point of pursuing a career. When Pepper asked Thea if she's worried, she'd said, "No. By 2032, I'll definitely have an apartment on a high floor."

My daughter is the greatest girl in the world.

All signs of life on Wisconsin seem to be limited to jogging. Outdoor summer exercise in DC is relegated to early morning and evening, with a midday workout being board-certified nuts. Pepper nudges himself to walk with more pace. Print journalists are not, as a general rule, morning people. They roll into work around ten, reading papers and drinking coffee before revving up their phone calls. Computers made showing up at all a lot more optional, and Pepper misses the early buzz of a crowded newsroom, the old wire machines clacking about the world-wide hubbub. He recalls that on May 18, 1980, the AP and UPI machines rang like slot machines. He happened to be nearby and raced in. He was disappointed to see it was only Mount St. Helens blowing up.

Walking past an apartment building annoyingly similar to his, he hears MSNBC leaking out of a second-floor window. *Maybe there's something to the whole Trump Derangement Syndrome. 6:30 in the morning and the town's already getting its fix. Then again, Mueller's probably been in the office for an hour already, his stone-jawed work ethic unstoppable. Unlike everyone else in DC, they say he wouldn't discuss his work with his mother. Then again, maybe his mother is a notorious gossip. Does Mueller ever make jokes in the office like a normal guy? Does he ever say, "Hey, Weissmann, I'll give you twenty bucks if you call Ivanka and tell her you subpoenaed her plastic surgeon. If it makes her flip, I'll go a hundred."*

Probably not. Those special counsel freaks keep their heads down and pound away. At this rate, Mueller will get Putin to flip, then close up shop. The media will report "the end of an era," as if there's not some American era ending every five minutes.

A jogger with a red headband and a black T-shirt with the only-in-Washington words across the front, "Gorsuch an asshole," slows his pace, jogging alongside. "Hey, Arnie," he says. "After reading your great article on the NFL kneeling rules, I officially retired as an NFL fan."

"You'll live a lot longer, my friend," Pepper says with grateful jauntiness.

"I was already turned off by the whole concussion thing."

"I hear you," Pepper says. "The NFL's biggest impact on society is that now dumb people donate their brains to science."

As the jogger laughs and then rumbles away, Pepper feels some buoyancy, warmed by the way a tiny dose of friendly yammering can goose his serotonin into hopefulness. Sometime in the '90s, his level of renown around DC settled into a pleasantly comfortable place. All the television appearances in which he inevitably made some wisecrack gave him an aura of approachability as a sports authority who doesn't take sports too seriously. People recognizing him on the street have almost invariably been jocular, usually to the tune of:

"Arnie! Think we can we kidnap Dan Snyder and sell him to the Skins for ransom?"

Or: "I hate to say it, Arnie, but your description of an ignorant sports fan fits me like a glove!"

Forgetting to walk faster, he thinks about the overall sweetness of the life he's made in this crazy town. He's a known quantity in Washington, DC, our nation's capital. He's made his own little dent on the cultural landscape of this worldwide center of power and stifling bureaucracy. Presidents and senators read his column along with normal people of all colors and creeds. They discuss his ideas, they steal his opinions. He has fans.

Amid all the good feeling, he remembers his upcoming meeting with the boss. Dark clouds gather, but Pepper fends off the feeling. *People in this town love me. I've been doing this for forty years. I'm a fixture. They can't fire me for one little joke.*

Can they?

At Starbucks, he's in line behind a gay couple with whom he regularly exchanges pleasantries. The taller one tells Pepper their air conditioner broke down last night. The shorter one says they're thinking of moving their stuff into Starbucks and just living here until Thanksgiving.

"You could do a lot worse," Pepper says with a smile.

"Oh believe me, Arnie, we have," says the shorter guy, his

diction more effeminate than his partner's.

Can a guy get woke enough to not notice that kind of thing? Not that it matters. Just... right?

Pepper feels grace in the sense of community he has with people whose names he can never remember, despite hearing the baristas call them out everyday. All the TV talk about divided America, how we've all retreated to our little bubbles... he loves his bubble. He wouldn't trade his bubble for any other bubble.

A ping rises from the phone of the shorter guy. He checks his screen and mutters to himself, "Oh, what else is new?"

"What's up?" asks his partner.

"There's an active shooter in Porter Falls, West Virginia. Wherever that is."

"It's in the southern part of the state, I think. By now, it should be bigger news if there's an inactive shooter."

Pepper orders a grande cappuccino and a classic coffee cake but is informed it's been discontinued. It's the third time he's settled on a regular choice of something sweet to start his day only to have it zapped from the Starbucks menu. Assuming symbolism he's unwilling to flesh out, he grabs a package of two shortbread cookies.

While the baristas concoct his drink, he stands behind a young black guy sitting at the bar, reading some news site on a laptop. Pepper finds it a bit reassuring the guy seems utterly unselfconscious, sipping coffee, not looking around in heavy dread of someone calling the cops on him for doing what white people do in a public place. Those two black Starbucks patrons cuffed in Philly just a few months ago, hauled off for getting together to drink coffee, another crisis faded as fast as it erupted, unresolved with life going on.

Pepper's thoughts keep doubling back to his predicament, and more specifically, his appointment with his editor, Linda Carlyle, which is hanging over him like sentencing hearing at DC Superior Court, only this punishment is to be handed down by fiat; no trial, no sentencing hearing. In the eyes of the public, and in the eyes of the corporation that employs him, he is already guilty. His sentence is the only question left.

Pepper starts doing some societal math. *What would be an acceptable outcome from the meeting with Carlyle? It's not like I'm Ted Bundy. Or even worse: said the N word. Alright, so I'm a dinosaur. I say things you're not supposed to say anymore. Let me sign the affidavit, bullshit my way through some Hail Marys and get this over with so I can knock out my next column about how the Terps will need to rely less on the running game after killing that kid at summer practice.*

He thinks about this for a minute. *Why should my good reputation go out the window for one little remark THAT I DID NOT EVEN PUBLICIZE MYSELF, OR CONSENT TO PUBLICIZE. Has anyone pointed out that whoever sent out that Instagram post not only stole my material, but violated the sanctity of the brotherhood of professional sportswriters? Not only should I keep my job, but there should be zero taint on my reputation. Just wait until they ask me to write a column pleading for forgiveness. I WILL NOT DO IT. I AM GUILTY OF NOTHING.*

And really, who among the dying-off population of readers is going to accept my apology? Sure, there would be a smattering of letters to the editor, one saying he was too quick to apologize, two or three offering maudlin praise for his owning up to the horrific nothing of which he's guilty, and the rest ripping him for being too arrogant, too thoughtless, too sexist, and too late. The whole culture of painfully honest contrition worked great for Tylenol, when some anonymous maniac laced their pills with cyanide. With unprecedented candor, Johnson & Johnson actually opted to tell the public the truth, sparking every MBA program to teach the strategy as a case study, a lesson that fizzled on graduation day. America wants to hear the conviction and punishment, the apology is time for a bathroom break. Hell, even God doesn't want to hear apologies anymore, despite all the pathetically pious assurances of mercy from a forgiving Almighty gushing out of our houses of worship. If God's so goddamn lenient, why couldn't he give Jane a break?

On his way back home, the light mood of his walk to Starbucks is nowhere to be found, the defense arguments he's rounded up since boarding the Delta flight, reduced to an over-all sense of powerlessness. *The NFL and NBA have changed the rules so there is no defense anymore and society followed along. Try to defend yourself, you're seen as defensive. Once you're seen as defensive, there's no defending yourself.*

In an effort to disperse his negative thoughts, he plugs his earbuds into his phone and hits random on his music library. Mid-song, he hears, "Any minor world that breaks apart falls together again..." The next song is a Jackson Browne dirge so dismal, Pepper scrambles to call up an off-beat podcast recommended by Thea. It's all international news, in-depth stories he'd be hard-pressed to find anywhere else. The first story is about a presidential debate in Brazil between a man and woman. The man, in an effort to paint his rival as unappealing, says he wouldn't even want to rape her.

There's no corner of the Earth for escape. He worries about Thea having decades ahead of her, the promise of her hearing about, reading about, and, God forbid, experiencing such global hell. Fleeing his apps, he calls her, knowing she's sleeping.

"Whoa, it's early! Are you okay, Daddy?"

"I'm fine, honey. Sorry to wake you. I just felt like hearing your voice."

"Aww. Are we still on for breakfast?"

"Absolutely. How about The Diner in Adams Morgan?"

"Perfect. 8:30?"

"Done. I love you."

"I love you."

And life breathes freely again. *See how easy it can be?*

Just outside his building, he comes face to face with the divorcee with whom he has exchanged eye-rolls but no words.

"You know," he says, "all this time, and I don't even know your name."

"You never asked."

"Well, there's that."

"Then again, I never asked either. Meredith Geiger."

"Arnie Pepper."

"I know. I read the sports page."

"Uh-oh."

"No, I like your column. Mainly because I usually agree with you."

"I like when people agree with me."

"Sorry to see you're in a little hot water."

"Oh, you heard about that too, huh?"

"Yeah. I read the thing about it this morning."

"I haven't seen the paper yet."

"It was nothing really, just a little Editor's Note with a vague description of your joke and a noncommittal 'we're looking into it' kind of thing."

"Strange that this would be the one day we finally have a conversation."

"A crisis, no matter how trivial, re-wires our thinking."

"You sound like you know what you're talking about."

"I'm a psychologist at the Pentagon. That said, I probably don't know what I'm talking about."

Pepper laughs, then breaks his rule about leaving well enough alone.

"So, you think my crime is trivial?"

"Well, I actually said your crisis is trivial. As for your crime, on scale of one to ten, with Al Franken at one and Harvey Weinstein at ten, you're a minus thirty."

Pepper is relieved until Meredith adds, "Of course, the scale is so out of whack right now that a minus thirty still falls somewhere between tasteless and disgusting."

How did being neighborly ever get a positive connotation?

Pepper's neck backs up and with blinking eyes he says, "Boy, my daughter's going to be so disappointed."

"Pardon?"

"Ever since I told her there was a divorcee down the hall, she's been bugging me to ask you out."

"I don't see why that option would be off the table."

"Well, Meredith, among my many character flaws, I shy away from people who find me somewhere between tasteless and disgusting."

"You? You're nothing compared to what's out there. Not long ago, I had a blind date. The second we met, he looked down at my legs and suggested I have cosmetic knee surgery."

"Cosmetic knee surgery?"

Pepper imagines himself on a date with Meredith, sitting in a restaurant as she focuses her psych expertise on him, trying to get to the bottom of a man who jokes about hysterectomies: The loss of subject's wife has awakened deep-seated misogynistic rage originating from a lifelong repulsion toward female genitalia arising from the prepubescent sight of his mother in the shower which gave rise to a repressed homosexual yearning expressed in frequent visits to locker rooms full of muscular, naked men. Ergo: his choice of a career as a sportswriter.

It dawns on Pepper that no matter what happens, the coming public psychoanalysis of him won't be limited to Meredith or her professional brethren. He can visualize people of all stripes, sick and tired of their own inner selves, happily taking their shots at his. Colleagues, strangers, hobbyists, all parsing his joke and projecting ignorant prognoses on him. "I'd always thought there was something a little off about him."

Imagine what people must be saying to Louis CK. I wonder if he even goes outside?

Pepper cranks up enough civility to look at Meredith and say, "Well, I've got to run."

"You mean, run away."

"Fine. I'm running away. From you. Because, in your terms, I present with a manifest fear of confrontation. In fact, that's how I got out of Vietnam, by telling the draft board I had a fear of confrontation. Okay? Satisfied?"

Meredith walks off in an unprofessional huff. Pepper immediately feels crummy for giving in to his instinct to toss

zingers. And yet, by the time he's in the elevator, he's thinking that, purely by virtue of being rational and fetish-free, he
should be among the six or seven most datable middle-aged
men in the nation. *Granted, it's not a highly competitive category.*
American men produce fewer and fewer goods, but boy, can we churn
out perversion. Our most creative artists can't compete with the ingenu-
ity of our degenerates, all of them normalized, as the pundits like to say.
No wonder it's without a trace of irony that news outlets report the latest
depravity in such vivid detail. "[Weinstein] then exposed himself, mas-
turbated, and quickly ejaculated into a nearby potted plant." Interesting
modifiers. Quickly. Nearby. Maybe that's the good news. He ejaculated
quickly and didn't tastelessly draw it out. The plant was nearby as men
haven't evolved to the point of whacking off from three-point range.

Nothing to worry about here, folks.

Pepper sits at his desk and charges his phone. He'd forgotten to do so last night; it's almost out of juice. Out of pure
nostalgia, his wall sockets still have child-proofing, left over
from Thea's toddler years. None of the kids he grew up with
got electrocuted or even wore seat belts. It's a miracle so many
sixty-year-olds are still enrolled among the living.

Pepper checks his emails, ignoring five from sports media
people, his head in no mood for well-meaning bromides. He
opens a sixth with the subject line "Thank-you so much!"

Hi Mr. Pepper,

I got your email address from the friend of a friend of a friend
of a friend who works at the Post and will remain nameless. The
reason I'm contacting you is because two days ago, I rescued
a terrier mix named Clara. I hate the name Clara but couldn't
think of one I liked UNTIL I read about your OH SO unfunny
joke about hysterectomies. That's when I decided to name my
dog Me-Too. Two syllables with long vowels divided by a hard
consonant! Perfect dog name! And I have you to thank!

Eat shit,

Clara Dempsey-Weinberg

Pepper's gut reaction is to marvel at the lengths to which this woman went to email him. The internet's warped edict that everyone's opinion matters has morphed into a bent form of home invasion, a victim without a crime. He pictures the woman now staring down at her inbox, dying for a response from him, a colloquy she can photograph and post on Facebook, leading to her viral moment in the sun. It won't happen. Poor Mr. Weinberg will come home to a livid wife and a baffled dog, the little mutt thinking she's better off back at the shelter with kooky but diligent volunteers lovingly feeding her kibble and the drivel that a perfect family will come around any day now.

Pepper remembers as a teenager seeing a photo of John Riggins when he played for the Jets, the wicked fullback with a Mohawk carrying a tiny rescue mutt, protecting it more conscientiously than any dopey football. The same Riggins who, as a Redskin, told Supreme Court Justice Sandra Day O'Connor at The Washington Press Club to "loosen up, Sandy, baby." They don't make them like Riggo anymore, the quirky athletes today trending toward carrying guns more than little dogs. Granted, their travel schedules make pet dogs impractical. Those who have them tend toward the Doberman-Rottweiler-pit bull varieties for protection against the overall derangement of sports fans, not to mention the groupies, ambitious women looking to get impregnated by someone with eight percent body fat and a no-cut contract. When Sports Illustrated wrote about all the NBA players having multiple kids with multiple women, Pepper wrote a column saying that groupies, like sports agents, should be certified by the players' unions. Even the greatest commissioner in the history of sports, David Stern, couldn't help calling Pepper to say he laughed out loud reading that column. A tiny smattering of women's groups was less amused, but that was two decades before America fell in love with moral outrage. Several years later, Pepper wrote a facetious piece about the NBA starting an affirmative action program to get work for more white players. Derek Fisher, former president of the NBAPU, ran over to him at a Wizards game to tell him how much the piece cracked him up. When five-time Pro Bowler Darren Sharper was sentenced to twenty years for multiple rapes, a list of the top fifty NFL players currently doing time raced around the internet. Pepper, only half kidding, suggested the establishment of a federal prison exclusively for professional and Division One athletes—You Da Man Quentin or The Pelican Bay Super (Sunday) Max or Jock-atraz—a facility offering uniquely focused rehabilitation programs that prepare inmates for the inevitably sad epilogue of most former sports stars. Well, of all people, Hall of Fame linebacker and acquitted murder defendant Ray Lewis called Pepper and said he not only laughed but thought Pepper could be onto something.

Amazing, Pepper thinks. *In this time of tyrannical political correctness, prison rape jokes are still acceptable. Prime time network sitcoms get canned laughs off prison rape banter without a drop of protest from the joke police. The horrors going on behind bars at this very second, and I'm the one who's up the creek? Maybe joking about sports has caught up with me, maybe the flippancy of all my words is now biting back. But then again, if being dead serious about the farcical world of sports is now a requirement, maybe it's time to get out, anyway. I made my reputation by poking the sports media's veneration of the game, the game, The Game. If their platitudes start breaking and entering into my column, infecting my bullshit detector, why go on? I couldn't do it anyway, not without unplugging a whole brain lobe. "He calmly stepped to the line and sank the free throw." Has anyone ever calmly missed a free throw? "The crowd is on its feet." Well, that's stupid. They paid for their seats. "The Orioles are desperate for an insurance run." Can't they buy one from Allstate? "Johnson was sidelined with an athletic hernia." As opposed to an academic hernia? "It's win or go home." Do the players have such bad home lives? "Hitting is contagious." If it's contagious, how come the other team doesn't catch it? "He worked hard the entire off-season." So, he really wasn't off, was he? "They're a very athletic* team." *Don't sports teams generally hire athletes?* "They traded him for cash and a player to be named later." *Does that mean they know the player, but his parents haven't named him yet?* "He's flirting with a no-hitter." *Did he get a date out of it?* "They made their draft choice, and the rest is history." *But when anything happens in the world, isn't the rest history?*

Pepper starts to get up when his inbox dings to announce a new email. The subject line sends heat through his face:

"Hey, Pepperoni!"

Trying to think of someone other than Wally Shockley who would call him Pepperoni, Pepper comes up empty. He debates opening the email, his ignorance of the cyber world inviting spiky questions. *If I read this, do I become an accessory to something? Would I be harboring or aiding and abetting a criminal? Should I call the FBI now? Is there a reward?*

His reporter curiosity forces him to open the email.

Bet you're surprised to hear from me! Was just reading the Post online (fugitives gotta keep up on sports too!) Saw you're in a bit of a jam...Look at us! Two peas in a pod! I have an untraceable phone...amazing what a few hundred million in stolen cash can buy! Call me!!!

Under the multiple exclamation marks is an absurdly long phone number with a 382 country code. Pepper quickly Googles. *Montenegro?*

His curiosity bumps to graduate level. Years ago, when Wally had gone on the lam, Pepper had written a piece about having an infamous fugitive for a friend. It wound up on the op-ed page, a nice, one-day furlough from sports. Now he thinks, *Hey, I'm a reporter!* His hands reach for a pen, a pad, and the phone.

"Holy shit!" Says Wally Shockley, "I knew you'd call! You're too much of a newshound to resist contacting someone on the FBI's Ten Most Wanted list, which I'm still on, as of this morning, by the way. I check every day as kind of badge of honor, although I really, really hate the picture they have of me. Ann took it in Sedona when we trying to keep our marriage together through a combination of rose quartz and the harmonic conversion. Guess the verdict's still out on that one, seeing as I've checked divorce filings on court websites without seeing my name on it. Poor Ann, her phone's probably bugged up the wazoo, her AOL account monitored by twenty-five different federal agencies, some financial feds checking out every withdrawal from the ATM. Hey, look. I didn't marry her, she married me! She asked. I said, 'Sure, why the fuck not?' Anyway, how the hell are you? It's so good to hear your voice!"

"Wally, I haven't said a word yet."

"Okay, now it's good to hear your voice."

Wally's voice, which always sounded like a 33-record played on 45, is now even more frenetic. An image pops in Pepper's head of Ray Liotta feverishly cleaning up his drug-infested house at the end of Goodfellas.

"Where are you, Wally?"

"Oh, come on, Pepperoni, you know I can't tell you that. I will tell you I'm not in Montenegro. Knowing you, you've already checked out the country code on my number. Suffice it to say, I'm somewhere outside America and living the life, baby. I'll also tell you that Trump was right about Africa being full of shithole countries. Couldn't wait to get out of there, although you're probably thinking that's a clue that I actually am in Africa. Which I'm not. So what's this shit you stepped in with the female population of the good old US of A? I mean, really, you of all people? The only guy in Chaparral High who didn't take his turn on top of Allison Wainscot! That's gotta be a mistake. Say it ain't so!"

"It's nothing, Wally. I just made a bad joke and it spiraled around the universe out of control."

"Obviously, if I know about it! I try to keep up on current events, but really, I do it out of habit more than anything else. I mean, what's the news of the world mean to me? Nothing.

I should only check to see if there's anything written about me. And I do! But somehow I can't stop reading about the shit storm going on back in America."

"It's a pretty crazy time," Pepper says.

"Tell me about it, Pepperoni! Meanwhile, I'm sitting here talking to you in a nice little house I bought with cash in a picture postcard little town where, like, four people speak English, so I don't have to listen to everyone and their ridiculously puny problems. I don't have to listen to anyone! Especially women, for Christ's sake! All my life, my mother, my two sisters, my wife, my three daughters. Holy shit! I've heard enough double X chromosome bullshit to last me nine lifetimes. I had a girlfriend until recently who I'd bang a few times a week, and I'll tell you, Pepperoni, for all I knew, she could've been telling me she was sent down to me from Neptune. I laid a few grand on her, hit the ejector seat, and that was that. 'Back to life, back to reality.' Who sang that? Oh, forget it, who really gives a shit? I'm living the life, baby. Not tied down to anything or anyone, packing unlimited cash. God, do you know how much people around the world just love American dollars? It's nuts. A picture of Ben Franklin is like porn to them. I flash a wad and it's like open sesame, advance to go! You can't imagine the high of living on the run with six phony passports. Shit, last year I had dinner with the US Ambassador to Greece! Me! A guy on the FBI's Ten Most Wanted List and the dork had no idea who I was! I'm living on the edge and killing it! I'm fucking Jason Bourne! Exhilaration every day, it's like totally primal, dude! I'm in touch with the primitive side of the human brain, the side that you and Thea—hey, I hope Thea's doing well, by the way—but what? Oh yeah, the primitive side of the brain. I'm the only person I've ever met who's managed to access the most basic levels of what it's like to be human. It's a fucking drug, man! The best drug ever! My animal senses are up! I'm seeing and smelling and hearing shit I never noticed before. Not that I ever put much thought into my life anyway, but still, I'm here to tell you, brother, there's more to life than picking up dry cleaning and ordering in from Grubhub. There's so much more, and me, Wally fucking Shockley, is the guy who's found it all! I'm, like, this visionary! This, this, this...guy! This ordinary guy who stumbled onto the truth through the sheer power of embezzlement. I'm the only person I've ever met who realizes that every minute of the day counts! Arnie...I'm so, so, so, so...fucking alive!"

Pepper pauses long enough to make sure it's his turn to speak. He exhales audibly, then gently says to his oldest friend, "Wally, maybe you should go to the nearest American Embassy and turn yourself in."

The explosion of bawling at the other end of the line, an adult male gurgling out the sobs of an abandoned child, is a sound Pepper will remember for life.

"It's okay, Wally. It's okay. Come home. I promise you, I'll find a way to be there at the airport when you arrive. I'll be the first face you see on American soil and it'll feel good to see a friendly face. You're a good guy, Wally. You did something ninety percent of men think of doing but they don't have your guts. You've been on the run for six years, you've learned a lot, you've experienced incredible things, but it's time to come home."

Listening and weeping, Wally finally says, "You think I can get into the same prison as Bernie Madoff?"

"It's not like applying to college, Wally, but maybe a good lawyer can swing it. And when you're there, I can ghost write your memoir."

"I like the sound of that," he sobs.

They talk a few more minutes, Pepper's paranoia waning but not enough to stop him from wanting to hang up.

"By the way, Wally, thanks for not ripping off my mother."

"That was actually a tough call."

They both, impossibly, laugh a little too long.

"Hey, Wally?"

"Yeah."

"See you soon?"

The sound of an exhausted man blowing his nose.

"Maybe. We'll see."

"Take care of yourself, okay, Wally? Remember I love you."

His call with Wally is another experience that feels, a minute later, like something that couldn't have really happened. And yet, an occurrence as bizarre as talking on the phone to an unraveling fugitive in a foreign country ends with a sense of, *Okay, what else do I have to do today?*

Pepper remembers that he should call his auto insurance rep. He goes into his office, turns on his desktop computer. Just then the phone rings.

"Mom! What are you doing up so early? It's what, six in the morning in Scottsdale?"

"I couldn't sleep. I don't sleep anyway, but last night I *really* couldn't sleep."

"I'm sorry. You were worried about me?"

"Well, yes, sure. But that's not why I couldn't sleep."

"Then why?"

"It's not important."

Getting his mother to talk is easy. Sarah Sanders she's not.

"Mom..."

"I'm just very aggravated. I bumped into Esther Mancuso in the clubhouse last night."

"Esther the Pester, as you call her."

"I don't know why I even talk to her. She's been my friend for forty years and I never liked her."

Pepper settles into his office chair for a twenty-second story that he knows will take fifteen minutes minimum. Sometimes, she'll spend a half hour describing in vivid detail her dinner: carefully describing each item on the menu, explaining why she rejected these choices over that, and how each element fared with her taste buds and gastrointestinal system.

It had been a globally warmed one hundred and five degrees in Phoenix during the day, but "there was a chill in the air by 6:30, so I put on a pair of slacks and the *Washington Post* fleece jacket. That jacket is a godsend."

"God didn't send it, Mom. I did."

"Hey, wise guy. Unlike you, I believe in God."

On January 8, 2011, Pepper's mom had a scratchy throat and decided against attending a meeting between constituents and Congresswoman Gabby Giffords. His mother saw that as a sign of God's existence. Pepper saw it as a sign of a sick world closing in.

"I know, Mom. It was a dopey joke."

"Yes. The second one you've made in two days. Sometimes, Arnold Pepper, you're a little too funny for your own good."

Pepper goes mute, mildly annoyed by how often his mother is right about stuff.

Stella Aronson Pepper broke the silence: "So how's my love, Thea, doing?"

"She's amazing, Mom. When did you talk to her last?"

"The day before yesterday. She said she was calling 'just because.' She is such a love."

Pepper's mother moved to Washington after Jane died and, for seven years, filled in admirably as a surrogate for Jane. Ever since, Thea's gone to Scottsdale for long weekends with her grandmother at least three times a year, one of the little, beautiful things in life Pepper tries to appreciate.

"So, Mom, what got you so agitated?"

"Where was I? Oh! So after dinner, that's when I see Esther in the clubhouse. I don't want to talk to her, but I exchange pleasantries, because what am I going to do, ignore her?"

"No. You may as well keep up good relations. You never know."

"That's what I was thinking. God forbid, I ever need her for something. Anyway, we chat a few minutes and then she looks at the *Washington Post* fleece jacket and says, 'I hear Arnold is in a bit of a pickle.'"

"Oh, great. How did she find out about that?"

"Like I've told you, she hovers around the men here, especially the rich ones. Not that they give her the time of day, mind you. But I guess one of them heard about your incident, somehow."

"Jeez, when retirees in Arizona hear about this kind of thing, I know we're living in the Too-Much Information Age."

"What?"

"Never mind."

"So anyway, she says she heard you were in a pickle and I tell her it's nothing. And..."

Muriel Pepper heaves a leaden sigh, a gesture her son has heard way too many times.

"Oh, God. And what, Mom?"

"Well, don't get upset. Esther is horrible human being. And let me tell you, her son never made anything of himself after failing out of dental school. Bouncing from job to job..."

"Mom! What did she say?"

In a somber tone reminiscent of Jim McKay announcing the deaths of eleven Israeli athletes at the '72 games in Munich, Pepper's mother says, "Well, after I told her your incident was nothing, Esther has the raw nerve to say, 'You'd think Arnold would be more sensitive about women considering his wife *committed suicide.'*"

Pepper puts his head in his hands. "I'm so sorry you had to hear that, Mom."

"You're sorry? I'm sorry you dragged it out of me."

"Don't worry about me. I can consider the source."

"Well, actually, that's the last part of the story: I considered the source, too. And I told Esther to drop dead."

"Really?" Pepper says, stifling a laugh. *Are you even allowed to say that in an assisted living facility in the state of Arizona?*

"You're damn right. I said, 'You know what, Esther? Drop dead.' And I don't regret it. Even though she reported me to the president of the condo board, and I may get fired from my position as social chairman for uncivil behavior."

"Social chairwoman."

"Whatever."

"You regretted running for that position the minute you won the election."

"That's true. But I would have preferred to leave the position on my own terms."

Pepper marvels at how even his elderly mom is infused with media language. *These days, everyone sounds like their own spokesperson.*

"Mom, leaving your position by telling Esther Mancuso to drop dead sounds like leaving on your own terms to me."

This time it is she who is goes silent. After a moment, she says, "You know what? You're right. Those *are* my terms. And I feel good about this now. Thank you, my love. You're such a brilliant boy."

"Oh, please, Ma."

Pepper gently ends the call with his mother. For some reason, his mind jumps backward to his conversation with Wally.

He was wrong about Allison Wainscot. I did try to take my turn with her as a secretly virginal high school senior, long after half my friends had taken theirs. Making out on the grass with her behind the football field, feeling criminal. Not long enough into groping my first breast— disappointingly small actually—Allison, bumping up against her reputation, wanted to stop. Funny, I have a long history with women who had just decided to stop expressing themselves sexually. Anyway, my palsied effort to change Allison's mind, showing her the unspectacular item she'd be missing, her involuntary shudder in response...I felt sick about it for weeks. It was genuine remorse, your honor.

Reflexively, he googles Allison Wainscot, and there she is on Facebook. A lawyer in Santa Fe, darker hair, still thin, still obviously proud of her deceptive cleavage, two grown sons, husband resembling El Chapo who likes skiing.

Deceptive Cleavage. Thea would find that a good name for a rock band.

There's a recent profile of Allison in a Santa Fe newspaper. Apparently, she attracted media attention for representing a white woman who sued a black woman co-worker after the black woman allegedly harassed the white woman for wearing hoop earrings, which the black woman viewed as "cultural appropriation." The white woman agreed to drop the case after the judge, a black woman, gave the white woman a lovely pair of cubic zirconia stud earrings, with the requirement that the white woman, in turn, give the black woman the hoop earrings.

Pepper imagines Allison reading about him in the paper this morning.

"Oh my God, honey, I knew this guy in high school!"

"Did you sleep with him?"

"No, he's the one guy I turned down."

Pepper finds the number for his insurance agent. Last night, before bed, he'd emailed all the information and promised to call.

Marlene Gingham picks up on the first ring and cheerfully says, "Good morning, Mr. Pepper! Are you okay? You weren't injured at all, were you?"

Pepper notes nothing in Marlene's voice indicating awareness of his little hysterectomy joke business. In fact, she sounds as interested and eager to please as usual; in a town that values power over fame, Pepper is as close as she comes to having a celebrity client.

After he assures her he is well, she jumps right in. "Boy," she says, "do I have a story for you!"

"Uh-oh."

"No. Don't worry. It shouldn't affect you, but you won't believe it. The man who holds the insurance policy on the car that struck yours last night? He's in jail."

In broad strokes: Apparently Emily's father, one Gary Blackstone, had berated his lovely daughter about her accident from the moment he began driving her home in his Bentley SUV. At a stop sign, Emily got so upset she bailed out of the car and took off running. Her father drove after her but lost her trail on a dark, money-infested street...

...where he was pulled over for an illegal U-turn by, not too coincidentally, the same officers from the scene of Emily's car crash, Angela Suarez and Conrad Hamilton. When Hamilton ran Blackstone's plates, he found a bench warrant had been issued for more than thirty unpaid parking tickets. Hamilton relayed this news to Suarez, who mentioned it to Blackstone, who mistakenly trusted his instincts by offering Suarez two crisp hundred-dollar bills, causing her to sternly instruct him to step out of the car and put his hands on the hood. At that point, Blackstone called Suarez a "loser dyke" and was promptly handcuffed and placed under arrest.

Sometimes, Pepper thinks, *life can be so beautiful.*

After Marlene hangs up, Pepper considers calling Emily to make sure she's all right. As a father, it feels like the right thing to do. Then he remembered what year it was. *The times are way too tricky to engage in concern for others, especially young women.* He calls Jillian instead and relates the tale.

"God, how much do I love that story?" Jillian says.

"I know. It's like the universe clicking back into place for one brief, shining moment."

"Yeah, with the emphasis on 'brief.'"

Pepper hears an ominous edge in her voice and reluctantly says, "Is something wrong?"

"Welllll," she says, with a level of non-committal unlike her usual brash self. "I did a deeper dive into the guy who wrote you that hate email. He's a sick hombre."

"He's done sicker stuff than waterboarding his coach with Gatorade?"

"You be the judge: Josiah Pitt Muldoon—that's his name— was paroled after serving time for being caught in West Virginia sodomizing an unidentified farm animal."

Growing immune to shock, Pepper says, "No one could identify the farm animal?"

"Yeah, that detail stuck out to me, too."

"Josiah Pitt Muldoon. Great name. Well, I'm glad someone caught him in the act because statistically, farm animals are notorious for underreporting rapes."

Jillian laughs. "I wish I'd let you keep that burner phone."

"Let the NSA listen in on my jokes. I don't care anymore."

"That General busted for talking to the Russians—"

"Flynn."

"Right. He probably feels the same way."

"I hope he gets shanked in the neck at Leavenworth."

"I know two cons in Leavenworth. I'll make some calls."

Back in his Subaru, headed for breakfast with Thea, Pepper puts his radio on scan, half-listening to eight-second tidbits all over the dial. Pop songs, news, Wall Street updates, and restaurant reviews lead to a local call-in show on which the host says, "It's a symptom. Arnie Pepper is just a symptom."

Pepper stops the scan on the all-talk station.

"Next caller: Greg from Tacoma Park, you're on the air."

Greg claims to be symptom as well. He describes himself as a fifty-eight-year-old man who friended his nephew's fiancée on Facebook because, he says, "They recommended her as a friend!" Greg thought he was just making a nice gesture, but his sister accused him of being a creep for hitting on his nephew's fiancée. Greg says he's now estranged from an entire wing of his family.

The radio host expresses total empathy. "Your sister should be ashamed of herself. You're better off without her."

The call-in number appears on the radio display, and Pepper dials it. The screener picks up, "Culture Klatch. What's your call about?"

"This is Arnie Pepper."

He is immediately put through to Phil Richmond, the host.

Pepper has tuned into "Culture Klatch" enough to know Richmond is a deep-voiced, thrice-divorced, former divorce attorney who handled the divorce of a top exec at Sinclair Broadcast group.

"We are so fortunate," intones Richmond. "Arnie Pepper himself has just called in. Good morning, sir. I've been defending you all morning."

Pepper remembers to turn down his radio.

"I tuned in to your show a minute ago by accident," Pepper says, "and that's all it took for me to call in and tell you that I don't need you to defend me."

"Oh. I'm sure you don't, Arnie, but every little bit helps."

"No. It certainly doesn't help to be defended by you, judging from your response to the last caller."

"What's your problem with my response to Greg?"

"Instead of blindly supporting him, you might have asked, 'Hey Greg, is it possible you're omitting something about your past that might have caused your sister to believe your friend request was creepy?'"

A moment of dead air.

"Okay, Arnie. I take your point. My bad."

"My bad? That's the best you can do?"

"Wow, this call has turned into a bummer."

"Actually, if you weren't such a charlatan, you'd realize this the best call you've ever gotten. Bye."

Pepper feels good. He gashed Greg's story just as he would have two days ago. Still a journalist, still miles above toxic media waste.

Pepper stands amid outdoor tables at The Diner, waiting for Thea. It seems busy for a weekday, but then again, he doesn't really grasp what people do with their lives anymore or when they do it. There are two al fresco tables with couples and one with a single guy hunched over a laptop. With the sun starting to muscle up, a man orders a mimosa, a drink Pepper assumes to exist purely to make morning alcoholism acceptable. The laptop guy looks up at him. Less than a day old, Pepper's low-grade paranoia about being recognized and scorned makes him look away. He imagines what it's like for Harvey Weinstein to go out for breakfast. Or anywhere beyond his front door. *Guy probably hasn't made eye contact with a stranger in months.* Pepper tries to visualize daily life for all the season's vanquished boldface names but as is the way of the world, intrusion hits from behind. "Hey it's you!"

Pepper does a drop-step spin and sees the kind of retiree featured on commercials for blood pressure meds, tanned and energetic in tennis clothes, deceptively alive.

"Arnie Pepper!"

Jesus. Can you keep it down, Pops?

"Good morning, sir," Pepper says in a near whisper.

"Been reading your sports articles for a hundred years. You like Serena in the US Open this year?"

"Bet on her losing in the finals after freaking out at the chair umpire."

Pepper is rescued by Thea's arrival. As always, when he hasn't seen her in a week or two, he's freshly struck by her radiance. He flashes back to when they saw Hamilton on Broadway in 2015. A woman looked (way) up at Thea and said, "My name is Faith. I own Next."

Lost, Thea said, "What's next?"

"Hello? The second biggest modeling agency in the world. I'd like to represent you."

"Thanks, but I'm just starting out in radio journalism and—"

"Radio?" Faith said in a tone someone else would use for leprosy. "Well, if you ever want to make ten thousand dollars an hour, here's my card."

Thea and Pepper watched the woman walk off.

"That was sweet of her, don't you think, Daddy?"

"Nice people in this city."

As he hugs Thea outside The Diner, he catches a woman looking at them with Jane Goodall-curiosity. She wears cherry lipstick a drag queen would find too loud. Pepper not only doesn't mind; he wishes Thea was mic'd up so everyone heard her say "Daddy."

"You look wiped, Daddy."

"I'm wiped but fine, honey. Really."

"Inside or outside?"

Pepper glances at the lipstick woman looking Thea up and down. He's remembers Jillian recently saying, "Sadly, I can confirm that women do eat our own."

Pepper had made the same observation, only with the pronoun "their." Now they can be a single person. On the radio he heard a gender fluid guest say, "They is a highly ambitious person." Later, he read an interview with the same person, but had to stop, too confused by the whacked-out pronouns. Used to be only sports fans who perverted pronouns: "We blew the game." Pepper always wants to respond, "No, they blew the game. You watched."

He looks back to Thea and says, "It's already so hot out."

"It's not the heat, it's the humiliation."

"Good one, honey!" *Nobody could ever say she isn't my daughter.* "Let's sit inside."

This time, Pepper doesn't debate his choice of seats, opting to face the wall, letting his daughter be open to the eyes of an undeserving world.

She's wearing a white tank-top with a big blue swoosh over a yellow tee shirt, shorts, and Adidas running shoes.

"Adidas shoes and Nike top? Isn't that a pimp violation?"

"Ha. That's so ten years ago. Pimp violations are happening now."

"Who can keep up with this stuff?"

"It's a complicated world, Daddy."

"You noticed."

"A long time ago."

It's another moment cuing Pepper into a meaningful talk with his daughter, another moment he lets pass. Instead he looks over at two women at a nearby table, one seated above a German shepherd wearing a yellow vest: ACCREDITED EMOTIONAL SUPPORT DOG. Everyone trying everything just to get through breakfast, no less their lives. God knows what she's been through and how many remedies she's already tested out. Time was, only your most intimate friends in DC admitted to seeking psychological help. Now, total strangers drop their damage in your lap.

Do you need accreditation for an emotional abuse dog?

"In Miami, I referred to Nike as the Greek Goddess of Sweatshops."

"Ha! I hope you wrote that one down."

"Oh yeah. It's been memorialized."

Thea spreads a napkin on her lap. "So, Daddy, are you worried about, you know, your job?"

"At this very second, no. But my outlook varies from minute to minute. Sometimes I'm worried about what my life is without the *Post* and in the next breath, I'm like, 'Do I really want to keep doing this forever?' I mean, driving over here, I was thinking about how, every time I attend a game now, no matter what sport, all I'm hoping is that it doesn't go into overtime so I can get the hell out of there. It even dawned on me that, in recent years, I kind of dread doing post-game interviews. I mean, interviewing the hero is great. But there's always a goat, some young ballplayer who just messed up in front of 35,000 fans and a zillion maniacs watching at home. These kids feel bad enough already without me asking, 'So what were you thinking when you made the play that ruined the entire season for you and your teammates?' Truthfully, I've hit a point where I feel too sorry for every losing athlete. It's supposed to be a better story for a reporter if local teams do well, but I can't look away from the miserable losers. I start imagining these kids from Dubuque or wherever going to sleep and replaying irreversibly terrible moments in their heads over and over. I mean, is that a good mindset for a sports journalist?"

Thea smiles in way that seems incongruous to Pepper.

"What?" he asks.

"I think that's the best mindset in the history of sports journalism."

His heart does a little flip flop.

"Considering how long you've been doing your job, it would be understandable if you were coldly objective about the human side of sports. But you're less cynical than when you first started. So that's pretty amazing."

God, she's so much smarter than me.

"Now you've nixed my best rationalization and I am worried about keeping my job."

"I can't see them letting you go. I mean, everyone's picking you to be voted into the Sportswriters' Hall of Fame."

"I've mentioned to you what bullshit the Sportswriters' Hall of Fame is, right?"

"Yes, you've denigrated it on several occasions."

A waitress comes over to take drink orders. Pepper gets more coffee, Thea requests water and some kind of tea with ginger and a powder that reportedly aids digestion, boosts your immune system, and gives you x-ray vision.

"Daddy, whether you keep your job or not, you'll keep writing and you'll keep getting published. This one incident shouldn't make people think of you as a writer who spent decades offending Washingtonians and everyone else in the world. I mean, it's not like when you were in Beijing and you wrote a column fat-shaming Buddha."

Pepper simultaneously laughs and gives her a look.

"Guess Buddhism's on my mind after yesterday's interview."

In conversations with his daughter, Pepper is always vigilant about capping the time focused on him. Feeling it's time to transition, he says, "So, how did that deal with the chain-smoking, Dalai Lama-hater play out?"

Thea weakly smiles. "Are you sitting?"

"Oh God."

"No. It's weird, but nothing to, you know, freak about."

"I repeat: Oh, God. But okay, lay it on me."

"After we spoke on the phone, Perry the Buddha came back. He smiled but it seemed forced. So I followed your suggestion to flash my Super Bowl XLVII pepper spray key ring. He saw it and asked about it. So I said, 'Oh, this? I got it from my dad. He's a sports columnist for the *Post*. Arnie Pepper...?' Sure enough, he says he's a fan of yours."

"I love this guy!" Pepper says. "Just kidding. Go on."

"Anyway, I turn my recorder back on, and we talk about the kids meditating. He's back to sounding placid and spiritual. He tells me that down deep, kids want to be silent, that they don't want to talk all the time and have to have opinions on everything."

"Sounds reasonable."

"Yup. So when the interview's basically done, I asked him if he's ever been to a Buddhist country, like, say, Tibet."

"Sounds like you were baiting him back into discussing the Dalai Lama."

"Yes. I was baiting him."

"Did he bite?"

"He said he'd never been out of the Eastern Time Zone in his whole life. But he said he's googled enough to know that if the Dalai Lama was suddenly called upon to go back to Tibet, he'd be so depressed he'd probably get the next flight to LA, apply for U.S. Citizenship and rent Eva Longoria's guest house."

"Sounds less whacko than his earlier outburst."

"That's what I thought, so I left it alone and thanked him for his time. But even though the interview was over, I had the sense I should leave on my recorder."

"Okay..."

"So just to make conversation before I split, I said, 'If your wife or son ever want tickets to a sporting event, don't hesitate to call.' He looks me in the eye and growls, 'My wife? Fuck her, cheating bitch.'"

"Jesus."

"And he launches into this whole story about how his wife, after giving birth to two kids, came out as 'a muncher' and moved in with some 'stone butch, hundred-footer, African American skank in Hyattsville.'"

"Hundred-footer?"

"A woman who you can spot as a lesbian from a hundred feet away."

Pepper shakes his head. "Amazing how, mixed in with the string of lesbian slurs, he goes all PC with 'African American.'"

"I know!" Thea laughs. "I had the same thought. So after ranting about how his wife is one of those 'deceitful bitches who switch sides like it's going from Colgate to Crest,' he doubles back to the Dalai Lama and how he's going to 'replace that potato-shaped Tibetan fraud' one day, that he's going to have so many kids in DC meditating that soon 'the world will be calling me His Holiness Perry,' that he'll have a worldwide following who'll "bow at my feet wherever they tread.' That he'll be the one who 'finally brings peace to this shithole of a motherfucking planet.'"

Pepper silently drops his head, unsure if it's the story itself, or hearing, for the first time ever, his daughter say the word "motherfucking," that's reinforcing the filthy hopelessness of life in general. He opts for the story angle. "So, we're dealing with a well-meaning megalomaniac."

"That pretty much—"

The waitress comes with the hot drinks and asks to take their orders. Pepper tersely says he needs more time to decide.

Do restaurants train waitresses to interrupt conversations at the worst possible moment?

Thea takes a sip of her tea and says, "I tried to sound compassionate by asking him how his son is handling his mom moving out. And he's like 'He hopes his mother *dies*.'"

Pepper flashes to those kids separated from their parents at the southern border, all the TV shrinks guaranteeing the cute little kids will be scarred for life. Dodging bullets and coyotes in Mexico feels so unnecessary when you can be permanently traumatized right here on the well-lighted, paved streets of Washington DC.

"What did you say to that?" Pepper asks.

"I tried to hide my disgust while feigning empathy. So I kind of shook my head and shut my eyes for a few seconds. When I opened them, he was blatantly staring down the front of my dress. His eyes were crazy wide, like a gecko. He whispered, 'Don't move!' then stood up and started untying the draw string from his peach-colored, knock-off Lululemons."

Pepper feels like he's dying of detail poisoning, wishing Thea would be so much less descriptive. But as a parent he knows he had to hear it all.

"I grabbed my Super Bowl XLVII pepper spray-key ring and said, 'Do not do that. If you drop your pants, I'll blind you. I swear, I'll spray this until your eyes drip out of their sockets.'"

"What did he do?"

"He offered me ten free private meditation lessons if I watched him masturbate."

"Oh my God, *Thea*."

"I held up my recorder and said, 'Look, I never stopped recording this conversation.' And then I headed for the door."

"Did he try to stop you from leaving?"

"No. But as I left, he called out to me and said, 'Can I ask you one question?' So I turned around like, *Okay, ask your one question.*"

Pepper, feels vital organs rising in his throat.

"With this really sad look on his face, he says, 'If you had to guess, do you think the Dalai Lama has fucked Eva Longoria?'"

Pepper stares into his cup of coffee. *Human inexplicability, a train that makes every local stop.* All he can think to say is: "The Montgomery County cops gave Jillian a 9mm Glock as a gift. She doesn't use it. Maybe...no. Forget I said that."

"Actually, I had a thought last night that if I were two degrees less sane than I am, and I had a gun, I might have shot the guy."

"I have that thought twelve times a day."

"Anyway, I'm talking to the powers at NPR this afternoon. I was up half the night thinking about how to play the story. I mean, maybe some of it's my fault. My outfit *was* kind of casual. Just a short summer dress."

"Oh come on, honey. It's a thousand degrees out. You don't need to wear a three-piece suit to conduct an interview."

"Yeah, I know. But whatever. I know I have to do the right thing journalism-wise, but if I get him fired, I'm not sure who it helps or who it hurts. The kids he helps—people aren't exactly stumbling over each other to help disadvantaged kids in this town."

Ping-ponging between Thea's humane deliberation and his animal urge to decapitate this perverted Buddha, Pepper looks around the restaurant where people are eating and reading and texting as if life is a cabaret, old chum.

"You know," he says, "when I wrote my series about parents of athletes—"

"Your extraordinary Pulitzer Prize-winning series."

"Precisely. Anyway, I went to Penn State to get a little perspective from Joe Paterno."

"The coach who looked like the dead guy from *Weekend at Bernie's*."

"Good memory!"

"Well, I kept up on the pedophile stuff that happened."

"That's my point. While waiting for Joe, I chatted with an assistant coach who later turned out to be that very pedophile, Jerry Sandusky. He was quite helpful, actually. I even quoted him! Who knew a monster was inside this goofy, affable assistant coach?"

"Daddy, it doesn't matter what they do. A-list actor, CEO, computer geek, coach, French Embassy attaché...I mean, you can barely call it deviance anymore when it's so everywhere."

"French Embassy attaché?"

"No comment."

Oh, God.

When the waitress returns, Pepper apologizes to her. "Sorry if I was snippy before. You caught us at a critical conversational moment."

"Oh, no worries," the waitress says. "Bad timing is the story of my life."

Another walking wounded takes their orders. Thea says, "So I see you've given up on egg whites."

"I figure I'm taking Lipitor, what's the point? Besides, you ever think about how many yolks are wasted every day? We could start a charity: Yolks for the Homeless."

"Good idea but don't say 'homeless.'"

"Huh?"

"Now it's 'People affected by homelessness.'"

"It's also the end of the world."

"Yeah, pretty much."

"Hey, at breakfast in Miami yesterday, I thought of a new dish for a really bad deli: Maalox, eggs, and onions."

"Good one, Daddy. Kind of like your other one: spaghetti and ultimatum sauce."

"I think Maalox, eggs, and onions is funnier."

"You ordered lox, eggs, and onions?"

"Yeah. Must be the one-sixteenth Jew in me from grandma's side. "

"I love lox, and I probably don't have any Jew in me."

"No, probably not."

Innocent chatter turns murky so fast, Pepper thinks. Like Wally on the lam, exhaustion sets in over his evasions.

"Do you think a lot about, you know, your DNA?"

"Less than I used to. A lot of times, I'd have questions about stuff I knew couldn't be answered but I'd call Grandma and talk to her about it, anyway."

"Really? I didn't know that."

"We kind of kept our talks to ourselves. Grandma felt you had enough on your plate, being a single dad and America's preeminent sports columnist, without having to spend hours answering my unanswerable questions."

"I'm not preeminent. But aside from that, honey, you know I would have—"

"I know, Daddy. I know you'd have sat down and answered any questions I had anytime, for as long as it took. But in a way, it was easier talking about this stuff with Grandma."

"She told Esther Mancuso to drop dead last night."

"I know. She called me on the way over here."

"Wow. I knew you were close but...Well, I'm very happy about that."

"I love her to death."

Momentum now carries Pepper to scary heights.

"I guess there's only so much Grandma could tell you about your mom."

Thea fields his surprising statement smoothly.

"Actually, she's got a lot of insights. A whole lot more than Mom's side of the family. In the rare calls I have with Grandpa Harvey, he can't even mention his own daughter's name to me without going to pieces."

"He's had it rough."

"That's for sure," Thea says. She gently adds, "First his wife, then his daughter."

Pepper is blind-sided. "You know about your Grandma Georgina's passing?"

"I didn't until last year. Grandma told me during my last trip to Scottsdale in February."

Seeing turmoil overtaking his face, Thea says, "Don't even

go there, Daddy. I swear, I'm not worried about it 'running in the family.'"

Pepper feels motion sickness while sitting still.

"Please stop. I see your head percolating. You have to believe me. You raised a happy, almost deliriously optimistic girl. You can't worry about me knowing this. It's information that doesn't hit me on any gut level whatsoever. That won't be me. Please, Daddy, you have to believe me."

The table shudders with quivering lips and eyelids.

"Your Grandpa Harvey now thinks Grandma Georgina didn't mean to, you know. That she was faking it, and something went wrong. Imagine convincing yourself that your wife died from an unsuccessful fake suicide attempt?"

"I guess people can get pretty creative when it comes to finding a way to just go on."

Pepper doesn't know where to take this crucial but unwieldy conversation. As another tongue-tied moment engulfs him, his phone rings. It's Jillian making a perfectly-timed clutch call.

"Hey. I'm at breakfast with Thea. What's up?"

"Oh wow! Put me on speaker."

Pepper taps the speaker icon and Thea croons, "Hi Jillian!"

"Hey sweetheart. I miss you."

"Me too. Wish you were here."

"I wish I were there, too. I'm just calling to let your dad know I've hit a new level in my fast break toward senility."

Pepper perks up. "Why? What happened?"

"I was in court addressing the judge and couldn't come up with the word 'dementia.'"

Thea doubles over in her mother's laugh.

Pepper says, "That reminds me of a joke. A doctor tells his patient he has both cancer and Alzheimer's. And the patient says, 'Well, at least I don't have cancer.'"

Thea howls as Jillian says, "Thanks, Arnie. That joke made me feel so much less alone. I've got to run. Bye-bye, Thea. Love you."

"Love you, too, Counselor."

Pepper hangs up.

The food arrives.

Pepper says, "So, honey, are you dating anyone?"

Thea says, "You know what, Daddy? Maybe we've hit our quota on new conversation topics for today."

Pepper nods. "Yeah, I guess. But I'm really happy about hitting that quota. And don't worry, I believe you."

For the next half hour, they talk about snow globes, sea salt, the new Supreme Court nominee who went to nearby Georgetown Prep, the pronunciation of quinoa, Geico commercials, Stephen Miller buying his suits at an Incel factory outlet, Thea being considered as a correspondent at a Trump rally in a red state, and a recent dog park incident in which the neutered Cronkite nevertheless tried so hard to hump a beagle named Rosie that Thea was sure, at any moment, she'd be getting a call from Ronan Farrow.

Pepper doesn't tell his daughter about his car accident, the jilted estrogen sprayer in the garage, the phone call with Wally, or the divorcee down the hall.

Pepper pays the bill and waits outside for Thea to emerge from the ladies' room. The lipstick woman is now standing out there, as well. Mid-fifties, wearing jeans pre-ripped by a designer with a made-up Italian name, she assertively steps up to Pepper. "How old was your daughter when you adopted her?"

When Thea was in grammar school, Pepper heard some form of this question several times from people madly confident of their baseless presumptions. He'd evolved from the edgy "Why would you need to know that?" to the benign "It's a long story." It's been years since he's dealt with such intrusions and now, in the afterglow of a memorably beautiful breakfast with Thea, a hit of indignation sets in.

"I didn't adopt her," Pepper says. "I designed her in my basement and manufactured her on a 3D printer."

As a modern American living life just hoping to be offend-ed, she boils. "Hey! It was just an innocent question!"

"Actually, I'm still working out the kinks. Think I should make her whiter?"

The woman takes an overdose of umbrage when a man comes over, puts his arm around her and says, "Holy cow, hon-ey! Do you know who you're talking to? This is Arnie Pepper! From the *Post*! Bill Pierce. Big fan for years. Hey, you think any team will pick up Kaepernick?"

"No, but he'll get a Nike commercial."

The woman shakes loose from Bill Pierce and storms off. Bill whispers to Pepper, "Menopause," and chases her down the street. *I wonder if it's possible to take out a restraining order against the entire human race.*

Thea taps him on the shoulder from behind and kisses him on the cheek. "Good luck today, Daddy. Whatever happens, we'll be fine."

We'll be fine.

Never has Pepper felt more love for the pronoun "we." *We'll be fine.* It's the greatest we in the whole wide world.

Eating and driving, driving to eat, driving back from eating. How much of life is taken up with that? Thirty percent? The AMA recommends seven hours of sleep. The NIH says a twen-ty-minute nap is rejuvenating. The ADA: brush your teeth for two minutes. The Heart Association: briskly walk for twen-ty-five. David Lynch: meditate for twenty. America: work your ass off the rest of the time. Pepper considers the upside of having time to sit around and do nothing, the major perk of being fired.

If I do get axed, I'll be ranked just below Billy Bush in all this mania. Cozying up to stars was his job. How's he supposed to react to one of them flashing his license to grab a woman's pussy? He laughed. Of course he laughed. Hell, Edward R. Murrow probably would have laughed, too.

With two hours before his meeting, there's nowhere to go

but back home. Pepper can't recall a weekday morning driving up Wisconsin Avenue. He feels like he's on the wrong side of the road, a low-hanging metaphor borne out when he almost runs over a jogger wearing a Caps jersey. Pepper waves: My, bad sorry!

When the Caps had won the Stanley Cup, Pepper wrote a fairly unoriginal piece about the victory being a moment of unity at a vicious time for a city divided by race, politics, and the technology that keeps people in their homes with barely a minute's exposure to fellow specimens of citizenry. The first letter in response to the column asked who anointed Pepper the great observer of sports sociology.

"We don't want your allegedly deep, poignant insights," the reader wrote. "You're there to interview Alex Ovechkin, period."

The ensuing 200 or so letters ran three to one in the same vein, typical of any column rude enough to connect sports and the real world. Even a series of solemn interviews he'd done with local sports figures in the days after 9/11 were met with venom from the same fang:

"Just inches above Arnie Pepper's terrorism article in today's paper, I noticed the word SPORTS. It was in big letters, so I don't know how he missed it."

Before email, a letter to the editor took some commitment, pen to pad or fingers to typewriter, a stamped envelope with a return address, a walk to the mailbox. Now a reader's id does all the work on vulgar impulse. Convenience and speed. Society killers. Pepper sometimes writes poisonous answers to nasty comments about his column but never hits send. He mentioned this to Thea once, and she called it distant gratification. He wonders how JK Rowling or Malcolm Gladwell deal with the opinions of the incensed masses but figures they're probably both rich enough to find anything funny. Pepper finds it all stupefying. *If you make a living expressing your opinions in a great American newspaper, it's galling to see everyone else doing it at home for an audience of zero. By rote, we acknowledge everyone's right to his or point of view, but who put the stamp of approval on saying those views aloud? When did "keep it to yourself" go extinct? Bloggers—people who can't get paid to write—don't even get out of bed to sound off on every- thing. Jesus, how could such a fun concept like democracy go so wrong?*

Pepper goes into thought dispersal mode once again, surf- ing through his radio presets. Howard Stern indulges his de- bauched limo driver, Ronnie; the classical station spins a hit single by Debussy; mellow rock on Sirius 32 trots out Joni Mitchell to warn us she's "seen some hot, hot blazes come down to smoke and ash." MSNBC Radio: "...confirmed dead, the situation on-going." POTUS on Sirius 124: "...why, ulti- mately, Kavanaugh will sail through confirmation." Classic rock: "...there was music in the cafes at night and revolution in the air." WTOP: "...destructive hurricane to hit—" '70's hits: "...Beautiful faces in loud empty places, look at the way that we live." BBC Radio: "...referring to Brexit as 'the beginning of the end.'" One of forty-four sports channels: "...don't want to talk about erectile dysfunction." '80's hits: "...and the dead sand falling on the children, The mothers and the fathers, And the automatic earth—."

Pepper silences the radio, annoyed by his bent toward hear- ing relevance in all the noise. His cellphone dings. *A text from Danielle Marino!*

Nice to meet you last night. Feel free to call me sometime to chat.

In an uncharacteristic show of spontaneity, Pepper pokes his phone and says, "Siri, call Danielle Marino."

There are three rings to change his mind before she picks up. "Oh my God, so strange you'd be calling now."

"Really? Why? Too soon?"

Pepper doesn't need to be a lawyer to know he's made the mistake of asking a question he doesn't know the answer to.

"No, no. Not at *all*. What am I, twenty-two?"

If this is fishing for a compliment, Pepper demurs. "Oh, I'm glad. I'm just, you know...why is it strange I called?"

"I was just talking to my son about you."

"I didn't know you had a son."

"I have a son in college and a daughter in grad school. Tyler's at BU. He's a sports nut so I told him I met you and he was like, 'You had dinner with Arnie Pepper? Awesome!'"

"These kids find everything awesome."

"Yeah. I hope you don't mind, but I told him about all the rigmarole about your hysterectomy joke."

That word again. Rigmarole.

"What was his takeaway?"

"His takeaway was that it's really hard to be a white male these days."

"Kids are awesome at making everything about themselves."

"Tell me about it."

"So what did you say?"

"I said, 'No Tyler, it's not hard to be a white male. It's never hard to be a white male. All you have to do to get by as a white male is not be an asshole.'"

Pepper is floored, certain he's heard the ultimate, most coherent statement on America's racial/sexual reckoning hurricane.

"Wow, Danielle. You must be the most incredible librarian ever."

Her laugh is a boom.

"Aren't you supposed to keep quiet in a library?"

"Yes. You're going to get me fired, Arnie."

"Then we may wind up in the same boat. Does dinner Saturday sound like a good way to celebrate either retaining or not retaining our jobs?"

"Yes, it sounds great. But not as a date."

"Oh. Really? Mind if I ask why?"

"Let's just say I'd rather date Jillian."

Pepper can do nothing but laugh.

"Why is that funny, Arnie?"

"It's not funny in any bad way." He laughs louder.

"Then how is it funny?"

"In college, the girls I met always wanted a date with Jillian—or Jerry, as she was known back then. Now it's forty-plus years later, Jerry is a woman, and girls I meet still want to date him. The circle of life!"

"So you're not mad at me?"

"I'm not sure why, but I'm actually kind of happy about it."

"If it's any consolation, your ask-out was extremely well executed."

"I guess my usual ineptitude is rusty."

Returning to his car, Pepper pulls out his notebook, jots down, "White male...not be an asshole."

How in God's name that line will ever wind up in a *Washington Post* sports column is beyond him, but it's too important to not record. Important? No, he thinks, *Danielle's statement was more than that. It was trenchant. That's the word for it. Trenchant. I've been aced out for a date with a trenchant woman by a transgender friend who can't remember the word "dementia."*

Sounds like a Cat Stevens song, Pepper thinks. Riding the elevator upstairs, he remembers seeing a comedian at Garvin's forever ago who, to the tune of "Moonshadow," played a guitar and sang, "I'm being followed by a huge Negro. Huge Negro, huge Negro..."

Got big laughs back then. Must've been the '80s, around the time he saw Pryor perform at DAR Constitution Hall, long before white people invented the term "N-word." Now, the '80s feels like a time when being human was something you could get away with. At the *Post*, writers have latitude on using "black" or "African American," often using both in the same piece. Pepper goes with Black—capital B—reasoning that those civil rights pioneers didn't willingly get savaged so they could be African Americans. Over the years, there have been newsroom debates on the subject, compromise being the practical result.

In 2009, Pepper joked that Obama should use his inaugural address to confirm the worst fears of racist America by saying "Axe not, what your country can do for you…"

The laughs in the liberal newsroom were definitely nervous.

Pepper enters his building's garage and backs into the parking spot where he'd encountered Jackson the night before. Again, he's taken by the strangeness of being in a familiar place at an unfamiliar time. *Wow, there are lots of open spots in the middle of a weekday morning.* The elevator takes him non-stop to the top floor, further evidence that he's not the only person who's been reporting to work all these years.

When the elevator door opens, Pepper's sightline is filled by a man holding a bundle of bedding, sheets, shams, and a duvet, all spilling out from his arms.

"Oh, excuse me," the man says.

"Do you need a hand?"

"Trust me, you don't want your skin making contact with this load."

The man is in his forties with reddish hair. Most of his body is blocked by linens, but Pepper gets the impression of a wiry, outdoor type, his presence in an urban condo out of place, his demeanor like someone who's forgotten how to deal with anxiety. The elevator door starts to close but Pepper runs his hand past the sensor to re-open it. As the man backs up a step, a sham falls to the floor beside him. He looks down, shakes his head, and gives up, letting the whole load drop. Pepper steps out of the elevator, the door closing behind him.

"Is everything okay?"

"Not really. Everything is pretty much horrible."

"Oh, I'm sorry. Is there anything—"

"You're Mr. Pepper, right?"

"Arnie."

"Charlie Drexler. I grew up reading you."

Pepper extends his hand, but Charlie says with a smile, "You don't want to do that."

"So you're Herb's and Lydia's son."

"Lillian. Yes. I assume you know about my father's health issues, considering that my mother sent out a press release."

"Hm. I briefly spoke to her this morning."

"When she called me last night to say my dad 'lapsed' into a coma, I drove in. I live in the Poconos."

"How's your dad doing?"

"Well, that's the problem. He's doing fine."

"I don't..."

"I met my mom in the lobby of the hospital, and we went upstairs to see my father eating scrambled eggs and watching MSNBC."

"Isn't that good?"

"At the moment, it was fantastic. Then my mom started telling him all about what she'd been through last night, with calls to the hospital, hearing about his coma, blah, blah, blah. Then she tells him about how late last night, some young man arranged 'an Uber drive' for her so she could get to the hospital—"

Oh God, Jackson.

"My mom describes the kid and how he 'pushed a few buttons on his phone' and the car 'came lickety-split' and the driver was 'a very nice Pakistani man' when suddenly, my father puts his hand up and practically shouts, 'Shut up, Lillian!'

"My mom and I kind of froze. We'd barely ever heard him even raise his voice. And then..."

Pepper watches as Charlie gathers himself to say something too absurd for words.

"Then, my father looks at my mother and says, 'I can't take this life anymore. I want a divorce.'"

Pepper blinks. "What?"

Charlie nods. "His exact words."

"Was he delusional? Maybe the coma affected part of his brain."

"No. He was as compos mentis as can be. I mean, get this. From his hospital bed, he'd already called his lawyer! Can you believe it? This eighty-four-year-old man came out of a coma with one thought: *I want a divorce.*"

Jesus, men never know when to give up.

"Fifty-four years of marriage," Herb says, shaking his head.

Pepper hears the elevator easing down the shaft. He pushes the button and helps Charlie gather the linens.

"Don't worry, I have antibacterial soap..."

The elevator door opens again. The linens inside, Charlie chuckles. "I guess there's a reason I moved my wife and kids to the Poconos."

"Hey," Pepper says, "running away from home is vastly underrated."

Charlie smiles. "So, how do you think the Wizards will do this year?"

"Put your money on the Wizards starting off one and ten... before things get really bad."

Pepper pours himself a glass of lemonade and slides open the glass door to his terrace. It's six-feet-deep with room for two chaise lounges, a small round table, and a good-sized Weber grill. He angles up the back of a chaise and sits. He's fairly sure he's only sat out here on weekends, which reminds him of grade school, when he'd gaze out the window of his classroom and see people walking the streets in the middle of the week. God knows what they were doing out there, but to him, they seemed so free.

It would be nice if there was some sun in his face, but the terrace faces west. Still, the limp air and oppressive heat feel oddly soothing. *This is nice*, he thinks, *being at home at 10:25 a.m.(!) while everyone else is out there clawing at each other to make America great in their own futile ways. What a concept: you can just be home. Write when you want or not at all, work out at the gym whenever or not at all. Go to Starbucks for a fifty-cent refill, mosey back, read. So this is what my neighborhood is like when I'm not here, full of people on their own schedules, students leisurely plotting on their phones, construction workers adjusting bandanas under their hardhats, women carrying rolled-up yoga mats, old men coming out of comas and dumping their wives.*

It's a strange new world just a few hundred feet under his terrace. Alone and aloud, he says, "I could possibly get used to this."

Pepper computes having a solid two hours before having to go to the *Post* for his meeting with Linda Carlyle. His mind reflexively goes analytical, assuming the decision on his future's already been made, guessing Linda and the higher ups have put some thought into this Serious Situation. Maybe the verdict has already leaked out across the *Post* newsroom, but he knows that when he wends his way to the sports section at 1:10 p.m., there will be no whispers behind him or vibes to pick up on—newspaper reporters are too hardened and cold, their prized objectivity having long ago outgrown the tells of childish emotions.

Not to belabor the point but, did I not list Monica Seles among the top five most fearless-in-the-clutch athletes ever? Yeah, the same scribe whom she requested as her first interviewer after that German psycho fan stabbed her during a changeover. Come to think of it, Steffi Graf, on whose behalf the psycho attacked Monica, never spoke to anyone about the incident except me. And I didn't even bring it up with her! I'm sitting around at some tournament in Luxembourg or Geneva and Steffi approaches me and starts talking on the record. Hell, I'm the go-to-guy for female athletes.

The landline rings. He decides to let it go to voicemail.

Please be the DNC asking me to waste more money for the midterms or that ditzy woman selling free cruises to hell or the predatory fake IRS agents or a Pakistani warning about a virus in my Mac or a carpet cleaner—just anyone who lives to be hung up on so I can revel in chaise heaven.

Because it's one of those ancient, home answering machines, he can hear the caller leaving the message in real time. "Arnie, it's Linda. All things considered, I think it's best you come to the office as soon as possible. I'll try your cell."

Before his cell can ring, Pepper texts Linda Carlyle:

On my way.

She texts back.

Thanks.

Then his cell rings.

Linda just texted. Why is she calling again?

"Yeah, Linda. I'm—"

"Hello," says the caller, "Mr. Pepper, it's Kristen Haynes again."

The rapid multi-media carpet bombing combined with Linda's strained voicemail momentarily gets the best of him. "Jesus Christ! Look: Whatever the hell bullshit you have on me now, my answer is 'No comment.' Alright? Got it?"

Pepper feels none of his customary regret at snapping. If anything, his rage spikes higher due to a modern inability to slam down a phone. Smack her down with the dainty "end call" button? Put her in her place with a meek fiber optic beep? You can't even hang up on someone anymore. Our humanity is all tech-smothered fever, snuffed zeal. Barely worth living.

"No, Mr. Pepper. I'm sorry. I was actually calling to tell you that I was fired."

And just like that, he wants to thank Steve Jobs personally for creating such a courteous product. But Jobs made the right move, dying before he could see the carnage he caused, a world beset by unintended consequences.

"Oh my God, Kristen. I am so sorry. I guess I've been a little frustrated. Can I call you back in five minutes? I have to get in my car and go to the paper."

He pockets his cell and kills the TV. A minute ago, he was a delighted shut-in. Now his preset drill of scurrying to the *Post* kicks in.

Walking to the elevator, he sees a mouse staring up at him, like: What are you doing here on a weekday? For a tiny vermin, he (or she) seems unafraid, in no rush.

"How'd you get up to the eighth floor?" Pepper asks aloud. The elevator door opens. The mouse flees.

Pulling out of the garage, a thought delays Pepper's call to Kristen. The voice mail message Linda left: "All things considered, I think it's best you come to the office as soon as possible."

What things are being considered?

Clearly some new factor has entered the equation of his career peril. Maybe, he thinks, Kristen will know. He feels only slight guilt at the idea of feeling her out for his own benefit during a call that should be all about her.

"Hi Kristen."

"Thanks for getting back to me. I didn't know who to call."

"Tell me what happened."

"Well, I made the mistake of telling my editor that I'd gotten that call from the woman you made love with at the Hilton."

There's something endearingly inaccurate in her use of the term "made love." Uncharacteristically, Pepper lets it go.

"So, I told him that her story, true or not, was irrelevant to your situation and I wouldn't include it in my piece. He said it wasn't my call to decide what is or isn't relevant, that it's for readers to decide. I argued that it would be like prejudicing a jury with testimony of an unrelated past incident."

"I'm biased, but journalistically, your instincts were absolutely correct."

"I know."

"But I don't get one thing. He's the editor. He could have included the incident in your story without your permission."

"I never told him the woman's name, and I refused to hand over my notes to him. So, he couldn't directly quote her or put in details that would make her seem credible."

"So, you stuck to your guns, and your editor fired you?"

"No, I stuck to my guns and he ran his hand under my dress and up my thigh and I hit him in the face with a stapler. Then he fired me."

Before he can respond, another call invades Pepper's phone. His mother. He disregards it.

"So, did you report him? Did you call the police?"

"No. I'm not doing that. I made a video of myself telling the story, in case I change my mind later."

"Later is no good. You have to do it today. Now."

"I know, but I'm not doing it anyway."

"Why?"

"Because I want...I want out."

"Out of what?"

"Out of this whole...thing. I don't want to be part of all the crap, another woman going public, a primly dressed statistic clinging to a lawyer I can't afford, telling my story over and over to some pseudo-sympathetic plastic bimbo on TV, being believed by one side, shit on by another, all to wind up being known as Stormy Daniels with a master's degree. Fuck that. Like I need to be more disillusioned. I moved here from LA to report on the whole game of power, ambition, and money and wound up spending half my life tip-toeing around women who can't stand me because I'm pretty, and men who relate to me purely through their little hairy dicks. Thank you, Nancy Reagan. I'm just saying 'no.' No to 'going public,' no to 'standing up for all women.' No to even telling my friends and family what happened so they can say, 'But Kristen, if you don't report your editor's sexual harassment, he wins.' Maybe that's why I'm telling only you. You're in sports, you know what bullshit winning and losing is. And in this hashtag game, nobody wins. I mean, is Gretchen Carlson on a yacht somewhere drinking champagne and thinking she'll go down alongside Rosa Parks in the history of defiant icons? The poor woman who said Matt Lauer locked her in his office using his remote control—is she feeling like a feminist heroine now? Somehow, I can't imagine that Andrea Constand wakes up every morning saying, 'I'm the woman who nailed Bill Cosby. Yay!' Or that totally pathetic woman who busted Al Franken purely so she could hold a press conference and be forgotten the next day. Actually, she's lucky to be forgotten compared to the women permanently stamped with the #MeToo label. They're young women and suddenly their whole future is about making the rest of their lives seem like something more than just sad epilogues."

"Kristen, most of the women who stepped forward are brave."

It takes several seconds before he hears, "God, did you have to say that?"

"Why? You think I'm wrong?"

"No, I think you're right. I know you're right. I was just hoping you'd back up my rationalization for not jumping right into the shit."

"No one likes a good rationalization more than I do, but—"

"I know, I know. The longer I wait..."

Pepper's phone announces another caller. It's Jillian. Pepper lets it ring.

"Look, Kristen, you'll overcome this. I mean, not to be un-PC, but you're a girl. A kid."

"I'm thirty-one. When I go home to LA, they look at me like I'm sixty-two. And by the way, don't say PC."

"What's wrong with PC?"

"It implies over-sensitivity in some people."

"Listen, Kristen, like I said last night: you ask good, well-formed questions. You're a good reporter. I can tell. Now granted, you know my history on this but, if I keep my job, maybe when things settle, I'll be happy to put in a word for you at the *Post*."

"Thanks. I really appreciate it but..."

"But what?"

"Things won't settle. Ever. Not here. At least not for me."

A rush of heat raids Pepper's face, like when you realize too late the car ahead of you has stopped.

"So wait," he says. "You're just going to give up? Just quit and call it a life? You're going to let yourself be defined forever by one night? Jesus Christ, I can't believe how you throw in the towel so easily, how fast you take the easy way out. 'Problem? No biggie, I'll just pull off the next exit and merge onto the path of least resistance.' And when you park yourself on the word 'coward,' then what? What's the next option? Swallowing a bottle of pills? You can rationalize all you want about this: 'Oh, I'm just a person who's really hard on herself' or 'I gave it my best shot so I'm not really a total sell-out.' But that's not what all this is about. It's about being too easy on yourself. It's about being a coward. Making one mistake and just bowing out? That's the definition of a coward."

Pepper's harangue dangles in the ether, the face on the other end of the line goes blurry in his mind's eye. He bumps up the AC without looking at the dashboard. When Kristen finally speaks, he's jolted as if finding someone hiding in the back seat.

"What mistake did I make?"

"What?"

"You said I made one mistake. What was the mistake?"

"No, that was...you didn't make a mistake. I just got...shit. I'm sorry."

Pepper hears a police siren over his speakerphone and Kristen muttering something.

"You okay, Kristen?"

"Yeah. Just...this call didn't go according to plan."

Pepper could tell her that nothing in the whole wide world goes according to plan but he's over his wisdom quota. He hears the flick of a match and wonders if she's lighting a cigarette or a joint.

Kristen inhales something and says, "You know, I had the TV on before, and there was something about an active shooter who a cop described as a white guy with an average build. I was thinking, 'Who's a white guy with an average build in America now? Chris Christie?'"

Pepper laughs. "That's really good. You should write that down. For use in future writing."

"Yeah, I guess. Anyway, thanks for kind of weirdly talking me off the ledge."

"What are you going to do now, Kristen?"

"I guess take a few more hits of a joint, then report my 'incident' to the #MeToo police. Not that I know who that is. It's not like my editor is a big enough fish for Ronan Farrow."

The call ends at a red light a mile and half from the *Post*. A short, boxy man with fright wig-gray hair walks by Pepper's Subaru, takes a bite of an apple, and promptly fumbles it to the asphalt. Pepper grabs his pad and writes:

Did Isaac Newton have a low center of gravity?

Pepper is taken by how his rituals hang in there on such an out-of-whack day. *But that's how everyone lives now—in epidemic cognitive dissonance, acting normal in a world gone bonkers. And really, what choice is there? We're vaguely aware that somewhere far over our heads, madmen are playing geopolitical tennis without a net. There's self-preservation in not looking up.*

He remembers the two calls he snubbed while talking to Kristen. His mother rarely calls his cell, so he chooses her over Jillian.

"Hi, mom. Sorry I was on the other line. Everything okay?

"Well, Arnold, I'm fine..."

"But?"

"But I have a story."

"Okay, but I'm not far from the *Post*, so you'll have to give me the short version."

She trims out some details on the way to describing her morning appearance before the condo board.

"It was like a courtroom. Esther on one side, me on another. So, they ask me if I'd like to speak in my own defense.

I stood right up and said clear as day: 'Look everyone, last night I told Esther Mancuso to drop dead. I admit that openly and honestly. In addition, I want to state for the record that what I said was wrong and unforgivable.'"

Pepper smiles, visualizing his mom reading from a prepared text written in her own hand.

"'Nevertheless, I feel I must at least mention extenuating circumstances. Esther made a comment that cast aspersions on my son, a Pulitzer-Prize winning journalist at the *Washington Post*, the same newspaper that produced Woodward and Bernstein, the two journalists who brought down President Nixon. In her comments, she had the gall to mention the tragic suicide of my son's wife. That, for me, was a bridge too far and prompted my rejoinder about dropping dead. Again, I was wrong. I hope Esther will accept my apology as I am readily willing to accept an apology from Esther.'"

"Very well put, Mom. I'm proud of you. How did Esther respond?"

"Well, everybody turned and looked at her. She got red in the face, stood up, started to say something, and—"

"And what, Mom?"

"And she dropped dead."

"What?"

"She just keeled over. Dr. Hudwalker, the retired dermatologist, tried CPR, pushing on her chest and this and that, but it was no use. Never sick a day in her life and boom, dead as a doornail."

Pepper focuses on the only thing that matters now, his mother's state of mind.

"*Mom.* It's not your fault."

"Oh please, Arnold. I know it's not my fault. I was civil and level-headed in my remarks. I said nothing inflammatory. Let's face it. Esther was always a hothead. Not to say I don't feel bad that she's dead. But in no way, shape, or form do I feel I'm to blame."

"Good. That's what's most important to me."

Pepper checks the time as he turns onto K Street.

"So Arnold, some story, huh?"

"Top ten most gripping stories you've ever told, Ma."

Muriel Pepper laughs and says, "Okay. I'm going to hang up now. I don't like you talking on the phone while you drive."

"I love you, Mom."

"I love you, too, darling."

Pepper's mom is at war with modern phones. Her success rate in pushing the OFF button when hanging up is around thirty percent. Instead of a hang up, Pepper hears a tone, probably his mom pushed the 3 DEF button by accident.

Then he hears his Muriel Pepper say to herself, loud and clear, "Poor thing."

Who is she talking about? Esther Mancuso or Me?

The *Post* newsroom, with its blonde wood walls, white desks, and black swivel chairs, is low-key as Pepper walks in. Most reporters are out on stories. Editors, still a couple hours from a rush of copy, are out to lunch; the copy desk people have yet to arrive. Whatever crisis is airing on cable news, it isn't enough to draw more than a small circle of people to the office monitors. *Then again, in this America, it would take Tom Brady and Taylor Swift being caught in a fentanyl smuggling ring to get reporters to crowd around a TV.*

Pepper quietly slinks his way to the sports section without his usual comradely greetings. Usually he feels like Ferris Bueller walking though the hallways between classes. "Hey, man," or "What's up?" or "Nice piece yesterday."

Hey, he tells himself, *buck up. Being ostentatiously cheerful might be unseemly, but this timidity is pathetically self-absorbed, as if the hyper-ambitious people of the Washington Post have the time or inclination to judge a beset sports columnist.*

He straightens his back and takes a long look around the newsroom.

I really do love this place. I know I doth protest too much sometimes. What else would I do if I didn't do this? Who would I be. How would I— Pepper turns around and finds his new friend, Jamal Khashoggi. Months earlier, Pepper had looked into writing a piece about how international professional basketball is one of the few ways in which hostile parts of world learn that Americans aren't all godless, decadent, capitalist pigs. *Post* columnist Eugene Robinson suggested he talk to Khashoggi, a dissident journalist who'd fled Saudi Arabia and wound up a columnist at the *Post*. One fascinating interview and a few lunches later, boom: Pepper had his first Saudi pal.

"Congrats, Jamal. When's the big day?"

"I can't say for certain. There are some complexities with the marriage license. How are you?"

"Never better," Pepper says, choosing not to gripe about his mess in light of what this guy's been through.

The sports section is a ghost town, no one around except for Drew Greene, a journeyman sitting in for Ken Minot, the full-time day editor. Minot is a warm, calm, astute, veteran newspaper man while Greene is a snarky, sporadically competent tool who has no idea Pepper can't stand him.

"Hey, Pepper," Greene says without looking up. "Carlyle is on some other floor doing whatever. She said you can wait in her throne room."

Just the way Greene calls everyone by their last names makes Pepper stiffen. He preempts any impulse to lash out if this creep comments about his situation.

"By the way, Pepper," Greene continues, peering at him over half-glasses. "Aren't you friends with that Walter Shockley guy who made off with half a billion dollars of poor peoples' money?"

"Wally? Yeah. It was a *quarter* of a billion. I grew up with him."

"Well, you can resume your friendship. He just turned himself in."

"Where?"

"Where what?"

"Where did he turn himself in?"

"At the American Embassy in Sarajevo. You know, where Yugoslavia used to be."

"I know where it is. I covered the 1984 winter games there."

"Why do you suppose a guy who successfully eluded authorities for all that time just ups and turns himself in?"

"Because I told him to," Pepper says.

Greene laughs, "Ha! Good one!"

Pepper wonders how someone with zero journalism instincts ever got to work in this profession, no less at the *Post. Maybe Greene is Carl Bernstein's eighth cousin, forty times removed. How he's kept working here is a bigger mystery, but then again, it's a question you can ask about a lot of people in America's work force.*

Last year, when the Redskins were in Dallas, Pepper mused aloud in the press box about how Jason Garrett continued to be the Cowboys head coach through so many years of failure. "Maybe he has a video of Jerry Jones romping with Russian hookers in a pool of pee," Pepper mused, and the gathered members of the sports media rumbled with laughter.

As he walks into Linda's office, Pepper thinks of that moment in Dallas. And of the countless times he and his colleagues have sat around tables or stood around bars or in locker rooms or behind batting cages, cutting up in just this way. *If you ask me, that pee joke was more offensive than the hysterectomy line.*

Linda's office prominently features a photo of herself looking positively gaga in the company of a beaming President Obama. What a smile on that guy! Pepper still can't believe we elected a black man named Barack Hussein Obama. In 2012, he should have given the Republicans a fighting chance by changing his name to Barack Hussein Wayne Gacy Nurse Ratched Obama. Still would've kicked their asses.

Greene pokes his head in and says, "Call for you, Arnie.

Should I transfer it over?"

"Sure."

Ten seconds later, the phone rings.

"Mr. Pepper?"

"Yes."

"Hi. Um, I'm Phil Hazelton, the man who had dinner with Les Moonves last night. We didn't meet, but I recognized you."

Pepper recalls the Stephen Hawking-looking guy from the FCC.

"What can I do for you, Mr. Hazelton?"

"This is awkward, but I read about your viewing parties at the Old Ebbitt Grill and was wondering how one gains entry."

Pepper gazes at the photo of a man who always takes the high road. Not everyone can be Obama: "Mr. Hazelton, can you find it in your heart to go fuck yourself?"

On the upside, there was a slam-down-able phone.

Jesus, where the hell is Linda? I had to race over here so I can sit and wait here fielding calls from closet cases?

Linda's office lacks the sloppy library of reference books you used to see in editors' offices. One of the upsides of everything being online, it makes for a neater workspace. She does have a row of (first edition?) hardbacks by Joan Didion. *Now there's a writer and a journalist.* The White Album. *One of the great book titles ever.*

Pepper edges toward fury at having to continue waiting for Linda, starting to read her lateness as vaguely passive-aggressive. *Rude. Can she not get up the empathy to realize his anguish over the last twenty-four hours? You'd think they teach that kind of thing in business school, treating your employees with respect.* Forty hours ago, he was carefree and casual, laughing and hanging out in Miami with other sportswriters. He cracked them up with an idea for a column in which he determines where Gronk stands in the succession to the American Presidency. Life was so sweet! *Who could have imagined then the scene now, sitting in the principal's office, waiting and stewing and being eaten away by the crap that happens only to other people.*

Don't let me hear you say life's taking you nowhere, angel...

God, Bowie was so great. All the wrong people are dying.

David Bowie? He's dead to me now. Ha, ha, ha.

Thea is into a band called St. Vincent, its lead singer a pretty girl from Waco or Tulsa or wherever who can wail on a guitar. Good for Thea, sticking with her gender. Her mom nearly fainted from reverence when we sat across the aisle from Chrissie Hynde on a flight to Chicago in the late '80s. Last year, Thea bought a vintage Pretenders T-shirt. If Jane could have lived to see that.

Drew Greene pokes his head in again.

"Pepper, there's a call for you from some girl who says she 'really needs to talk' to you."

"Tell her I'm in a meeting."

Greene shrugs and leaves. Pepper thinks to himself that he's not in a meeting. He's just waiting to be in a meeting. Linda is keeping him waiting.

I'm giving this bitch another minute to get here, and then I'm out of here. The nerve, keeping me waiting like this, treating a Pulitzer Prize winner like some desperate freelancer trying to sell a story about an eight-year-old hot dog-eating prodigy in Bladensburg. I've made the Best Sportswriting of the Year anthology eight times! I'm a shoo-in for the sportswriter's Hall of Fame, for Christ's sake! Maybe I'll be voted in right after being fired. How funny would that be? Like when Taxi got a load of Emmys right after one of the retarded networks cancelled it. Yeah, that's right: retarded. I said "retarded" and I'll say "retarded" all I want. I should write a novel about an effeminate freshman retard and his butch gypsy prostitute girlfriend who run a politically correct kiddie porn ring out of a campus safe space for white nationalists. "I'm Terry Gross, and welcome to Fresh Air. Our guest today is Arnie Pepper, author of And Keep Out!, *the repellent novel now number one on both the* New York Times *and* Amazon *best sellers—"*

"I'm so sorry, Arnie."

Linda walks in at an even pace, which Pepper finds annoying until he sees that she's being trailed by Security Chief Brenda Williams, who is carrying a manila folder. In one instant, Pepper feels like a defendant watching the jury come back with a verdict. In the next, he wonders if Brenda is there to rough him up if things get ugly. He looks to see if she's packing heat.

"As you can imagine," Linda says, going to her chair while motioning Brenda to have a seat, "Marty had to be consulted on this situation."

Actually, it's flattering and daunting that the executive editor had to be consulted on this situation. Pepper maintains a blank look as Linda settles in, then steals a glance at Brenda. Her face, a bit over the top in its grimness, strikes him as a sure sign he's being fired.

"It's all so sick and yet all-too-familiar," she says.

Pepper struggles to not look totally lost.

"But we're a news organization, and these are the times we live in."

He imperceptibly nods.

"I mean, the unforeseeable consequences are breathtaking."

Sounds like a bit of an overstatement, but okay.

"And it's no one's fault."

I kind of thought it was my fault, but okay.

"It's not your fault, Arnie..."

If you say so.

"...and surely it's not Brenda's fault."

Brenda? Who would think it's Brenda's fault? And don't call me Shirley.

"If anyone's to blame, it's Shep Smiley."

Who on God's green Earth is Shep Smiley?

"If Smiley doesn't post your joke on Instagram, none of this happens," she says. "And besides, what sportswriter goes public with press box talk?"

Sounds a bit like Trump attributing his pussy grabbing line to locker room talk, but I'll take it.

"Not to excuse your statement like Trump excused his pussy grabbing stuff as locker room talk—we can argue the semantics another day. Today, we have to deal with serious ramifications."

Finally, words stumble from Pepper's face: "Yeah, it's all kind of a drag."

Brenda's head cranks toward Pepper. Linda's face twitches. Bad choice of wording?

"Kind of a drag??? Arnie, what the f—"

Mid-expletive, Linda reinterprets Pepper's cluelessness.

"Wait a minute, Arnie, have you consumed any news coverage in the last few hours?"

In his best impression of stupidity, he says, "Linda, unless firing me is a much bigger international crisis than I'd assumed, I have no idea what you're talking about."

She nods understandingly, as if remembering how daft boomers like Pepper take inexplicable breaks from media.

"Brenda. I think it's best if you fill Arnie in, okay?"

Brenda Williams, so reassuringly genial on the phone the evening before, now resembles Angela Bassett playing the movie role of a warden after a prison break.

"Mr. Pepper," Brenda begins, "after your call last evening, I read the threatening email you received and touched base with our tech people. They tracked down the sender and got back to me with rather concerning results. The email was sent from a North Carolina man named Josiah Pitt Muldoon."

Icicles form on Pepper's spine but he makes no indication of having heard that name from Jillian just hours ago. Brenda touches a tiny silver cross hanging around her neck, then takes three pages of printed copy from the manila folder.

"Mr. Muldoon had a long prison record and was currently on parole for a violation that required him to register as a sex offender. He was forbidden to leave the state of North Carolina, although it's being reported that Mr. Muldoon was given a waiver to attend the Unite the Right march in Charlottesville."

"Oh my God," Linda says, "I hadn't heard that tidbit. He was quite a specimen."

Pepper fixates on the word was, the ominous past tense.

"After reviewing the terms of Mr. Muldoon's release, I felt certain his menacing email to you was a clear parole violation and alerted local authorities in Northern North Carolina. They assured me Mr. Muldoon was very much on their radar as a dangerous individual. I got the sense they were looking for any opportunity to apprehend him. This is where the story is less well-defined. The police secured a warrant for Mr. Muldoon's arrest. Unfortunately, he was tipped off, whereupon he packed a long rifle in his car and drove to the Virginia town where he grew up."

All Pepper can do is brace himself for the body count.

"...shooting from the public address announcer's booth above an outdoor high school athletic facility, the same high school from which Mr. Muldoon was expelled fourteen years earlier."

Expelled for water-boarding a coach with Gatorade. Which isn't technically *water*boarding...

"...overlooking a dairy farm just beyond the grounds of the high school, shooting several cows, six of which passed away."

Four people shot qualifies as a mass shooting. How many cows?

"...when one stray bullet went through the window of a driver's ed car. The student driver, Millicent Flood, was age seventy-eight. It was literally her first time behind the wheel. She passed away instantly."

In 1981, night editor Cal Bingham admonished a twenty-two-year-old Pepper, "Never write 'passed away.' People don't pass away. They die."

"...the shoulder, another officer took a round to his hand. When Mr. Muldoon finally ran out of ammunition, he dropped his rifle, and drank several ounces of Drano from a Washington Redskins souvenir water bottle."

And there's your past tense.

Brenda folds the pages from which she read. She looks at Pepper and then Linda, who says, "Thanks Brenda. I appreciate you coming along with me. If I had to recite that story..."

"It's my job. Which I probably should get back to now."

Pepper wants to give Brenda a hug, Instead, he solemnly shakes her damp hand before watching her forlornly walk off.

"She'll be okay," Linda says, "she's seen a lot in her day."

Pepper silently agrees.

"As for you, Arnie..."

Pepper nods at appropriate times as Linda outlines the now laughably anti-climactic verdict on his employment at the *Washington Post*. His "long and distinguished career" will not be undone by one joke which, "depending on whom I've consulted, was at best 'kind of funny but not okay,' or at worst, 'inappropriate and beneath the dignity of a *Washington Post* columnist but ultimately not a fireable offense.'"

Somehow, the words "not okay" burrow into Pepper's head and settle alongside the main takeaway: He will not lose his column. He will not be on probation. He will not be suspended without pay, but his salary for the next month will be donated to a charity to be named later. He will go to high school and college journalism classes and talk to students about gender sensitivity. An editor's note to be placed in the Sports Section will simply state that the matter has been handled in-house and is considered closed. Pepper will write an apology to circulate only among newsroom personnel, along with a public apology in the form of a column that will offer "no self-exoneration or mitigation whatsoever" from his insensitive remarks.

And then there was the last bit: "If you object to any of these conditions," Linda says, "your job status at the *Washington Post* will be subject to reconsideration."

This last feels a bit over the top, but in sum, Pepper has no objections, no comments, no human feelings at all. His litany of defense exhibits, defunct. His self-righteous militancy, gone. He would describe himself at this moment as comfortably numb, but he can't stand Pink Floyd. He still has his job but feels hollowed out. *Am I ditching my principles to save my job? It was only a goddam joke.*

Linda un-crosses her legs and drops her feet to the floor, close together like Greg Louganis on the springboard. Pepper hazily focuses on her shoes, black leather flats, tapered to pointy toes.

"There is one more condition," she says.

Pepper looks up to her face, half-listening.

"You will be forbidden from covering, or writing anything related to, women's sports for one year."

It takes a moment to sink in.

Wait. What was that? Did she just say what I thought she said?

Suddenly, the titanium membrane normally separating Pepper from his true emotions is perforated.

No writing about women's sports? That's the journalistic quarantine to which I've been assigned? Confined to a half-way house of all-male sportswriting? Sequestered from being in the presence of female athletes? As if I can be a threat to women merely by typing the words 'she' or 'her?'

"...After a year," Linda continues, "we'll reassess."

Mutinous rage blows unhinged words around Pepper's brain: *Absurd, warped, senseless, unjust, moronic, pompous, wishy-washy, arbitrary, gratuitous, self-righteous, counterproductive, disingenuous—*

Bullshit.

"And that's pretty much it, Arnie."

Pepper feels his neck begin to twitch. Only when his list of adjectives reaches the tip of his tongue does a shred of survival instinct kick in like an air bag to dam the flow.

In lieu of telling Linda and his own better angels to shove it up their asses, he takes a deep breath, drops his shoulders and finds his inner mute button.

Suspecting his face might rat him out anyway, he stiffly

looks away, his eyes landing on the photo of Bill Buckner: *Balls rolling through the legs of good men everywhere you look, our errors frozen, framed, signed and permanent.*

After being excused from the principal's office, he walks through the newsroom. Over the past twenty-four hours, he'd imagined this moment dozens of times, assuming he'd be feeling something. Sadness from the end of a forty-year era as a newspaperman, relief from the end of a two-day era as a sexual pariah. It's neither. Just more personal history all unpinned.

Unavoidable glimpses of TV monitors reveal BREAKING NEWS graphics, police tape, an interview with a man in body armor, a sheet over a corpse beside a burgundy-and-gold water bottle. Reporters at their desks look up or don't look up as Pepper passes. Some nod to him. A few say, "Hey, Arnie." A young editor walks by and says, "Arnie, if the Nats don't get rid of Gio Gonzalez..." Two reporters drink coffee, one complaining that an editor deleted the phrase "sociopath of least resistance.'" From three-point distance, Pepper sees Gene Robinson. They nod to each other as a copy aide who looks fourteen bumps into Pepper and says, "Excuse me. So sorry. My first day."

Stopping at a water fountain, Pepper thinks of texting Thea, but remembers she's probably working and opts instead to email her. No words of reassurance come to mind, so he holds off, then notices an email in his inbox from Emilygurl@gmail.

"Hi, Mr. Pepper. Just wanted to thank you for being so nice after our car accident last night (all my fault!) and also wanted you to see my last Instagram post. Emily."

The Instagram post features a mugshot of Emily's father under the words "Hahahahahaha!"

Pepper hydrates and resumes his walk through the newsroom when Phil Rucker approaches him and quietly says, "First, I'm glad you're still part of the family."

There are no secrets in the newspaper biz.

"Thanks, Phil."

"Second, we're holding your story about the White House official's Muslim joke. Not because it's not a great story, but because your source begged us to hold off. She felt if the story broke now, it could more easily come back to her. So Ashley made a great deal with her: We'd hold off in return for the promise of the woman being a reliable off-the-record source for the foreseeable future. On balance, having her as a source is the real prize. In fact, I think, over time, we'll have a lot to thank you for, Arnie."

Pepper nods, then says, "Hey, I assumed the bald official who made the Muslim joke was Kelly but it dawned on me it could've been Miller. Did she confirm who it was?"

"No. She just said, 'There are a lot of bald shitheads in the administration.' But other sources confirmed which bald shithead it was."

Pepper waits for the name, but Rucker's too savvy to spill it. Pepper feels the twinge of not eating at the adult table, of being mired in sports, the sandbox of journalism where he can't write about women for a year. He and Rucker share smiles of understanding and head off in opposite directions.

Pepper takes about ten steps before an unfamiliar reporter introduces himself.

"Arnie, we haven't met. Jamie Franklin."

"Oh. You're working the Old Ebbitt Grill story."

"How'd you know?"

"Purely by chance, I drove by there late last night and saw a bunch of cops. One them told me you'd already been there."

"Yeah. Pretty crazy. Anyway, sorry about this, but I'll have to be calling you about the situation sometime today."

"No apology necessary. Is the story going anywhere?"

"Yeah, it's going to Crazytown. Turns out, the phony video party rumor was traced back to a pastry chef recently fired by the Grill."

"Why was he fired?"

"He spit in Bryce Harper's crème brulee."

"Well, Harper *has* been slumping lately."

Franklin nods. "And yet he got off to such a good start."

Resuming his slog through a newsroom dedicated to reporting on the sinkhole of 2018, Pepper thinks of how America isn't a country. It's a whole world, Washington DC having nothing in common with Washington state, North Carolinians a different species than North Dakotans. A hurricane in Houston may as well be in Jakarta for all a Minnesotan cares, insider trading on Wall Street strikes a Nebraskan as a problem on Krypton. Not even the regularly scheduled mass shootings hit us the same way, X percent hugging their kids, Y percent buying more guns, Z percent—people like Pepper—reflexively praying, *Please let the shooter be a Rush Limbaugh-loving white guy.*

The anesthetic for all of it is supposed to be the beaten-to-death cliché of sports being a safe haven. Then your team holds your city hostage, your kids' role model punches a woman five feet away from a hotel security camera, your MVP thanks Jesus and then tweets about fags, spics, and bitches. Welcome back from Camelot.

Maybe, I haven't been covering a sandbox my whole career. Sitting in press boxes attaching import to pointless games, traveling wherever freak athletes compete, bringing a spouse along to share the experience and getting both devastation and a perfect daughter for my thoughtfulness—maybe I'm Ben Bradlee and Nelson Mandela rolled into one glorified typist.

The elevator stops at the fourth floor to pick up two unfamiliar men in suits. As they enter, one says, "I so don't want to go outside now and sweat my ass off."

Pepper says, "It's not the heat, it's the humiliation."

The men look at him quizzically until one says, "Oh, you're Arnie Pepper, right? Love your column."

"Thanks."

"How do you think Alex Smith will work out for the Skins?"

"I think midway through the season he'll break his leg."

Pepper walks out into the lobby and says hello to Nate Weatherly, a security guard who played nose guard at Howard thirty years earlier.

"Hey Arnie, you doing okay? I was worried about you due to, you know..."

"Thanks, Nate. It worked out okay. Sort of."

"No harm, no foul, huh?"

"It was a judgment call."

"Incidental contact."

"The refs let them play."

"It didn't affect the outcome."

At a loss for another cliché, Pepper says, "Let's grab lunch sometime, Nate."

"Love to. In fact, I wish I could do it today. I got two guys out sick and can't leave my post for a second."

Pepper stops at the bakery for a non-happy hour baguette. A new batch is steaming hot. He buys two with the idea of giving one to Nate. The cashier, wearing a T-shirt covered in block letters: I WOULD HAVE ACCOMPLISHED SO MUCH WITHOUT YOU, says, "Do you think the Nats will re-sign Harper?"

"Put your money on him signing with Philly for $330 million."

The cashier shakes his head at the world and mumbles "thanks" after Pepper drops a bill in the tip jar.

Just outside the bakery, a homeless man with inexplicably Mormon-like white teeth asks Pepper for five dollars. Settling for two, the man jaywalks across K Street, unconcerned with oncoming traffic. A mid-size Infiniti stops short, the driver exhaling frustration. Pepper wonders how, among all the cars in the world, someone chooses a mid-size Infiniti. It's a safer thought than estimating when the homeless guy's luck will run out or if two months in traction would qualify as good luck.

An obese cloud covering Northwest DC looks like the mothership in *Independence Day*, a movie Pepper's seen fifty times in channel-flipping chunks. It always bugged him that the pretty, black, single mother dating Will Smith was an exotic dancer. *Why did the writers do that? Because at the time, they could? Pretty pointless, considering she was never shown dancing naked. Or at all, for that matter. Actually, they made a sequel. Independence Day II? Codependence Day? Whatever. Maybe they updated her status, made her some big city ballet director or an owner of a Pilates studio or Secretary of Defense.*

Reentering the *Post*, Pepper sees Nate talking to someone familiar.

Thea runs across the lobby and envelops him in a hug.

Over Thea's shoulder, Pepper sees Bob Woodward walking into the lobby, his Trump book soon to hit bookstores. His publicity tour will inevitably goose the president of the United States into calling the greatest reporter ever an enemy of the people.

Pepper lifts a hand to wave at Woodward, who gently smiles at the hardened newspaper man unabashedly propped up by the consoling arms of his daughter in the lobby of the *Washington Post*.

"...I called you, and you weren't home, and you didn't pick up your cell, so I called the *Post* and they said you were in a meeting so, I don't know, I just thought I should be here when you came out because, y'know, I was worried because, no offense, but you're not that great at defense when it comes to, y'know, defending yourself against...you."

A weak breeze from Maryland limps through the intersection at K and 14th Streets. Washington DC has a certain aroma Pepper's never been able to place—charred wood and Play-Doh?—not unpleasant until it bulks up over the summer, plops down on his shoulders and seeps into his shirts. Thea decelerates her steps to her father's pace. She says she's meeting with higher-ups at NPR in an hour and a half.

"It's a pretty tough call," he says. "I can't wait to hear what they say."

"You first," Thea says. "Aside from the headline about your continued employment, tell me about the meeting with Linda."

It doesn't dawn on Pepper that the tables have turned, that now it's his daughter limiting the conversation time spent on herself, allotting the lion's share to her father.

He rushes though his recounting of the shooting in Virginia, glossing over or outright omitting details that would make it into the thinnest reporting of the events. Of course, Thea had heard the news. She just hadn't made the connection.

"Jillian had given me a heads up, but I thought he was the same as all the other trolls. But yes, indirectly, I guess I had a hand in a mass shooting."

By the time they drift into McPherson Square, Pepper is done recounting Part One of the meeting—Brenda's presentation—and is onto Part Two, the upshot of his own personal and professional travails. This part of his recitation is exhaustive, with richly detailed descriptions of Linda's attitude, clothes, voice, posture, office, where she sat, how she crossed and uncrossed her legs. Pepper could be telling the story alone in a confessional booth considering how he doesn't even register his daughter's total silence.

At first, there's flatness in Pepper's monologue, no editorializing in his descriptions, no caricature in his voice. He tells his story as a journalist, an admirable effort that starts fraying when he gets to the reviews on his comedic sensibility.

"Linda told me that some editors actually thought the joke was funny. But ultimately, they all agreed it was 'not okay.'"

On the words "not okay," Pepper flips up his hands and twaddles two fingers to add eye-rolling quotes. His voice sops the words with prissy derision. Thea says nothing. Had he been paying attention, he would have realized—since when did Thea—the millennial master of the one-line comeback, listen to one of his stories in complete silence?

"So, in essence," Pepper continues, "I have the complete freedom to write about any subject in the whole wide world—

except women. Pretty exorbitant freedom, don't you think? Half the population, off limits! Apparently, after weathering years of blatant racism, Serena Williams will be discomforted by Arnie Pepper holding a recorder up to her! If I mention the giant slalom to Mikaela Shiffrin, it could now be misconstrued in myriad perverse ways. Catching up with Maya Moore's sabbatical from basketball? Well, obviously that would require the presence of an armed guard. Because I made a joke that was *not okay.*"

A drizzle starts falling, too faint for a fixated Pepper to notice. Thea checks the sky for darker clouds ahead, then refocuses on the sidewalk.

"I mean, the sheer prudishness of the terminology is enough to make you question your own liberalism. 'That's not okay.' 'That's so inappropriate.' "That's not funny.' 'That's over the line.' 'That's sooo offensive!' 'That makes me uncomfortable!' I used to have mixed feelings about political correctness, thinking it was stultifying but worth it just to enlighten the masses. Now, the whole PC thing makes my skin crawl. Jesus, you can't even say 'PC' anymore."

Thea considers steering her father toward the Hamilton Hotel where they can borrow umbrellas meant for guests. Actually, she thinks she wouldn't mind checking in. Alone.

"Get this: The estrogen spray kid told me that making a sexist joke is a gateway to sexual predation. Where do they come up with this crap? And the woman down the hall—the one you wanted me to ask out?—I finally talked to her this morning and I won't even go into her take on my situation. Suffice to say, the word 'disgusting' came up but she *still* wanted to date me! It's like repulsion was the attraction!"

Thea rolls her head against tension in her neck.

"Christ, the whole country is buried in their phones, searching for some tidbit they can be offended by. You know who was probably—no, undoubtedly—the person least offended by my joke? The wimpy NBA player who was the actual butt of the joke! He hasn't publicly responded because he's a professional basketball player pulling down twelve million a year, who doesn't care what some sportswriter half a country away says about him. Athletes themselves take their careers less seriously than the fans sitting at home! NBA players get bounced from the playoffs and happily go to Cancun while their fans go into mass morbid depression. And that's a microcosm of the whole country, an America where everyone takes everything the wrong way."

Drizzle evolves into showers. Near the end of the square, Thea gives up on deciding on where to go next.

"How did we get so prickly, so...judgmental? Maybe we all try getting out of jury duty because we're on permanent jury duty just by sitting at home and handing down sentences to total strangers we read about on Facebook. And believe me, if my punishment leaks out—which it will because no can keep their mouths shut anymore—the vast majority of readers will whine about how they let me off with a slap on the wrist, that I should've been canned altogether. It's like everyone who's not popping Fentanyl is taking Moral Outrage Oxycontin, anything to make us feel better than someone else. Out of all of human nature, we've settled on the basic human need of having someone to dump on. 'How does that guy get his name in the paper everyday? I have plenty of great opinions on sports and that shlump Pepper has a public profile instead of me? Well, hallelujah!! *We finally have the chance to dump on him, let's party!*'"

Thea watches a young mother literally dragging her toddler son along, a hoodie tied over his head, the toes of his mini-Adidas Superstars scraping the sidewalk. The kind of DC day when people just give up. Even a jogger, soaked to the bone, has slowed to the walk. He notices Pepper and calls out: "Arnie Pepper! Love your work. Think Tiger has another major championship in him?

"Put your money on Tiger shattering his T12 and L1 vertebrae a few holes into next year's Masters. He'll never play golf again. Okay, pal?"

Pepper resumes talking as if the interruption never happened.

"The one saving grace of all this is that, I can assure you, if or when it gets out that I'm banned from reporting about women athletes, plenty of them will speak out. When you get right down to it, it's an insult to women! Like these sublime physical specimens are actually delicate flowers who need protection from a guy they've known and trusted for years because he made a joke that wasn't 'okay.' They won't stand for it. Lisa Leslie, Candace Parker, Mia Hamm, Martina, Billy Jean, Breanna Stewart, Brittney Griner, Lindsey Vonn...believe me, they will make it known that they think my punishment is totally idiotic."

"You want to bet?"

The sound of Thea's voice kills the volume on all else. Pepper finally notices the rain, its droplets dangling from his daughter's eyelashes, just above a vehemence he's never seen in her walnut eyes.

"What?" he asks. He's not sure where this is going.

"Those women will not comment on your situation. They will *never* respond to your situation. Period, full stop. And you know why? Not because they're timid or offended or lacking in principle. Because they are part of the society in which we live—unlike you."

Pepper waits for the missing "Daddy" at the end of her sentence. It's not coming.

"Do you know what you sounded like to me for the last twenty minutes? You sounded like some holier-than-thou zealot who thinks the 2018 shit parade of modern life doesn't apply to you. Think again. This is the world now and you've *finally* gotten your first taste. And by the way: You really dodged the bullet here. You only got a *tiny* taste. A totally insignificant, next-to-nothing taste. I mean, with all that's going on around us, do you honestly think that your twenty-four-hour ordeal is worthy of a mortifying, batshit rant to your daughter in the middle of the street in a downpour?"

Pepper's eyes bulge. He s feels like he's going to throw up.

"All those imaginary readers whom you arrogantly assume would resent your light punishment?" says Thea. "They'd be right. You *did* get off easy—with *less* than a slap on the wrist! You still have your job! You still have a voice. You still have a daughter who'll go out to breakfast with you. Harvey Weinstein, Louis CK, Matt Lauer...they all have daughters who probably wear wigs, sunglasses and fake mustaches to have breakfast with their fathers in public."

Pepper's knees go weak. Rain runs down his face, dripping from his nose.

"Look around: lives are being ruined left and right for crimes that didn't exist ten years ago. And yes, some of it is bullshit, and some of it is justified, but guess what: It doesn't matter either way, because that's the way it is. Just because you're sixty-one years old, it doesn't mean you're grandfathered in with old rules shielding you against the present. Really, you're not even shielded from the past! Now? Today? There aren't ex post facto laws protecting you from prosecution of past sins! You think everyone's prickly and whiny and judgmental and out for blood? Tough shit. That's where we are. All of us. Except you. You think you're above it all, that you don't have to get with the program. How you can be a writer for a great American newspaper and somehow be blind to—"

Wearing down, Thea gets a sense she's belabored this point enough but can't quite stop. "Look, look, look: What I'm saying is, you're acting as if you went to sleep last night in 1995 and woke up twenty-three years later. But you're not a parolee who's just experiencing the outside world after spending his entire adulthood in prison. You shouldn't be so blind that you need to play this much catch-up. But if you want to catch up, do it fast because right now, 2018 is just begging to eat you the fuck alive."

Pepper looks stricken.

Thea apologizes immediately: "That was unnecessarily

harsh. I'm sorry."

Pepper feebly raises a hand. *No. Don't apologize.* It's all the communication he can muster. It's not "eat you the fuck alive" or "tough shit" ringing in his skull. But "mortifying" plays in a loop. One word, and he's wrecked.

"You know," Thea continues, choosing her words carefully now. "I didn't tell you this before but when I first heard about your joke, my first reaction was to laugh. I wasn't offended at all. If anything, I was embarrassed by how funny I thought it was. Realistically, it was the kind of crack you've been making for years. But within thirty seconds, I was also like, 'Oh, wait, this is not good. This could be big trouble.' I didn't know how big because the rules are even too fluid for me, a twenty-five-year-old who's supposed to be in the front car of the PC train.

"But now, you'll be happy to know, I've come to one conclusion in your favor: The punishment the *Post* handed down is mild...but ridiculous. I honestly think it would be smarter if they relegated you to *only* covering women's sports for a year."

Jesus, how did I not come to that conclusion?

"Of course, it's not my call to make and, more importantly, it's not your call to make. The *Washington Post* is full of very smart people, and even if we question their decision, we should accept it, because they could be right, and we could be wrong or visa-versa. Either way, you and I, of all people, should know that life is unfair, but if you hang around, you can still steal a game here and there."

Pepper's breathing kicks faintly back to life, even while he feels like a child who's been spoken to on a child's terms... sports.

"Okay?"

Pepper nods.

Thea angles him back toward McPherson Square. They walk a silent stretch, a moment of dead air that feels worse to Pepper than the conversation he's just had. Right now, he'd welcome the kind of toxic small-talk that America runs on. Trump, the weather, "How about those Redskins?" All to be avoided with Thea on the jolliest of days, she being someone who sees the evil of banality.

Finally, somewhere between groping and hemorrhaging, Pepper speaks.

"So, do you still think my hysterectomy joke was funny?"

The out-of-leftfield-ness of the question doesn't faze Thea.

"Well...let me put it this way," she flatly says. "I find it less funny than when I first heard it but, hopefully, less funny than it will be someday in the future."

Pepper considers the ancient dream of "Someday we'll look back on this day and laugh." It doesn't seem possible, but then, it never does.

"Not to spastically jump from subject to subject but, your reference before to how we can 'hang around' and 'steal a game.' You thought it best to make your final point with a sports analogy?"

Without condescension or levity: "I know my audience." Then Thea finally smiles. It strikes Pepper as a patient kind of smile she'd give to an airport Hare Krishna.

At the end of the square, Thea calls an Uber; it's there in minutes. Pepper kisses her cheek and shuts the passenger door, then sets himself in the direction of his own car.

He's walked about a half a block when an ambulance streaks past, siren blaring someone else's hell. Cars compete to trail the ambulance, drafting like bicycle racers, another sport Pepper has impassively watched for over 39 years.

The thought of 39 years hangs in his head.

Time flies. Even worse, it flies coach.

A usable joke he doesn't jot down.

About the Author

After graduating from the University of Maryland, Peter Mehlman, a New York native, became a writer for *The Washington Post*. He slid to television in 1982, writing for *SportsBeat with Howard Cosell*. From 1985-90, he returned to forming full sentences as a writer for numerous national publications, including *The New York Times Magazine*, *GQ*, *Esquire*.

In 1989, two years after moving to Los Angeles, he became a writer for the iconic TV show, *Seinfeld*. Over the eight-year run of the show, Mehlman rose to executive producer and coined such well-known Seinfeld-isms as "Yada Yada," "spongeworthy," "shrinkage," and "double-dipping."

In 1997, Mehlman joined DreamWorks and created *It's Like, You Know...*a scathing look at life in Los Angeles. In recent years, he has written screenplays, novels, and humor pieces, many of which were collected in his book, *Mandela Was Late*. Mehlman has appeared on-camera for TNT Sports and the Webby-nominated *Peter Mehlman's Narrow World of Sports*. He's the creator of the lifestyle brand Bravely Oblivious. He lives in Los Angeles.

Also By Peter Mehlman

It Won't Always Be This Great, A Novel

Mandela Was Late: Odd Things & Essays From the Seinfeld Writer Who Coined Yada, Yada and Made Spongeworthy a Compliment

About the Publisher

The Sager Group was founded in 1984. In 2012 it was chartered as a multimedia content brand, with the intent of empowering those who create art—an umbrella beneath which makers can pursue, and profit from, their craft directly, without gatekeepers. TSG publishes books; ministers to artists and provides modest grants; designs logos, products and packaging, and produces documentary, feature, and commercial films. By harnessing the means of production, The Sager Group helps artists help themselves. To read more from The SagerGroup, please visit www.TheSagerGroup.net.

Artifex Te Adiuva

CPSIA information can be obtained
at www.ICGtesting.com
Printed in the USA
LVHW041941300820
664591LV00010B/1623